"YOU WANT SOMETHING THAT DOESN'T EXIST ANYMORE."

Kate struggled to keep her voice level. "You want it to be like the fairy tale. He takes her off to his castle and they live happily ever after...."

He stopped her from saying more with a hungry kiss.

"That's right," he said. "It's an old-fashioned love story we both wanted once. Almost as much as I want you now. Just as much as you want me."

It was true. She did want him. Making love would not solve their problems, but it would comfort them. It was a time when they were both completely free, not caught between two worlds, two conflicts.

Perhaps for the last time, she reached out her arms and her heart and loved him.

ABOUT THE AUTHOR

Ann Salerno was born in New York, but her family was constantly on the move. She credits much of the material in her six romances to the fact that "they really got around." Ann and her daughter now live in Albuquerque, New Mexico, where "it's hot as blazes, but lots of fun—the perfect combination for a writer." It must be, because Ann has written four Silhouettes—two Special Editions, two Desires— under the name Ann Hurley, as well as one Temptation and one Superromance under her own name, Ann Salerno.

Books by Ann Salerno

HARLEQUIN SUPERROMANCE
195—RAIN OF FLOWERS

HARLEQUIN TEMPTATION
58—FIRES AT NIGHT

These books may be available at your local bookseller.

Don't miss any of our special offers. Write to us at the following address for information on our newest releases.

Harlequin Reader Service
P.O. Box 52040, Phoenix, AZ 85072-2040
Canadian address: P.O. Box 2800, Postal Station A,
5170 Yonge St., Willowdale, Ont. M2N 6J3

Ann Salerno

Rain of Flowers

Harlequin Books

TORONTO • NEW YORK • LONDON
AMSTERDAM • PARIS • SYDNEY • HAMBURG
STOCKHOLM • ATHENS • TOKYO • MILAN

Published January 1986

First printing November 1985

ISBN 0-373-70195-0

Printed in Canada

And so the spring buds burst, and so I gaze,
And the rain of flowers falls, and so my days . . .

CHAPTER ONE

"WE'RE READY TO START, KATE," Fran whispered urgently to her boss as she hurried past her into the crowded side gallery.

Katherine Cleary took a deep breath and gave the long, linen-draped buffet table one final glance. She carefully crossed the highly polished tiles of the main gallery's floor to straighten a sagging yellow chrysanthemum in a *raku* bowl. The ancient piece of ceramic was over a century old and perfect; the floral display was a few hours old and already looked as if it would not last the evening.

Before she slipped into the next room for the official opening of the show, Kate quickly surveyed the newest acquisitions and smiled faintly to herself. Her job was still exciting, albeit nerve-racking, even after four years. She savored the quiet yet strong sense of pride she felt, as if tonight were the first of her shows as curator of the Cutler's Oriental graphics collection. Seeing the six new works, set like precious jewels on the stark white walls, caused her smile to widen.

Her personal and private pride showed only in the erect posture of her tall, slim, gray-suited figure. Her excitement danced deep in the Irish-green of her eyes and painted color over the cheekbones of her pale, oval face. Even so, she presented a calm, cool, collected picture.

She smoothed imaginary wrinkles out of her gray suit and counted the number of guests. The Cutler was full.

"So good to see you... I'm very glad you're here...." Kate meant every overworked phrase as she shook hands with some of the hundred local patrons. "Yes, I think so, too. Thank you."

"It's a miracle," an elderly man declared, vigorously pumping her hand. "On this year's budget, too! The lithographs are exquisite, Dr. Cleary."

Kate nodded agreement and remembered his name and business in the nick of time. "Sell lots of lawn mowers, Mr. Garber, and help us next year and I promise to do even more."

"Ladies and gentlemen, welcome to the Cutler Museum of Oriental Art, now the eighteenth largest collection..."

Kate glanced quickly at the director as he began the evening's formal opening. Marcus Cutler Holman would not be able to resist the temptation of a captive audience. She may have planned the show from the calligraphy on the invitations to the lighting in the gallery, but his speech was one detail Kate had no control over. It took effort but she restrained herself from peeking at the gold watch on her slender wrist as Holman continued to drone on. When he finally announced her, Kate was more than ready to speak.

"Really, she needs no introduction. I believe she is the youngest but I know she is one of the loveliest..."

Kate winced inwardly. At twenty-eight, with
torate in Art History from one of Japan's mos
tigious universities, she was painfully aware she did
not fit a largely conservative business community's
picture of a curator. Holman's introduction of her was
an embarrassment. Her severe crown of dark braids,
her tailored clothes, even her minimal use of makeup,
was supposed to allay lingering suspicions that she
should be older or male or plainer in order to do a
good job.

Holman's introduction went on and on, until Kate
was uncomfortable with the praise heaped upon her.
He finally said her name and she took his place, eagerly and gratefully, waiting until the applause died
down. The faces turned toward her were mostly
friendly and familiar ones. There was hardly a con-
tributor to the museum she had not personally buttonholed—in a nice, restrained way—for a donation.
After four years of knocking on their doors Kate could
have sworn she had the splinters in her knuckles to
prove it.

"To all of you and to our successful marriage of
Western business and Eastern Art. May the honeymoon never end!" Kate held an imaginary champagne glass aloft and toasted them, promising that the
real bubbly would follow shortly.

There was an appreciative collective chuckle from
the crowd. Counting heads with a quick sweeping
glance, Kate returned smile for smile and kidded them
about their discovery that "curator" was just another way of saying, "pickpocket for culture."
Whenever she met a Cutler patron on the street, she

added wryly, he or she instinctively reached for a checkbook and not for her hand.

"Such reflexes have been responsible for meeting the yearly challenge of growth for the Cutler, not me." Forgetting her public persona, she really smiled, treating her guests to the rare sight of Dr. Cleary's girlish, hated dimples.

The loudest laugh came from Morris Yashima, the bank's vice president and Kate's staunchest supporter, personal as well as financial. Her eyes sought him out to offer a special thanks to a special friend but stopped abruptly and unexpectedly. The man to Morris's left was staring at her in a way that made her forget her next line entirely. She met his fierce black eyes momentarily and got the impression of a marvelous, classical Japanese face. But the intensity of his fixed gaze was so strong, Kate had to look away to continue.

"With...without your support, these lovely new offspring of ours could never have been purchased to enrich this home for art, to enrich our lives with their beautiful, enduring presence."

Her slim, unadorned hand gestured toward the main gallery. The dark, narrowed eyes of the man followed the hand and returned smoothly to her face. Kate found herself meeting his eyes again and again as she hurried through her remarks. She wasn't sure if there was more challenge than approval in his scrutiny, but she was drawn toward him.

There was something fascinating about him, a strange and yet vaguely familiar quality. Kate knew she had never met him before; she wouldn't have forgotten those eyes or the way he watched her—like a tiger watching his prey. But he was sitting next to Morris and that clue gave her the answer while she mechanically finished her part in the ceremony.

Good, she thought with relief. *No, great!* He must be Morris's nephew, Cass Yashima. There was no sign of the other V.I.P. she had sent a special invitation to, hoping to widen the circle of wealthy benefactors. Arnold Whelan-Jones hadn't bothered to reply, but Cass Yashima had even been interested enough to turn up. A nibble like this was worth pursuing and Kate deliberately headed his way through the press of bodies.

While she accepted the handshakes and compliments, she tried to dredge up pertinent facts on the younger Yashima. The write-up in *Business World* was a good but brief profile of the founder of Sunco Electronics. Morris hadn't said much more than that Cass was a hometown boy, born right here in Riverside, and a UCLA graduate. Oh, yes, and that since Sunco's head office was in Los Angeles, Cass hardly got back here to see them anymore.

Kate decided on and readied her standard "native son" appeal. A small burst of nervous energy pushed her past a knot of people, and she homed in on Morris Yashima and nephew with both genuine pleasure and determination. The thirty-five-year-old prince of microchips was too good a prospect to lose, and Kate Cleary felt like a winner tonight.

She had to bend slightly to kiss Morris's cheek, but when she straightened up and offered her hand to Cass Yashima there was no disparity in height. She was forced to look once more, even more closely, into the most arresting, mesmerizing eyes she had ever seen. In their incredible darkness, Kate saw herself—a reflection as clear and sharp as in a mirror—and she was suddenly transformed into a very small, slightly startled-looking image.

"A marvelous show." Morris beamed broadly at her. "A marvelous turnout. And, Kate, you look . . ."

"Marvelous," finished Cass Yashima with a smile. "My uncle told me stories about your legendary efforts for the Cutler, Dr. Cleary. I was glad to take the chance to meet the museum's miracle worker in person."

Kate retrieved her hand and gave Morris a scolding look. "I have no idea what your uncle's been telling you. Mostly lies, I'm sure, but thank you on several scores. For accepting the invitation and for bolstering this curator's sagging morale at the end of a long, long day. Now, if after you've seen the exhibit, you still have nice things to say, I'll be truly complimented."

The words came out evenly but Kate was aware of being horribly uneasy. She decided it had to be the haunting, inexplicable familiarity of Cass's face. Nothing else could account for the uncanny feeling she had.

Even when he smiled and his face was relaxed and open, his strong, uncompromising features matched the intensity of his eyes. Kate chatted about the show as she studied the hard, angular shape of his jaw and the straight, thin, rather long line of his nose as Cass turned to Morris. Somehow, she recognized the slightly dimpled cleft at the very bottom of his chin and she had known that up close his wide mouth would have a full bottom lip, a top lip barely bowed.

But how? Recognition without an apparent reason disturbed her.

"Morris also warned me about your modesty, but it isn't necessary," Cass insisted. "I want to know how you arranged to get those fine lithographs under market value."

"Go ahead," urged Morris. "Brag a little, Kate, about your Japanese contacts. You're allowed to gloat a bit tonight."

"Brag yourself. I couldn't have finished the first show, much less a fourth, without you helping me to mobilize the big money in the community, Morris." Kate resolutely dismissed the notion that Cass Yashima was familiar to her and looked around for Fran without success. "Now, if I can find my secretary, I could show you both some very exciting material on new artists."

Cass chuckled, a deep, quiet sound, and exchanged a smile with his uncle. "You're planning next year's show tonight? And I assume that somehow I'm included in these plans, right?"

"You and Sunco," Kate said eagerly. She heard someone calling her name over the noise of the room and tried to block it out. This was a perfect opportunity to involve Cass and she must not lose it. "I know you have an interest, personal and corporate, in some fine art. I just happened to see those prints on loan from Sunco the last time I lectured at your alma mater, Mr. Yashima, and if that generosity could be slightly diverted to include us . . ."

"Cass," he said and touched her arm.

The single syllable, the single touch and the look of the man stopped her cold. The sensation of warmth seemed to travel up her arm and lodge in her throat with a vengeance. Forty or fifty people tonight had grabbed her hand or her arm or pecked absently at her cheek and it hadn't stopped her brain from clicking away or her jaw from moving. They were all contributors and she was supposed to think "pocketbook" first, last and always. And she had been rattling on, thinking of him as fair game—very, *very* fair game— yet the sound of his name made him a man. A very, very attractive man.

Kate tactfully shrugged off his touch and covered the gesture with a small, dry cough. "Yes, of course. Cass. Well, I was hoping you would have time while you were in town to really see the Cutler. This acquisitions show can't possibly give you an idea of the scope and the depth of our collection. We need..." *Oh Lord, we need to stop staring at each other like two kids at a high-school dance.*

"To discuss this in greater depth," Cass said agreeably. He gave a soft laugh as if the idea appealed to him and nodded. "I have two or three days in Riverside. Will I get a personal tour and a little speech about preserving my heritage?"

His tone of voice told Kate she was being teased, very gently but deliberately, and instead of being annoyed at having been so transparent, Kate found she was enjoying it. "You will get a hard sell that would put a Santa Monica used-car salesman to shame, Cass." She liked saying his name and looking right into his piercing eyes under straight black brows. In a minute she would forget "pocketbook" and think about the physique under the expensively tailored navy suit. "My own homage to certain ancestral ties is drinking green beer and marching in the St. Patrick's Day parade. I have to convince you that yours is to loan us, give us, promise us..."

"I could be convinced over dinner," suggested Cass. "Morris tells me the Cove's food is pretty good. How about tomorrow night?"

She was sure her mouth must be hanging open. Talk about hard sell! How he had jumped from a tour of the Cutler to a dinner date awed her a little. It wasn't a new experience to have a prospect for museum funding try and make an appointment something more; what was new was the blatancy of this man. Everything about Cass Yashima seemed businesslike but the way he looked at her. Well, things weren't what they seemed.

"I don't, as a rule, mix business with pleasure, Cass. If there're less than fifty men wearing name tags eating rubbery chicken, I consider it a social evening." She was grateful when a couple bustled up to distract her with a question on one of the works. It would give her time to let her subtle refusal sink in. His interest was flattering and the attraction between them was unmistakable but Kate had learned by now that a man's charm in California had nothing to do with his job skills or his willingness to write her a generous check.

As the couple moved away, Kate shifted her gaze back to Cass and found him studying her with what looked like amusement. Morris had disappeared entirely in the interim.

"I came on like a visiting fireman," he said. "I didn't mean to, Dr. Cleary, but I'd enjoy your pitch for the Cutler much more over a steak and I'll listen very carefully between the courses. Your priorities are clear, believe me.''

Maybe, Kate thought fleetingly, she should get to know him, rather than worry over where she had seen him before. And maybe her priorities were clearer to him at that moment than they were to her. It had been a long time since she spent an evening alone with an interesting, handsome man.

''Kate,'' she insisted. There was no earthly reason she should say no. Hadn't she desperately wanted a shot at enlisting this man and his fortune? The rule she had spoken of had only been a way of putting off the invariably misunderstood local tycoon who wanted to pour out his marital sorrows intead of listening to the Cutler's financial woes. Cass Yashima was a man married only to his work, according to *Business World*. ''As a matter of fact, I don't imagine the clatter of salad forks will be nearly as difficult to talk over as the chatter of our normal weekend visitors. Yes, thanks, the Cove will be fine.''

The suggestion of amusement on his face became a sudden laugh and he looked boyishly pleased, almost relieved. ''Then, no more shop talk tonight. I wanted to hear about your finagling the lithographs but it can wait. Tell me about you, instead, over a glass of good California champagne.'' He didn't wait for her to agree, turning her with a light touch on her elbow toward the main gallery and the buffet.

Although she could hardly feel the contact, it managed to spark a strong sense of his physical presence and his self-confidence. There was as much force in his golden fingers as there was power in his eyes. It shouldn't shake her or surprise her; she dealt with influential people all the time. But there was a difference; she could feel it. And the feeling had no name.

There was no hope of talking anything but shop as they strolled into the milling mob in the next room. One guest after another stopped Kate to comment on some aspect of the opening or to say good-night.

"So glad to see you here again. I can't tell you what the Cutler owes you, how much of this night is really yours," Kate said with the ease of four years' practice. She caught the flicker of annoyance crossing Cass's smooth, golden face after he heard the phrase repeated for the sixth interruption of her conversation with him. The small show of impatience, however carefully controlled, was noted and warmed her more than the overcrowded, stuffy gallery. He was definitely interested in more than her professional plans for the Cutler.

Morris was at the table and offered them both wine, refilling his own glass and setting down the empty bottle with a satisfied grin. "Well, was I right about Kate's ability to ambush and trap the unwary visitor? Are you a signed, sealed and delivered patron or not?"

"Not," admitted Kate with a dramatic sigh and a self-deprecating wave of her hand. "Your nephew is going to be a full-scale project, it seems. I told you, Morris, all that advance publicity you indulge in was going to backfire. Cass wasn't fooled by our mutual admiration society act or my stab at buttering him up."

"A restaurant *is* a better place to butter someone up," Cass pointed out. Kate ignored the curious look Morris gave them both and tried to change the subject to keep the conversation running smoothly. Her insistence on separating her personal life from her demanding schedule was well-known to Cass's uncle; she would have to put up with a good ribbing soon enough, as it was.

Her name was trumpeted again and Fran rushed up, a little breathless and a lot agitated. Someone had to see Kate right away, she wheezed anxiously, and jerked her head toward an elderly man standing with Marcus Holman. It couldn't wait another second. Arnold Whelan-Jones had arrived and he never waited.

"Cass, this is Fran Murata, my secretary and resident hysteric," Kate said calmly. "The last time she was in this state I had to catch a large frog some third grader had let loose in our teahouse display. Morris, will you find a wet sheet to wrap Fran in while I go see what's loose this time?" She glanced at Cass and extended her hand but before she could excuse herself, his fingers found hers and gripped them tightly as though he was restraining her.

"I'm afraid Arnold Whelan-Jones is yet another large frog," he said in a voice devoid of humor.

"Kate," wailed Fran, looking back over her shoulder. The edge of panic in her voice sounded very real to Kate. Marcus Holman was scowling in their general direction and frantically signaling with his program like a Boy Scout gone mad.

"All right, all right," muttered Kate under her breath as she started for the odd couple. Both her special invitations had yielded results unexpectedly. The absolute last reaction Kate would have expected was irritation, but here she was, stalking along the perimeter of the room, fighting down the annoyance she felt at what should have been a heaven-sent arrival. The Cutler had just hit the big time—*maybe*.

If she hadn't been quite so dazzled by Cass Yashima, she told herself with a trace of embarrassment, she would have spotted the celebrated philanthropist. His face did not startle her or require any introduction or thought; it appeared with great regularity in her trade journals, in newspapers and museum bulletins.

Perhaps it was the accumulation of tension or the strain of the night as a whole, but Kate was seized with the most horrible feeling that she was going to burst into hysterical giggles. Cass had obviously recognized Whelan-Jones, and the image he'd planted in her brain had taken root. *Another large frog. Oh God, he does look like a frog in a gray silk suit.* She forced herself to think about something else: how glad she was that Whelan-Jones had found his way from San Francisco, his recently publicized philanthropies, the real-estate empire that made it all possible.

Without prompting, Kate could reel off the biggest of the well-known private collector's contributions to other museums and universities. There were Whelan-Jones scholarships in fine art and a Whelan-Jones room in Chicago's Oriental Institute. Her letters and calls on behalf of the Cutler had never been answered and tonight's invitation had really only been a last-ditch attempt to arouse his interest—a letter to a Santa Claus that she couldn't quite believe in.

Well, here he was, out of the blue, and sailing toward her with one hand thrust out before he even reached her. Except for being short and stocky, Arnold Whelan-Jones looked nothing like Santa Claus,

she noted as she fixed her widest smile firmly in place.
He was a remarkably fit man for his sixty-plus years.
A fresh tan glowing above the white shirt collar and
the springy, hurried step of a much younger man made
him appear more attractive than Kate had expected.

"It's a great pleasure to meet you," Kate murmured.

"It might be," responded Whelan-Jones cryptically as he seized her hand. "That's up to you, according to your boss. I want ten minutes, Cleary. Just
ten minutes alone with you." He gave her a fast head-
to-toe appraisal and fixed his very cool faded-blue
eyes, magnified by the lenses of his glasses, on her.

Kate cleared her throat and hung on to her composure. "You may certainly have ten minutes, Mr. Whelan-Jones, but I don't think I can tell you much about
our pledge and purchase program in that short a
time."

"I don't want a sales talk and I didn't come to see
the show," said the elderly man bluntly. "I'm here to
see you."

Gribbet, gribbet, a small inner voice whispered,
causing Kate to bite her lower lip hard. She suspected
she did not like Arnold Whelan-Jones but unless she
was completely crazy, she'd better be willing to listen
to him. He could help the Cutler immeasurably and
her pride and personal tastes had to be tempered by
common sense. If it brought one gift from Whelan-
Jones's own enormous, priceless collection, she might
be willing to kiss him and see if he turned into a prince.

Taking his arm, Kate cheerfully steered them to a
relatively quiet spot. "I'm delighted to give you as
much time as you like. I only wish you could find a

minute or two to allow me to explain our endowment setup before you leave."

"Not necessary," Whelan-Jones declared. "I've already spoken to Holman. I need your attention and an answer immediately."

Kate just nodded agreement. She didn't trust herself to speak. All her years in Japan had instilled in her a distaste for brusque, overwhelming behavior. But this was America and bluntness and brevity, even to the point of rudeness, were acceptable business.

She concentrated hard on the man as he ran through his discussion with Marcus Holman. He knew Kate was planning to take her long overdue vacation in Japan for eight weeks and that fit nicely with Whelan-Jones's plans. Kate started to explain all the personal reasons for her trip but the great patron of the arts interrupted her before she got two words out.

"You can still see old friends and what all. These sales I'm talking about won't take more than a few weeks. You *have* heard about the Tokyo auctions, I assume?"

"I have," Kate began, hanging on to a smile with difficulty. "But I couldn't—"

"These works I'm considering bidding and buying, I want you to examine, authenticate and appraise." His eyes flashed with pale lightning and his staccato, harsh delivery actually picked up tempo. If Kate didn't know her own biography she wouldn't have been able to make heads or tails out of what he was saying.

He cited her particular credentials, her fluency in Japanese and her professional contacts in the field. Arnold Whelan-Jones let her know he had gone to a great deal of trouble to find out about her, and he wasn't expecting any more difficulty, in the form of a refusal. Kate wondered when anyone had last denied this man anything.

"You'll save me half the work by previewing everything," he summarized, ticking each point off with his fingers. "Finally, you're my insurance policy. There's always a chance of forgery or fraud. I don't want to miss a single fine investment but I won't be taken, either."

"Under different circumstances, I'd say yes for the opportunity of attending the sales themselves," Kate said. She repeated as quickly as she could all the considerations that outweighed any possibility of being his technical aide. No amount of money could be as attractive as her plans with Fran to visit Fran's grandparents and all of Kate's friends, faculty and fellow students from her university days. She and her secretary had waited and looked forward to this trip for more than a year.

Arnold Whelan-Jones didn't bother to disguise his boredom and peevishness with her. "You haven't heard my offer," he said flatly. "All your expenses paid and an honorarium of two thousand dollars at the conclusion of the sales. And the bonus I mentioned to Holman for the Cutler. You'd get first choice, Cleary. Pick of the litter from the works I buy." He slowed down for emphasis but it was necessary; Kate was short of breath and steadying herself on the back of a folding chair. "I'm going there with slightly over one million dollars."

A giddiness seized her as though she was a child who had been offered the key to a candy store. Whelan-Jones damned well knew the biggest single contributions to the Cutler were in three figures; he was offering her the choice of works which, minimally, ran to several hundred thousand dollars. She gave in to the impulse and laughed in disbelief.

"I take it your answer is a resounding yes," Whelan-Jones said dryly and glanced down to check the large gold watch on his thick wrist. "Eight minutes," he noted with satisfaction when Kate exhaled audibly. "I'll be sending you the particulars tomorrow. Schedule, catalogs of sale and a letter of confirmation."

"This is so generous of you," gasped Kate, glad she could still speak intelligibly. "This means so much to the Cutler and to me. I'm sure Mr. Holman thanked you."

Whelan-Jones was already eyeing the door. "Holman's an ass," he said loudly. "If his mother wasn't born a Cutler, he'd be pushing a broom here and not running the place. Good night."

Kate stopped trailing him and stood still, torn between shock and amusement. Since she had been freed of the relative isolation and safety of her academic ivory tower, she had encountered some odd characters, but Arnold Whelan-Jones was a stunner. She hadn't sold him on the Cutler; he'd sold her on a bonus, like a side-show barker at a carnival.

The crowd was much thinner as she circled the room. The small, hot patches of excitement were nearly cooled on her cheeks but Kate drank a final glass of champagne to wash down the bubble of guilt and confusion rising in her. Fran would be disappointed and hurt by the change of plans, but Whelan-

Jones was a man who could neither be anticipated nor refused.

That thought led to thoughts of another man, yet Kate could find neither Morris nor Cass Yashima in the small number of stragglers. What a night! The previews usually produced a sense of exhilaration and she felt it. But there was also a numbness, a confusion she hadn't expected. What had she committed herself to? A dinner date and a change of vacation plans. It had gone spectacularly well—better than she dreamed—and yet she was unnerved. The careful, cool facade she cultivated as Dr. Cleary was completely lost.

"Take a bow," ordered Marcus Holman into Kate's ears, making her jump. "It was the best show we've ever had. From the glassy eyes, I already know what happened with Arnold Whelan-Jones. Great, I was praying you'd accept. Now get him to write us into his will."

"It'll be in tomorrow and I'll talk to Fran about rearranging my leave." Kate stood at the door with Holman and helped him usher the last guests out. "I don't want to even think about her reaction. I feel as if I've made history tonight and I can't explain why. I'm going home and sleep for fourteen hours straight."

"Ride?" he offered happily. "Or just a raise? The board is voting next week and there won't be a problem, I'm sure."

She declined the ride but the raise was very good news. On the short walk to her apartment, she decided the entire evening was a case of good news. She had met two totally intriguing men who were totally different and had engineered an all-around triumph for the Cutler. It didn't take a genius to figure out why her feet didn't hurt even after a whole day and night in high heels—they never touched the ground once.

CHAPTER TWO

"I'LL MANAGE," Fran said in a tiny, resigned voice. She twisted the ends of her black bangs together, a nervous habit, and fiddled with the stack of mail on Kate's desk. "It really is too good a deal to pass up. It's just...well, you know..."

Kate rubbed her temples to forestall the headache from too much sleep or too much champagne. "I know, but we both have to think positive. You'll be sipping tea with your grandparents and telling them all about your wedding plans. I'll be right across town working for Mr. Whelan-Dealin' as his—talk about a way with words—'legs.' Tokyo is big, Franny, but it's not as if we're going to be at opposite ends of the earth."

"I guess not," said Fran without much conviction.

Kate launched into a description of her meeting with Whelan-Jones to distract her secretary. No matter how many assurances she gave Fran, both of them were aware Fran would really be the stranger in a strange land. It was her first trip to Japan and her first meeting, face-to-face, with her paternal grandparents. Now, Fran would have to handle the two weeks pretty much on her own.

"He talked about buying Hiratsukas and Hiro-shiges as though we were going to run down to the su-

permarket and pick out some nice lamb chops,''
exclaimed Kate. "I wanted to step to the side before he
machine-gunned me to death with words. I don't think
I ever met a man who talked so fast or raised my
hackles as much."

Fran stopped yanking at her hair, which Kate took
as a good sign, and actually giggled. "I've heard gossip from certain board members who know Whelan-
Jones from other projects. Did you ever hear him
called '3P' for patron, philanthropist and pirate?''

"Philanderer," amended Kate. "When his wife was
alive, it was for philanderer. And the way he in-
spected me, I expected to find a purple stamp on my
hip when I got undressed last night. Choice. Grade
A."

The notion of the elderly man as a lover boy who
talked a mile a minute tickled them both. "Wait until
he asks you to go to San Francisco to see his private
collection of woodblocks," snickered Fran, dabbing
at her moist eyes.

Kate shuddered and had to rummage around in her
desk for a tissue, clutching it until the wave of silliness subsided. "Oh, but, Franny, he got to me one
way. I was almost drooling last night thinking about
that commission. When he offered us first choice of
what he buys, I almost strangled myself trying to accept. He gives a print here, a scholarship there and the
world fawns on him." She pushed a recent journal toward Fran and flipped it open to an article on Whelan-Jones. "In spite of my 'art belongs to the people'
lecture, I was ready to kiss him in greed and grati-
tude."

"Speech number thirty-eight by Kate Cleary," intoned Fran. "The private collector should make his treasures accessible to the widest possible audience."

"Well, it's true," Kate retorted defensively and took back her magazine. "People like AWJ buy up everything they can get their hands on, dole out what they want and hoard the rest as financial investments. I don't approve; I'd rather see art handled the way Sunco does...loaning out Yashima's private collection as part of a corporate program. It's good publicity and public relations—"

"Yes, indeed!" interrupted Fran. Her eyes twinkled at the mention of Sunco and Yashima and she lifted a dark eyebrow at Kate. "Speaking of good things, I saw you playing hostess with Morris and Cass Yashima, too. He's quite a hunk, isn't he?"

"Morris is in his late fifties and married," Kate said with a perfectly straight face.

"Come on," groaned Fran. "Give me a break! You know very well who I mean. I saw him and you met him. Don't try and tell me you weren't interested. I pumped Morris for every scrap of information I could. Cass Yashima is not married, has never been married, travels all over for Sunco. He goes to Japan three or four times a year," Fran said, plunging on without pausing for breath, "has a seventeen-room house in Costa Mesa, likes modern as well as traditional art, owns an interest in some race horses, second-generation American..."

"What's his shoe size?" Kate asked laconically, glancing up from papers on her desk. She hadn't missed a word. Shaking a finger of warning at Fran, she advised her petite friend to practice and polish up more maidenly virtues if she was going to Japan. "I'm used to you calling them as you see them, but your grandpa and *Obasan* Murata will be shocked if you describe David as a hunk."

The mention of Fran's fiancé brought forth a wide, white smile. "David is not a hunk. He's a sweet, quiet, slightly nutty man, not a world-shaking heart-breaking dynamo like Cass Yashima. If he could only get away from the hospital and go with me, I'm sure my grandparents would love him." She shrugged slightly, thinking about her solo trip, and swept up Kate's handwritten notes for typing. "Anything else?"

Kate almost told Fran she was having dinner with Cass tonight, when she realized the question had nothing to do with men or Cass Yashima, in particular. It annoyed her to be preoccupied with thoughts of him when there was so much to do, so many things that took precedence. She waved Fran out of her office before the rehash of the preview turned into a hen party. Since she had hired Franny two years ago, their relationship had grown into a strong and close friend-ship, but now was not the time for a heart-to-heart about men.

She knew what Fran would say, anyway, if she con-fessed how fascinated she had been by Cass. Every single man who walked into the Cutler or attended a civic dinner Kate spoke at was a candidate for ro-mance, as far as Fran was concerned. It was always advice like "get with it" and "go for it" when a man showed interest in her. And when nothing came of it, Fran always had something to say about Kate's pick-iness and her very un-California-like attitudes.

Falling in love was a simple matter, Fran said. Of course, not everyone literally fell in love the way she had. A determined medical student had never run into Kate's bicycle, told her he loved her while he was examining her knee damage, and moved in with her within six weeks the way David Townsend had with Franny after one Sunday in One Oak Park.

It wasn't that easy or simple. Kate flipped listlessly through the correspondence on her desk and opened the glossy pages of an auction catalog. How long had it been since she was with a man she could really talk to? How long had it been since she was physically attracted to someone? And even when she pondered and counted backward, she did not come up with the same answer. Where was one man who wanted her, mind and body? Nowhere. And a man she wanted the same way?

The door opened slightly and Fran stuck her head in. Kate marked a page with her finger as if she had been studying the offering with real interest. "Forget something?" she asked.

Fran flashed a truly wicked smile. "Eleven and a half, maybe a twelve...D width. You might want to comb your hair, boss. You have a visitor, a Mr. Cass Yashima."

"Here? Now?" She stifled a groan and grabbed her purse off the floor. *Really professional, really lovely,* she thought as she glanced down at her usual Saturday attire. Weekends were for catching up on her paperwork, not for tour groups or school children or appointments. Her jeans were expensive but they were jeans and the less she looked at her hair, pulled back into a thick, black, unruly ponytail, and her once-good, now-faded shirt, the better she'd feel.

"Okay, show him in...no, wait," ordered Kate. She felt with her toes under the desk for her sandals and stuffed the brush and mirror back into the purse. She looked about as old and competent as one of the college students who worked at the museum's gift shop, but it would have to do. The sandals seemed to have been eaten by the carpet; she ducked under the desk to find them. A barefoot tour of the Cutler would *not* do.

"I can't wait," Cass announced from the doorway. "I said dinner but you said personal guided tour. I decided to be greedy and get both."

Kate came up, clutching her shoes, and grazed her head on the edge of the desk. She said a short, unlovely and unprofessional word and Cass laughed.

"Well, if you feel *that* way about it, we can skip the whole thing."

"No, no, no!" Kate straightened, rubbing her forehead with one hand and motioning him in with the other. At least, he wasn't all suited in tie and white shirt today; they would blend in with the Saturday crowd nicely. Last night she would have sworn he was the kind of man who slept in a three-piece suit. Well, he wasn't and he looked awfully good in jeans, boots and a plaid shirt. "I wouldn't miss this if I had to do it in a bathrobe and tap shoes with a slight concussion."

"Oh, do you need first aid or will just a kiss make it better?" he asked with a dazzling smile. Fran, who had been watching all this from the door, made a sound like a snort and giggle combined and disappeared so fast she might have evaporated.

"I'm fine. I'll live," Kate said, thrusting her feet hurriedly into the sandals. She came around her desk with as much dignity as she could muster and led him out into the reception area, brushing by Fran's desk. She completely ignored the knowing tilt to her secretary's head and a most unmaidenly leer.

The Cutler was filled with families and college students on the weekends. There was a slightly larger than usual crowd as people filed in to see the acquisitions show Cass had already previewed. Kate chose one of the smaller side galleries to start in and as they strolled past the inked scrolls, she began to explain all the changes the Cutler had undergone in the past few years.

The museum had been more a warehouse than a showplace when she accepted Holman's offer to curate the graphics collection. Priceless works were stored alongside gaudy, cheap, mass-produced paintings and displayed without any rhyme or reason. Her first year had been a race to catalog and cull, organize and show the best of what was lying around. The campaign to get the public interested in coming and supporting the Cutler came later.

"I remember what a dismal, empty place this was," confirmed Cass. He paused and studied the flowing, graceful brush strokes on a Chinese landscape. "When I was in high school, no one came here unless it was an assignment or he needed a quiet spot to make out with his girlfriend and didn't have a car. The Cutler had a lousy reputation in the art world and with our parents."

"We're still not number one but we're trying," Kate said, with a sigh. She gave him a long, appreciative glance while he was studying another work and decided not to ask how many times he'd been here as a teenager, and whether his motives had been school or sex. She started to speculate about what Cass had looked like then: probably just as tall but leaner, less muscled, less width to the shoulder and chest, perhaps not quite so lean in the hips and long in the legs. Had his mouth been as sensual looking then or sweeter?

"Let's see the woodblocks," he suggested, stopping short in front of the next room. Kate bumped him, felt the length of him against her and the unexpected pressure of his arm against the side of her breast and moved away quickly. "Sorry," he said under his breath and waited until Kate went in ahead of him. "Morris told me that *ukiyo-e* was your area of expertise. I'm very partial to the classic prints myself."

She muttered a few things about her doctoral dissertation on the fabulous Japanese woodblocks and explained why the Cutler showed so few works from that area. "I decided it was better to display only the very best examples we had and buy only the best." She was feeling skittish and silly, edging slightly away from him, but when she walked next to him, their legs and hips kept touching and she was afraid she'd go blank.

"That's a good policy, looking for the finest and then, getting it. I don't settle easily, either," Cass said quietly, but he was staring at her, not the Utamaro they were standing near. "This one is superb."

All the depth and power of those marvelous black eyes were clearly focused on her, her mouth, her face. For a second, Kate thought he was going to lean over in the deserted room and kiss her, refresh his memories as an adolescent, and her mouth went dry. She could practically sense the distance between them closing, the air growing warmer with their body heat and moving as they breathed. His eyes flicked past her and up to the print and the second dissolved instantly into the next.

"Yes, it is an excellent one of his famous women," Kate agreed, somewhat throatily. "There's a blue-clad geisha with a veil which should be hung with this print, but it's rarely offered for sale."

"It will be. Soon." His voice sounded flat, gruff as Cass mentioned one of the auction houses in Tokyo and the sales. He was hoping he'd have time to see it and a lot more between contract talks in Japan but, he explained, he wasn't personally interested in buying art this trip. "Of course, if the Cutler wants it badly, I could look for it and call you if it's a good edition ... and the price isn't sky high."

The surge of excitement filling her wasn't entirely due to the news of an Utamaro offering. He was going to be there! There was more than a chance of seeing him in Japan; the auctions would only draw, at most, a hundred serious dealers and buyers. Kate refused his offer with thanks, confiding the bare bones of her arrangement with Arnold Whelan-Jones. There wasn't a shadow of doubt that Whelan-Jones would bid for the rare *Blue-Veiled Geisha* print and under their agreement, Kate could choose it as the Cutler's share of the bounty. What a stroke of luck, she exclaimed. Especially since the museum's annual budget for purchasing was exhausted.

"A stroke of luck," Cass repeated dully and then gave his dark head a slight shake as if he were disagreeing with himself. The corners of his mouth grew visibly strained and he started to say something but stopped. "Maybe. How about us getting a cold drink before we go on?"

Abruptly, he turned his back on Kate and started for the garden café. Kate was so surprised by the sudden, unexpected shift in atmosphere that she was unusually slow to respond and had to hurry to catch up with his quick strides, her sandals slapping on the polished floors.

"Hey, wait a minute! Cass?" She slipped up behind him, irritated and puzzled by his behavior, and touched his arm. His sidelong glance was filled with turmoil but his handsome features stayed composed. Kate felt tremendous tension in the muscles of his forearm and a heat like anger rising through the thin cotton fabric of his shirt. "What's wrong? Please tell me."

"Nothing," he said far too quickly. His step shortened and slowed. "No," he amended just as fast, "there is something but it's none of my business. Iced tea or lemonade?"

A few minutes later he picked up two glasses and gestured out at the sun-dappled patio with his chin. Since he added nothing else, Kate was struck with an unpleasant thought. Everything had been going so beautifully until she mentioned Japan and her plans. It occurred to her that the prospect of seeing her again might not have delighted him as much as it had her, and he might be too nice, too polite to say so. Her lemonade promptly lost its taste. She pushed the drink aside and toyed with the crinkled straw wrapper, avoiding his eyes altogether. Without being awkward or rude, there must be a way to shelve his dinner invitation, made so quickly last night, and give him a graceful out.

"I could give you a raincheck on tonight," Kate offered finally when, in contrast to the babble and laughter around them, their silence became oppressive. "The next time you visit Riverside, we could... I mean..."

"I know what you mean," Cass said and reached across the small table to pick up her hand. He held it lightly, cradling her fingers in his larger hand. His lips twitched once before they compressed into a thin line. She sensed he was weighing the wisdom of saying more and she waited. "I *do* like your tour and I *do* want to have that dinner with you. Very much, unless you've changed your mind. And I'll understand if you have. I tend to be moody, I know."

"That's not it," protested Kate. "I said something back there about us getting together for cocktails or a dinner in Tokyo. It was a little pushy sounding, wasn't it? Well, believe me, I didn't intend to come on that way. I've adjusted nicely, thank you, to being back in the free-and-easy U.S.A. but I don't think I'll ever be as aggressive as California women, if you follow me."

She kept staring intently at the tabletop, her thick eyelashes almost touching her undoubtedly flushed skin. A man like Cass ran into a million predatory females, especially in the wealthy, "beautiful people" circles he must travel in. One more tigress, scenting money and power and real virility in him, would be commonplace and annoying. Admittedly, she was interested, but not quite bold or brave enough to do what they did. Kate lifted her hand slightly and started to get up when Cass's fingers closed tightly but not painfully in capture.

"Oh, I believe you," he whispered, so softly Kate almost missed the words. "I follow you, too. Now, sit down." When she did and met his eyes, the same look and tension was there as when she thought he was going to kiss her. "I don't see it happening, but I wouldn't mind at all if you were the hungry lady type, not just an eager curator."

The strange feeling came back, flooding Kate with images and thoughts of him she could not know, and it was suddenly mixed with desire. She knew his mouth and wanted to taste him, to see this very look of his deepen, darken with passion. She recognized the way he touched her as if his hand was an old friend who remembered her very well. And she had seen him somewhere, sometime. She had to have seen him to feel this way so quickly, so inexplicably!

"No, I'm not a hungry lady but it will be a different story about eight o'clock," Kate managed to say with an artificial lightness. "I only wish you'd tell me a few things, honestly."

"Anything," Cass promised. His thumb stroked gently back and forth across her knuckles, a soft pendulum to mark time until they were alone. But when Kate repeated her question about what had gone wrong back in the gallery, he grimaced and hesitated before he answered. "I have no right to comment on or criticize what you do, Kate. I know how much I resent people giving me advice, good, bad or indifferent, on how to run Sunco. There are times I've done the wrong thing just to be my own man and make my own decisions. Let it pass, okay?''

If he hadn't been uptight about her, there was another possibility and Kate couldn't restrain herself. "It's Whelan-Jones," she guessed and the answer showed only in his eyes. "You *did* know him last night and you don't like him." She pressed a bit harder, wanting to know everything he did. "Our arrangement? You don't like something about it."

"*Anything* about it," corrected Cass vehemently, "starting with Arnold Whelan-Jones. He's everything the media writes about him, but he's a lot more they don't print. I'd prefer it if you checked him out with a few people you know you can trust, that's all. Before you sign on his pirate ship!"

Too late, admitted Kate. She was quick to add that she had heard the stories about Whelan-Jones and she wasn't entirely a fool or a schoolgirl. Yes, she was going to get the arrangement in writing and even then, she was going to be cautious.

"Good," said Cass without much emotion. "And, remember, I'll be somewhere in the wings for most of those few weeks. You can . . . I want you to call me if there's trouble or it begins to look funny. Will you do that?"

"I might do that," was as far as Kate would commit herself. She wasn't used to relying on other people to rescue her and she didn't have much respect for women who needed a man to save them. The deal with Arnold was made and she hadn't had her arm twisted; if she ended up with egg on her face, she asked for it. "Let's go see the teahouse and the silk screens and call it a day."

They couldn't get near the teahouse—the authentic and ancient reassemblage from Japan was mobbed and the sheer number of people traipsing through it destroyed the very serenity and simplicity it was supposed to demonstrate. The room with the silk screens was better but they hurried through. Sitting together in the garden had been too close, too intense, and Kate was vaguely uncomfortable slipping back into her guide role. She knew Cass felt the shift, too. He held her arm and said very little, asked no more questions, but she was conscious of him watching her every second.

"Here," he said as they were walking back to her office. He reached into his back pocket and handed Kate a white business envelope, folded and sealed. "Signed, sealed and delivered. It's amazing how much you've done and I can see the potential of the Cutler. You really took on a mess and cleaned it up, Kate."

She wasn't sure whether she wanted to laugh or cry. There was obviously a check—a generous one, all prepared in advance—and all her effort, while not wasted, wasn't needed. Why bother with a tour and a dinner if he was convinced before he got the red-carpet treatment?

"I like you," Cass said simply, seeing the bewilderment on her face. "I want to see you while I'm here. Morris told me you were bright and beautiful and, for once, a banker's word is as good as gold."

"Thank you," Kate replied, fingering the envelope but not opening it. "For both gifts, Cass. The Cutler's and your honesty. The truth is usually harder to get out of people around here than their money."

"The truth is worth more." He stroked her cheek with the very ends of his fingers, which left her tingling as though she had passed too close to fire. "Did I tell you everything you wanted to know, honestly?"

"Not everything," Kate confessed slowly. The heat in her cheek began to spread downward until she felt it flare secretly deep within her. Perhaps Holman was right to insist she take her long-overdue leave. She was working too hard or going crazy or both if a small, intimate gesture produced such a wave of sensation. "I know you. I know you and we never met before..." Kate said quietly and then, more loudly. "How... where do I know you from? Go ahead and laugh if you want to, Cass, but I have this strange..." She searched and gave up on finding the right words to describe the mystery.

"You do know me," he confirmed. "Don't worry and wonder about it, Kate. You, of all people, would know my face." He dropped his voice and said a single word, the name of a famous woodblock artist, and instant understanding lightened the green of Kate's eyes.

"Sharaku!" Kate laughed and the giddiness passed. The print-master's name conjured up the vision of a special face with frightening clarity. An ancient actor's face and the one in close proximity to hers were the same. Her finger moved up in the narrow space between them as if she were tracing the dark red lines of stylized Kabuki makeup on Cass. "But it's you, too."

The resemblance faded when Cass smiled. He was smiling when he told Kate the actor was a direct but very distant relative. "Morris thinks that print explains my interest in Japanese art. He thinks it's a case of possession by an ancestor's spirit because I'm the rebirth of his image. Silly, huh?''

Kate shivered and shook her head. "No, it's fantastic! I wish there was a way to work a picture of you and a slide of that print into a lecture. We don't own the Sharaku but I can contact Boston Museum.''

"I'll have my office in Los Angeles send you a slide. The Sharaku is the print I outbid Whelan-Jones for about a year ago. Sunco lent it to Boston, but Arnold was convinced it belonged on his walls. He won't forget that loss soon.''

"Oh," was the only word Kate came up with. Whelan-Jones hadn't struck her as a man who forgot much or took a loss with a shred of good grace. He wasn't an especially gracious winner, for that matter.

"Feel better? Saner? Now, you know where and how you know me and by eight o'clock, you will be ravenous.''

"I will have a hearty appetite and about a hundred other questions, I think." Kate stepped reluctantly through the open doorway, keeping her gaze fixed on him for one last look. Cass said goodbye and walked off down the hall without a backward glance and Kate waited until he disappeared at the corner before she went into the reception area. Having the puzzle of last night solved did not eliminate all the disturbing feelings he had stirred up.

"So?" Fran's bark was impressive, coming out of such a small frame. She should have been long gone for the day.

"So what?" countered Kate blandly as she put the Sunco contribution on Fran's desk and penciled a note to accounting on it. She wanted to hold on to the day, sort it out and contemplate the evening without Fran's words of wisdom.

"You are my best friend and sometimes I hate you," moaned Franny. "Didn't you learn useful, real things—man and woman things—at school in Japan? What about Cass?"

"He's very interesting. He likes me. That's all." Kate unlocked the door to her office and ducked in as Fran slammed a file drawer in frustration.

"For a Westerner, you are positively...inscrutable," hollered Fran. "You need help, Dr. Katherine Cleary. You need someone to take you in hand and explain how these matters proceed in the modern world." She opened and shut another drawer hard for emphasis.

"We're going to dinner tonight," Kate yelled back from her sanctuary. "Good enough?"

There was no more noise and no answer. When Kate got curious, she came back out and there was no Fran. The white paper standing on the secretary's desk was the only evidence that Fran had been there to hear Kate. Fran had printed GO FOR IT in big block letters and slipped away.

CHAPTER THREE

"GET OFF MY BED," Kate said irritably.

Her hand trailed over the hangers in her closet again, rejecting a long black dress, a red-and-gray silk shirtwaist and settled on her best tan suit. When she held up a clinging crepe blouse patterned with hundreds of black, tan and green butterflies, her silent, disobedient critic lifted his head.

"I'm glad something meets with your approval," she commented. "Wait until you have to munch those hard little red stars for dinner tonight! No sharing a frozen mystery meat meal, no tuna salad tonight...regulation cat food. Now, will you get off my bed?"

Tomadachi was unmoved, unimpressed. He rolled himself over into a fat orange knot and tucked his tail across his eyes. Three years ago, when Kate was returning from her last Japanese trip, he was only a bedraggled kitten greeting her on her doorstep. He had looked as if he needed a friend, so she dubbed him with the equivalent in Japanese. Friend? He was now the prince of all he surveyed.

"You are a typical male," she announced to the placid, furry lump and was ignored.

The thought of typical males made her speculate on her date. Cass seemed different, looked and acted differently than the usual male who drifted in and out of her life lately. The link she felt with him was bothersome because she still couldn't put a label on it.

And all on the strength of seeing him twice and an eery resemblance to an old print, she thought with a trace of disgust at herself and her flights of fancy.

It would be an evening of small talk and perhaps a pass. Nothing more. She steeled herself for disappointment.

Dressed except for her accessories, Kate fumbled with one of her diamond-and-pearl earrings, the ones her parents had given her when she received her doctorate. She was still fumbling when the doorbell buzzed impatiently. Tomadachi finally stirred himself at the sound and jumped down from the bed, padding to the front door.

"I'll answer it, if you don't mind," Kate muttered, shooing him aside. She opened the door with one hand and clutched her ear with the other.

"Oh, no," Cass said with a faint smile, taking in her strange pose. "I was planning to talk your ear off during dinner, not before. Here, let me..."

His fingers were cool, touching her ear lightly. There was a certain ease, almost familiarity he exuded, turning her sideways as if he performed little services like this often. It took a second or two for him to close the stubborn back firmly over the gold post, but his hand lingered longer, brushing away a long wisp of hair.

"Thanks. I'm all set to go."

"I'm not," Cass replied stepping into the room. "You don't mind if I just look, do you?"

He was surveying her apartment as quickly and efficiently as he fastened an earring. One sweep of the silvery carpet, the stark and simple furnishings and what hung on her walls obviously told him what he wanted to know. Even Tomadachi, one of the few spots of color, was noted and Kate got a nod as if she had said something Cass agreed with.

"You have two worlds," Cass remarked. "You must really miss Japan to bring it back here."

"I had two homes," Kate countered as they left. "I'm pretty sure Morris, that old gossip, filled you in about me so I won't repeat the tired history of Kate in the Far East."

"I want to hear it," he insisted. "I'm determined to find out all about you, in fact."

She was not quite used to his directness but she tried to match it, talking about her unusual life. As they drove to The Cove, Kate unraveled most of the skein of her background. She was born at the American military hospital in Tokyo and grew up a typical officer's brat, eating pizza and listening to the current stateside rock and roll hits. Untypically, however, she stayed in Japan and embraced their art and culture, winning a place at the wildly competitive Tokyo University.

"You know," finished Kate thoughtfully, studying his handsome profile, "there's a paradox here. You're a Yashima from California and I'm a Cleary from Tokyo. You achieved the American dream using traditional Japanese war strategies. On the other hand, I combined Japanese culture with American dollars and came up with a success."

"You think we're very different?" asked Cass with a glance toward her. He parked and took the keys, juggling them in his palm as if he were weighing his words. "I think we're more like mirror images of each other, Kate. You felt you knew me and it goes further than a modern man in the image of an ancestor far away and long ago. I saw you at the opening show and there was much more than my natural attraction to a beautiful woman. I had to meet you. I had to know more about you. Don't ask me why or for what. Maybe I'll come up with the answer tonight."

Her notion of small talk began to fade. The Cove's interior was dim and cool and quiet. Cass asked the waiter to seat them near one of the fireplaces, and he watched Kate sip her Scotch for a while without comment. There were hushed murmurs all around them but she was more conscious of the hiss and pop of the burning wood, the rise of sparks behind Cass. The whiskey burned pleasantly in her throat and when he reached for her hand, her fingers were warm.

"We share a love of art," Kate said tentatively. "Besides that, I can't think of anything similar. I don't know a microchip from a marshmallow."

His voice came out of the shadows, deep and sincere and slightly troubled. Cass took a breath and stroked her fingers, one by one. "I made up my mind I didn't care how strange what I want to say sounds. There's something I've been meaning to ask you.... Are you comfortable with who you are? Do you sometimes feel you're trapped between two places? Do you know what I mean?"

"Yes, I do," whispered Kate. He was trying to voice a dilemma she wrestled with alone: the fear of fitting in nowhere. "There are great cultural differences between here and Japan, as well as in the worlds of art and business. Since I've always been a dreamer, an impractical romantic, I prefer to think it's possible to live in two worlds at once. Anyway, I work awfully hard at it."

"Ah, yes. A workaholic, like me," he added. "You could be describing either one of us. I can add another conflict we share, I suspect: what we wanted versus what we got. You might laugh, but I set out to be a 'silicon samurai.' I wanted to build an empire honorably, gloriously in the modern arena of power."

"You did and you're rich," Kate said bluntly. "Sunco is expanding all over the world. Isn't that enough?"

She didn't mean to sound as cynical as she did. Cass wasn't complaining about being wealthy any more than she would whine about her job, she realized. There were still things she wanted, unfulfilled dreams, that she wasn't prepared to share on such short acquaintance. It was risky to confide too much, too soon. Cass was used to taking risks, perhaps.

He shook his dark head at her and gave the waiter orders for two dinners, without consulting her. It was either another dumb coincidence or they were on the same wavelength. He hit the right entree. His black eyes were slightly more guarded and wary when he resumed their conversation.

"No, I'm beginning to feel what I have is not nearly enough. The trappings are right for a feudal lord and wrong for me. I've got a big, close family and I almost never see them. I'm going to sell the house because I don't really live in it. I'm usually off waging a paper war for Sunco somewhere. But as powerful as you may think I am, I just found out that when I see a real danger, a situation in the making, I may be totally unable to do anything about it.''

Kate took her hand away and toyed with her fork. Playing dumb was not a ploy that appealed to her. "Do you mean a situation concerning me?"

"You...Arnold Whelan-Jones...me." Cass paused to move his steak knife as the plates were set down in front of them.

This time, Kate didn't care if she was being silly or easily spooked. She shivered and felt her flesh crawl at the sight of Cass holding a knife and talking about Arnold. It meant something, omen or premonition. She put a fork into the shrimp bisque and brought it to her mouth, chewing mechanically. She was drawn to Cass and frightened by him.

"There's nothing dangerous about selling my expertise for a few weeks," she said to break the silence. "It's more inconvenient than anything else. I heard your little warning this afternoon and I'm aware—"

He interrupted her, almost angrily. "You're not! If I thought it would do any good, I'd tell you to forget those sales."

One of the logs behind him broke open and the resulting flash of light startled her. Bright orange flames illuminated Cass before the fire died down a bit.

Kate saw him clearly again—the intensity and mystery of the man—and she felt herself respond to him as a woman. But he was telling her what to do and her resentment also flared. "You yourself said you had no right... I was hired as a consultant by a rival of yours. I don't even know if you and Whelan-Jones hate each other because of business or the Sharaku print but it doesn't matter."

"If I thought you'd go for it, I was perfectly willing to bribe you with an offering from the Sunco collection to retract your agreement with him." Cass let his words sink in for a long minute before he continued. "I told you I had some strange things to say. You're looking at me as if I'm crazy."

"You're being dramatic, that's all," Kate replied curtly. "You were right about us being alike in certain respects. I have a touch of the theatrical about myself when I'm lecturing."

He pushed the plate away and leaned forward. "Ouch, that stung! A sharp tongue, a sharp mind...but it won't stop me. I'm not kidding. Arnold's capable of hurting people if it serves his purpose and I feel...close, protective of you, let's say. My lecture is over."

So was the meal. Her appetite had fled and Kate did not want to pursue the subject of Whelan-Jones. A conversational shift back to Cass's plans, Kate's ambitions was more interesting, anyway. He had a few days before he was supposed to fly to Washington, D.C., to negotiate a government contract and the gist of their talk indicated to Kate that Cass wanted the time with her.

"We're both always on the go, I see," teased Kate. "I only have until the twenty-third to whip things into shape before I leave."

Cass jerked his thumb toward the next room where The Cove's small band was playing. "Well, we don't have a minute to waste. Let's make plans for tomorrow while we dance."

It was an invitation she was not able to refuse. Kate wanted to know what it would feel like to be held by him. Dancing close was a nice, acceptable way to test their chemistry in a public place, not her apartment. She draped her suit jacket over the back of her chair and stood up.

His arms gathered her in easily and didn't clutch at her. "Golf...tennis...a drive down to Costa Mesa," recited Cass softly into her ear. "What's your pleasure?"

This is, Kate thought as their bodies brushed together in the press of other couples on the dance floor. "Nice" was an understatement for the feeling she got and "acceptable" was far short of the truth. Cass moved very well, very smoothly.

"I'm not much for games," murmured Kate. "Your uncle wanted me to take up golf. He claimed it would make a new, relaxed woman out of me and then spoiled it by telling me how many deals are made over the eighteenth hole."

Cass chuckled and his fingers tightened slightly, sliding along the silky material of her blouse. "I'm not much for games myself. I've forgotten how to play. And I don't know why you would want to be a new woman." He pulled back and gave Kate his deeply hypnotic stare. "You're pretty impressive the way you are."

"Thank you." Only when she averted her eyes from his did she manage to speak again. "A drive, a walk through town...we can even recapture our carefree youth and chase a Frisbee in the park."

"Or we could make love..." His lips grazed her temple and came to rest in the thick, black wing of hair swept back over Kate's ear. "Don't go tense on me, Kate. I'd rather say it than have it hover around us like a shadow all night. I'd be a liar or an idiot if I claimed my only interest in you was intellectual."

She heard herself laugh, throaty but relaxed. "Clearly, you're not either one of those. It's just that it's different . . . and a little exciting to hear a man say we could make love, so simply, so unadorned."

"Only a little exciting?" He brought Kate nearer with the pressure of his hand on the small of her back. "I'll have to do better, then." His voice dropped to a caress. "I want you, Katherine Cleary."

"Please don't. An easy, quick affair is not my style. Let's go, Cass."

Kate stopped moving and stood there, still in his grasp. She raised her hand and laid it on his mouth. She could not deny she was sorely tempted to make love to him. His breath was fiery. The skin she touched was smooth and surprisingly soft.

But he didn't let go of her arm or her waist. "I wasn't talking about anything easy or quick. I was merely telling the truth. I want you. Is there time or room in our lives for each other?"

The music swirled to a halt and the smattering of applause covered her "I don't know" but not her confusion. Cass led her back to the table and held her jacket while she slipped her arms into the sleeves. Kate felt her cheeks flush and wondered what was happening.

She could have put down any Good Time Charlie with alacrity. She could have handled any of her male peers, intellectually and socially. With Cass she was at a loss. If he wasn't asking to spend the night in her bed, what did he want?

When they stepped into the night air, she sighed and let the breeze cool her fevered thoughts as well as her cheeks. Smoothing a wayward strand of hair back in place, Kate stole a sidelong glance at Cass.

Definitely different and not disappointing, she decided, but he was intimidating. Honesty didn't have to be brutal or touched with arrogance. He knew now she wasn't unwilling to see something develop, to consider taking a lover, but if there was a genuine affinity, it wouldn't hurt to allow it time and room to grow.

"I'm sorry if I scared you," Cass said as if he read her mind. "Coming on strong and making yourself clear is a prerequisite in business. And damn it all, Kate, I don't seem to do anything but business. Every bit of energy, every minute of time is Sunco. I eat, breathe, sleep the company."

"Who owns whom?" she asked and hit a nerve somewhere. Cass looked away this time. She wasn't unsympathetic; her four years at the Cutler didn't match his ten years building Sunco but she'd devoted at least as much effort to her field. It did tend to shut out every other possibility.

Cass killed the engine in front of her building and held the door for her as she got out. Despite the late hour, Kate didn't want the night to be over. Not yet. He walked her up to the front door and waited while she fumbled in her purse for the keys. The soft yellow light from overhead was kinder to them than the fire had been. Kate turned and looked at him, debating the wisdom of inviting him in. She might not want him to leave.

"Another cup of coffee?"

"Sure."

She introduced him—in two languages—to the cat. It was wise to start practicing for the trip. At the sound of her voice Tomadachi raised his head from the black-and-white tweed cushion. He examined Cass and yawned widely, exposing his pink tongue, mottled palate and a set of sharp, wicked teeth.

"He doesn't care for me," laughed Cass. "Or he simply doesn't care." He sat on the couch and scratched the cat over his nose and behind his ears.

Kate stuck her head around the divider from the kitchen. "He bites. He's not into electronics or finance, just fish. Unless you own interests in mackerel, watch out! I have to farm Tomadachi out while I'm gone and it isn't easy to find a babysitter he likes. My secretary's fiancé, David Townsend, is the lucky man. David will smother him in sardines, and Elmo, the parrot, will provide his amusement."

Tomadachi growled his approval and walked regally up Cass's chest to dance on his shirt front. Cass grinned at Kate.

"That's right. Make a liar out of me," grumbled Kate. She brought two mugs of instant coffee out and handed one to Cass. Glaring at the cat, she sat down and sipped hesitantly, watching them over the rim of her cup.

"The auctions run two weeks. Three weeks, tops." Cass gently lifted Tomadachi and set him down on the couch. "You didn't mention any plans for the rest of your leave."

"Mostly rest and relaxation. I want to meet Fran's grandparents and find out how they know my father.

There are old classmates to visit. The most important mission is to spend time with Yoshio Sabusawa, my favorite teacher. He recently retired because of his health. He's more than a former teacher; Yoshio was mentor, advisor, friend...you get the idea."

"Lover?" Cass asked evenly.

Kate laughed until moisture collected in the corners of her eyes. "Oh, no...sorry... I wasn't expecting that! No, Lord, Yoshio is about seventy-six, skinny as a bamboo pole...and every inch as straight and rigid. Never married. A living saint, I'd say."

"You have dimples and you look about nineteen when you laugh like that," Cass said. He put his cup down and took hers away, setting them carefully on the end table behind her. The stretch brought him very close, his arm extended across her body and the pressure of his leg increased. "I was curious if there was a man you were involved with over there. Someone from the past you haven't shaken completely?"

Her eyes widened, their green suddenly brighter with understanding. "No one. I've still got ties there, but none that are heartstrings."

"That's a relief. There's room in both our lives."

His fingers moved to the back of Kate's neck and began to draw her steadily toward him. There was no hurry to the movement and she didn't resist. *Let it happen,* she thought fleetingly. Prolonging this moment seemed very important to Cass and pleasant to Kate.

"And no rush?" she asked cautiously. The darkness of his eyes was not frightening now but soft, a velvet night to sink into.

"No rush," he promised.

As the space closed, she was aware of the smallest, strangest things. The scent of coffee mixed with a trace of her own perfume and him—brandy, smoke, aftershave. The muffled tick of the kitchen clock fell into syncopation with her heartbeat and the sound filled her head.

His face, first in incredibly sharp detail, came closer and closer. Inches away, he stopped, a blur. His hand slid up her neck to cup her cheek, to tilt her head fractionally. There was the warmth of their breath mingling, the warmth of his hand—the most fragile of connections.

Kate looked at his mouth, anticipating his taste, eager for the kiss.

With the care of a man examining a priceless porcelain, Cass moved his thumb over her lips. He traced the finely sculpted edge of the top lip, slowly, very slowly. At the corner of her mouth, his thumb trailed to the fuller bottom lip, just as slowly and precisely.

Kate sat still, almost hypnotized by the electrical touch. Just her lips, just his thumb. Over and over, Cass stroked until the exquisite sensitivity of her mouth made it part, the tip of her tongue moistening the pad of his thumb. More touching, more stroking and it became wildly erotic, difficult to sit still. Her hips wanted to move in little circles. She wanted more.

"Kate..." he said hoarsely and then his mouth was on hers.

They connected instantly. Leaning into the embrace they struggled to hold each other as close as possible. Their tongues mated in the dance of desire. Kate was stunned by the wave of hunger flowing through her and she responded with the same boldness he showed.

His hands explored her, until they returned to hold her head steady while his mouth twisted, slid on hers. With the same quickness it began, it ended. Cass broke the seal of their mouths and swayed backward as if staggered.

"My God, for a beginning..." Cass touched her lip once more and she was not sure if her mouth or his fingers trembled. "That was a flying start, wasn't it, Kate? I don't think I could stand it if you say 'thanks for a nice evening but don't bother to call.'"

Her blood was still roaring in her ears. Slowly she exhaled the air lodged painfully in her lungs. "You're right," she said quietly, getting off the couch. "That was special... and I won't say 'don't bother to call.'"

She wouldn't have guessed there was so much hidden fire in them both or that they could release it so easily with each other. Something else they shared, another secret link. Kate walked him to the door, grateful she hadn't said more, surprised she wasn't asking him to stay. He was special. He wasn't like any other man she'd met. When Cass left, she chained the door and rested her forehead on the hard, unyielding wood. She was almost afraid to sleep and dream of more.

THE NEXT MORNING Kate shuffled to the front door, raking her fingers through her hair. The combination of too little sleep and too many dreams was as bad as a hangover. Bleary-eyed, she checked the clock before she peeked cautiously through the crack in the door the security chain would allow. "Cass? Is that you? Oh, no...you look so..."

She closed the door, slipped the chain off and re-opened it, blinking and giggling. "So...so..."

The rest of her comments slipped away in helpless laughter as he swaggered in and tipped a high-crowned straw cowboy hat at her.

"Shucks, ma'am, I thought no one in these parts knew Lefty Yashima. Well, a fast-drawin', hard-ridin' man takes the eye and word spreads."

His drawl was nearly perfect. The yoked shirt, his jeans faded to a pearly blue, one thumb hung in a belt loop and his slouching stance all contributed to a convincing picture of a cowboy.

Kate shook her head, disbelieving. "They swept through here earlier, Marshal. You just missed them but they swore they'll burn my barn if I told you they went...that-a-way!" She leaned against the wall, crossing her arms tightly over her midriff to contain her laughter. "Lefty Yashima."

"C'mon, gal, and throw on a petticoat. Boots wouldn't hurt, neither. We'll saddle up and run them to earth." He did a neat bow-legged turn around the living room and pulled the drapes back, the blinds open.

"What is this?" asked Kate weakly. "I mean, be-sides Sunday and seven in the morning. Not Hallow-een, not a regular meeting for us Bronco Billie fans, is it?"

Cass grinned and pointed out her window. "We agreed we needed fun last night. Great idea, but a drive or a walk is pretty darned old hat, pardon the expression. Get dressed . . . no, give me a kiss and get dressed and let's ride, partner.''

"We said, if I recall, we weren't much for games.'' She crossed the room to stand next to him. Her face ached from a smile that wouldn't quit, not even when she realized what a kick he was getting from seeing her in a morning mess. "Okay, it might be Halloween. I look like the wicked witch, right?''

Maybe witches with wildly flowing tresses and fraying silk robes were in demand. Cass kissed her hard enough to wake her up completely. With her vision cleared, nerve endings alive, Kate caught a glimpse of the street below.

"Horses,'' she rasped. "There are two horses down there.''

"Shoot, honey, we can't cover any ground on goats, can we?''

"Horses,'' she repeated. "But I don't . . . I never, ever rode . . . Cass, there aren't any horses around here.''

There was a stable. If she ever rode a horse, she might have known about it, about the bridle path around One Oak Park. While she protested she didn't have the proper wardrobe, the slightest inclination or sufficient guts to ride, Cass pushed her toward her bedroom.

"Anything goes, as long as your butt's covered, as business types are fond of saying. You don't want sores.''

"I don't want a horse. Big damned things,'' wailed Kate in mock terror. "Big feet, big teeth.''

"That reminds me," Cass hollered through her door. "We'll hit Jolly Burger for breakfast. They've got a ride-up window."

Kate hopped out, bent over to tie her sneaker and howled at the vision of the two of them clip-clopping up to place an order. Her jeans were dirty, so she was stuck with a mauve-and-black jogging suit but Cass gave it the nod of approval. He wasn't as sure about her impulsive choice of headgear from a long-past costume party.

"It's in the spirit," she said of her hat as they went downstairs. Five neighborhood kids were gathered around the horses. They giggled when Kate's huge white plume flopped in her face and one of the horses shied away.

"Grab him," shrieked a child.

Cass clutched for the reins, tied loosely to a litter basket. Kate grabbed Cass's arm. "You ride these beasts?" she asked with trepidation.

It turned out he did. After Cass got her up on the horse—the sweet one, he explained—Kate did, too. She wasn't sure if it was more fun riding or seeing the expression on the girl's face when they collected the egg and cheese specialties down the road.

"Finish it while we're on the way to the park." Cass leaned over and kissed a smudge of grease and cheese on her cheek. "You're getting the hang of it, Puss-In-Boots. God, that hat!"

Her "umph-umph" reply was supposed to slow him down but he pretended not to understand the full-mouthed protest. Kate set off, gamely, still chewing.

"You wanted to be a jockey?" She stared at the spread of his shoulders under the red-and-blue plaid shirt and snickered. Her mare made a whiffling noise bobbing her head in agreement. "I could understand wanting to be a vet. All kids want to be a vet, I think. I understand wanting to be a cowboy. But a *jockey*!"

"I didn't know I was going to grow when I was twelve." Cass indicated the sun-dappled gravelled path and waited for Kate to ride next to him. "Morris, my dad,...they're short. You may have noticed. I was all hot to be a world-class jockey, but hitting six feet put a damper on my plans! Then, to make things worse, I was too short to make the basketball team...well, too short and not quite quick enough, truthfully."

Kate found the ride fun, the talk revealing. He was a natural competitor, driven to excel. It wasn't just money that Cass wanted, it was whatever glory and honor were available. She noticed a lot of similarities between them.

She had confided her ambition of being recognized as the foremost authority in her field. The fact that she was not Japanese was a definite disadvantage which she was determined to overcome. She was driven to excel and she wouldn't turn down glory and honor if they were given to her.

Nodding sagely, Kate heard all about his horses. She wasn't sure there was any difference between a three-year-old filly and a four-year-old except for a year, but Cass obviously knew the difference and loved to talk about them.

"But those are race horses, right? You don't ride them, do you?"

He pulled up and got off, stroking the neck of his brown gelding. "No," he said, "I don't do a whole heck of a lot of anything but push paper lately. But that might change.''

With a minimum of help, Kate climbed down to flop on the grass and rub her behind until circulation was restored. ''This is fun,'' she admitted as Cass settled himself next to her. ''I thought you were Fran at the door. She's supposed to drop over a box of slides today so I can run through a lecture I'm giving this week.''

He tickled her with a long blade of grass. ''Forget the museum. Let it go, Kate. Let's both concentrate on something else for a change. Us. What a great day it is. Anything but what we have to do, or should do.'' The blade of grass jabbed her under the chin.

''You could talk me into it,'' muttered Kate, searching frantically for her own plume to defend herself. She got in one swipe which set him sneezing before he pinned her down on One Oak Meadow.

''I did not,'' Cass said fiercely, ''have only verbal persuasion in mind.''

She liked his weight on her and the gleam in his eyes. *This is fun, too,* she thought right before he kissed her.

It was a magic day. The most ordinary conversation was made extraordinary because something good, something great was happening. When strangers walked by and smiled at them, Kate knew they had recognized the magic between her and Cass.

She had found Cass without looking for him, but she looked now, noting how many times she could finish a thought for him, anticipate a kiss before he leaned over to deliver it. And he watched her as if she were a rare-earth element newly discovered. He touched her with a scientist's awe, an explorer's daring and a lover's gentleness.

How does love happen? she thought dazedly, before the day was over. Not so soon, not so swiftly, her personal unwritten rule book would probably say, but she wasn't about to flip through and review the page.

If Cass was willing to move closer to an unknown land, an unmapped country in his heart, so was Kate. It was fun, it was a voyage long overdue for both of them and the risks seemed well worth it.

Kate reached over him and snatched the last piece of pepperoni pizza from the cardboard box.

"Mine," he moaned, poking disconsolately at the sausage and onion remainder.

"The race is to the swift," she mumbled, "and the sneaky." Plucking a thin pepperoni slice off and holding it aloft, she waggled it seductively at him. "I could be persuaded...if the terms are right."

The terms were right. His kiss was more persuasive than any she had known. The rest of the pizza grew cold during the negotiations.

"This is the best deal I've ever had," whispered Cass. "What's the bottom line and where do I sign?"

She laughed with difficulty, licked her greasy fingers and kissed away a tomato smudge on his chin. "As long as you're here, as long as I'm free, let's be together and see what happens. Whatever we're building doesn't seem to have any plans to follow, any production date to meet...."

"Or much of a market nowadays," he finished for her. "But it's nice to know it's still out there...."

"What?" she teased, thinking he wouldn't answer. They had discussed a million things today with a million more to go, but feelings were unspoken, growing silently inside, waiting to be shared.

Cass smiled, his eyes smiling, too. "Romance. The kind with flashing lights, sirens and bells and puffs of smoke...." His smile widened to a grin. "The kind with no interchangeable parts and no deposit or return...."

"Sounds good," Kate said softly. "What's the warranty like?"

"Oh, what a careful shopper," Cass exclaimed. "Leave that mess there and come back here. I'll read you the fine print.... For the life of the product."

CHAPTER FOUR

HE REGARDED THE TELEPHONE in his uncle's study as if it were a venomous black toad. It had to be done, but that didn't make it any easier. Predictably, the worst glitches in a computer program come when everything seems to be perfect, running smoothly. The real screw-up on contracts show up when everyone is whipping out pens to sign them. Cass sighed and reached for the receiver.

"You're leaving for Los Angeles?"

His aunt's voice was a welcome interruption. Any excuse to put off calling Kate was welcome.

"Can't be helped, Minnie. I can't go to Washington and sell them on something that doesn't work right."

"It's done all the time," Minnie Yashima said sarcastically. "And this was such a nice visit. You were like you used to be, fooling around..."

Fooling myself, he thought. A thirty-five-year-old man necking in the park, playing afternoon basketball, looking forward to a quiet, romantic evening. The image of Kate, in all her loveliness swam before his eyes. She hadn't minded leaving work early. She acted as if she were playing hooky, savoring the thrill of being naughty, somehow.

So, in effect, he had fooled Kate, too. The past couple of days—and nights—probably convinced her that this was the way it was going to be. Seeing each other, talking, holding, touching, reaching toward something really good. And it was good. They were getting so open and free while he could feel the man-woman tension between them grow, tightening down like a heavy metal coil being compressed inside. Soon, that force would have exploded like a spring but brought them closer, not driven them apart. He started to dial, not wanting to think about how that would have been—his hands learning every inch of her, his body joining with hers, giving them both the ultimate pleasure.

The phone rang and rang without her answering. He let it ring, knowing she was there, counting the hollow sounds. Nine, ten.

"Katie... I'm sorry I got you out of the shower." He heard the regret, the note of bitterness in his own voice. When he closed his eyes he could visualize her standing, damp and shivering, shifting from foot to foot. He could imagine the fragrance of her body. "About tonight... I can't make it."

It was unrealistic of him to think he ever could. Cass used his polite and distant tone but he was aching underneath. She sounded disappointed and asked when she would see him again. The real question was why would she want to? This was the pattern of his life, the blueprint he'd drawn up, and he must have forgotten to draw a door to let himself get out.

"No, it's very unlikely I could be back before you leave. This is about those electrodes implanted in paraplegics. The belt computer seems to be messing up sending signals to their legs.... If it had been a snag with video games..."

What? Would he throw away a huge deal on video games to taste her lasagna recipe and let her big orange cat watch them make love afterward? Maybe. Kate had taken him nearer to a feeling he was hungry for. This whole long weekend gave Cass a taste of freedom, a way to see himself through someone else's eyes.

"Yeah, I liked it, too. The next time Holman introduces you at one of the chicken and frozen peas dinners, ask him to mention your jump shot... Well, it wowed me, Dr. Cleary."

He laughed but the heaviness was back in his chest. The playful, relaxed feeling was ebbing fast. His thighs hurt and by tomorrow, he'd probably be stiff and sore and the archetype of the middle-aged businessman who acted like a kid.

"I can't."

His flat refusal to stop by, say goodbye in the flesh, came out harsh, strained. She was just too tempting. He'd reach for her and might not be able to stop, able to leave. If he ever made love to her, he didn't want it to be a hurried, clumsy afterthought, the finishing touch to a relationship.

For once, the effort to be cool was costing more than letting his feelings out. A mask of stony composure and an air of control worked better across a bargaining table than along a heart-to-heart phone line.

I don't want to hurt you, Kate—taking more than I give. I hurt already, wanting more than I can have. But he didn't say it.

"We'll see each other in Tokyo."

The muscles in his hand were tight when he hung up. His palm was damp and left a slick mark on the phone receiver. It wasn't over. Staring blankly at the bookcase, he let the little war rage inside himself for a few minutes. Absolute, unshakable confidence that he would manage to be with Kate again fought with the fear that he was courting disaster.

"WHAT A BEAR YOU ARE!" Fran dropped the last pile of letters in front of Kate for her signature and stepped back in case her boss wanted to throw things. "Tell me it's that time of the month or you've got the pre-travel jitters, but tell me something!"

"It's not. I don't," snapped Kate. She scrawled her name on the bottom of the papers without reading them. Raising her head, she caught the bewilderment on Fran's face and put the pen down on her desk. "Okay, I've been grumpy. Instead of the airport, I should lumber off to a warm cave and hibernate until spring."

She had been prone to uncharacteristic displays of temper over minor problems. Everyone walked cautiously around her but Fran. Bawling out a security guard and a new technician in Restorations was not her style and although she apologized later, Kate felt mildly guilty.

"Want to talk about it?"

"Not much to talk about," said Kate, signing yet another letter. "A minor depression moved in like a weather front. I went up to San Bernadino to see my parents before I left. My father issued all the standard warnings and my mother cried."

"There's more to it," said Fran sweetly.

Kate smiled in spite of herself. Fran's love for detective stories was getting out of hand.

"How about my having to reject a check for two thousand dollars from the Japanese American Citizens League? They scrape the money together because I'm going to be where the action is, and I have to say no because Arnold's rules forbid me to act on anyone's behalf but his. A bummer, Fran."

Her secretary's nose wrinkled as if she smelled something off. "A minor upset. That one was worth about five minutes of swearing. You traded off their gift for whatever Whelan-Dealin' lets you drag home and he's taking one point two million dollars to spread around."

Fran answered the flashing light on Kate's phone and informed her David was outside, raring to drive her to the airport. Kate's luggage was in the trunk; her cat was ensconced at Fran and David's apartment chasing Elmo in glee.

"We'll see each other in Tokyo," muttered Kate, gathering her things to leave.

"Of course we will. I'll call you the second I arrive—"

"I was quoting Cass Yashima." Kate made a face as they left. David greeted her with a wide and friendly grin. Kate just kept on talking. "I wish you could have heard his delivery. An invitation carved in ice."

"Ah! Eureka! Elementary, my dear Watson," chortled Fran Murata, a delighted Miss Marple. "The real reason for your less than sunny disposition emerges. *Cherchez* the man."

Kate settled for giving her a dirty look but no denial. She confided what a puzzling man she found Cass to be. All her jokes with Fran about finding two men, one who appealed to her mind, one who appealed to her physically, haunted her a bit. Cass was like two men, she complained.

"For the most part, he was wonderful. David, don't snicker! I mean it. He was tender and considerate, interesting, stimulating..."

Fran was closer to David than Kate. She did the honors and swatted him. "But what...? You found out he's an axe murderer?"

Kate took a thin, folded strip of paper out of her purse as she explained about Cass's quick and cool departure. "It was like talking to a different person. Almost brusque, a trifle icy. Then, when I was stewing about a brushoff—"

"And taking it out on your secretary," interjected Fran, looking over the paper. "Did he send you this poem? If that's what you call rejection...well, you're weird."

David groaned and grumbled about what deep trouble Fran would give him now. He asked if a fledgling doctor could get by with "roses are red, violets are blue" and a pizza of her choice. He also took a peek at the poem and demanded one of them translate the Japanese characters for him so he would, at least, have a chance to crib it.

"Cass didn't write this *haiku*," explained Kate. "It's famous. It's by Issa. And, yes, it's romantic but it's also a riddle. 'The same old village, here where I was born, every flower I touch—a hidden thorn.' Okay?"

"You," both of them said in a chorus. "He means you."

Kate made a low, menacing noise in her throat and put the paper away. "Brilliant. I knew *that*. But how? Why? I didn't wound him. I didn't hurt him. I . . . I'd better shut up."

She was glad to see the airport and sorry she'd mentioned anything about Cass. The only person who could interpret it completely wasn't there.

Neither was Arnold Whelan-Jones. Kate picked up her ticket at the JAL counter and checked through, looking in vain for him. She waved Fran and David away with last-minute instructions and hugs and listened to the flight being announced for the second time. She spotted him seconds later.

"There you are! Glad you could make it," mumbled Kate under her breath.

He hurried up, moving as if on wheels, and barked an order to one of the two men following him. "I never miss a connection or a good-looking woman," he said, grabbing Kate's arm and tugging her through the boarding area.

They were the last passengers on the jumbo jet. The steward was waiting to close the massive steel door. Arnold looked happy, sliding in ahead of Kate to grab the window seat, talking a mile a minute. The plane was beginning to roll out slowly and Whelan-Jones was already getting down to business, shoving a sheaf of stapled papers into her hands. Arnold was not interested in knowing how to bail out over water or how to use an oxygen mask; he was intent on his daily schedules for the next few weeks.

Kate scanned the first page. "You give new meaning to the phrase, 'getting his money's worth,' Arnold. We'll need roller skates to cover this much ground. I had plans to go to the bathroom once in a while, to sleep the usual eight hours—"

"Do I look like a sugar daddy?" he asked cheerfully. "I push myself hard and nobody who works for me slacks off. Clear? Only two women in my life have managed to get the better of me: my mother and my wife. They're both dead."

"Succinctly put," said Kate, thinking about how long the flight was. She unsnapped her seat belt when the light went off and asked the stewardess, formally and politely in Japanese, for aspirins to go with her drink.

"Sorry to interrupt you two," Cass said from behind them. He came into the narrow aisle and balanced there, watching Kate with obvious amusement. "Small world, Arnold."

"Shrinking every second," the older man complained. "And seeing you, my tired circulation picks right up. I assume I'll be bidding against you again. The timing of your trip isn't an accident."

"No accident," Cass replied with a grin. "Even choosing this particular flight was intentional. Kate, there's no one sitting next to me. Why don't you join me?"

"I'd love to," she said before Arnold could draw breath. She craned her neck to watch Cass return to his seat, feeling her oppressive mood evaporate. It was as if the day was just starting over.

Before she could get up, however, Arnold restrained her. His fingers wrapped around her wrist and his expression told Kate he was not amused.

"A few things we ought to get straight, first. You work for me, Kate. If you've got something going with

Wonder Boy, it better be off hours and strictly fun and games. You two can be Bill 'n Coo, for all I care, as long as it doesn't slow me down or cost me a cent.''

Whelan-Jones dropped her hand, opened an attaché case on his lap and didn't look up at her again. Kate understood she was being dismissed, the hired help taken to task. She would be wasting her time to make some caustic retort and it was unlikely anything she said would pierce that tanned, wrinkled hide, anyway. The man was a boor and a bully but this was his show.

"He's amazing," she whispered, dropping down next to Cass. "Is it natural to be so crude or do you think he has to practice?"

Cass laughed and didn't answer until he had kissed her. The light, moist reunion of their mouths dampened some of the fire of anger in Kate, and rekindled other sparks. Nine hours of sitting side by side with Cass, letting their legs touch now and then, their mouths meet and part casually, promised to leave her as limp as one of the hot, damp towels the stewardesses were passing out.

She took an *oshibori* and dabbed at her hands, temples and throat. "You must have done some fancy footwork to finish in Washington and take this flight. I'm flattered, I'm grateful . . . and I'm happy."

"I aim to please, ma'am," he drawled in his Lefty Yashima voice. His eyes told her he was happy, too, among other things. "I wish I could ride shotgun for you constantly but it's not possible. Are you going to be able to handle Arnold?"

"Handle him, yes. Stomach him, no," she chuckled. They heard Arnold's loud comment that he didn't want wet rags flapped at him; he wanted another drink and quick. The stewardess fled past them, a frozen and bleak smile on her face.

"Just don't underestimate him," cautioned Cass. "He's tough and he's smart, to give him his due."

Kate smiled, her confidence unshaken. She was raised as a military brat, used to biting the bullet and taking what came. She was intelligent and her lack of business smarts was offset, she felt, by her familiarity with the art world. Her growing suspicion was that Arnold needed her to help him present a better face, to lend him respectability and credence.

"I did my homework," she said. "AWJ's made two buying expeditions before and neither one was especially fruitful. He alienated people; being a mover and shaker is fine unless, like an earthquake, you're destructive. He's clever enough to hire me to ensure the desired results this time."

Cass nodded agreement and changed the topic. He didn't find Arnold as fascinating as the opportunity to pick up where they had left off. On the surface, they were talking about what they had been doing, how Cass had fared before the Veterans' Administration. But it was an act, Kate realized.

They sipped cocktails brought by a woman in a brocaded kimono and drank in the sight of each other. She put her hand on his arm, not to emphasize a point but to feel the reality of warm skin under a shirt sleeve. He put his fingers on the inside of her wrist, leaning toward her to see the cloud-shrouded Pacific Ocean below. It was clear he was savoring the pressure on her shoulder and breast more than the view.

"Not much space to maneuver in these flying box-cars," he said. "Or privacy. As big and crowded as Tokyo is, we'll be more comfortable there." He took Kate's tray down and rested his hand on her thigh. His fingers began to open and close slowly, bunching the material of her skirt together, making a whispery sound on her stockings. "Won't we?"

She could feel the little shock waves travel up and down her leg, reach into her lower back and settle intimately between her thighs. He was asking a very direct question and inspiring deliciously wicked answers, physical and verbal. She didn't feel like being shy or coy.

"I'm quite sure we will." She moistened her lips very deliberately, provocatively and shifted her legs so her skirt rode up another inch or two. If this was seduction, he should know it was a mutual decision.

He knew. He understood. His lips twitched, his eyes took on the gleam of polished ebony. A look as palpable as any caress passed between them and something was resolved without words. He made her feel incredibly sexy, capable of doing anything, anyplace, anywhere. Cass shifted his hips, straining against the metal buckle of the seat belt.

"I could get distinctly uncomfortable if we keep this up," Cass whispered. "I don't suppose you'd like to hear a few novel ideas I'm having about how to ease a sense of confinement, how to break a lot of airline rules and regulations?"

"Do they involve asking for blankets after dinner? Pretending we're both too exhausted to sit upright, rustling around?"

They were still laughing, huddled together in private conference, when the meal arrived. Kate ran her fingers appreciatively over the decorated lacquer box she was served, wondering why whetting one appetite had sharpened another. She was starving. But instead of the typical disappointing fare, she had been handed a treasure trove of delicacies. There were no soggy, reheated vegetables; she picked out fresh bamboo shoots, rosy jewels of crab and shrimp with her chopsticks. Even slivers of asparagus and tiny fancifully cut radishes were exotic, presented to tempt her.

"Wait until you see all the fast-food franchises on your way to the hotel," said Cass. "There are as many fried chicken and burger restaurants as sushi bars. Three years since you visited? Brace yourself for a shock."

Kate was more engrossed in her rice roll with toasted sesame seeds than a discussion of how Westernized Japan was becoming. It wasn't her point of view, no matter what she saw or would see. Modern skyscrapers sprang up next to market sidewalks and temples that held ground when Tokyo was Edo and the site of the shogun's castle. Superficially, change was sweeping and progressive; but she herself had never seen a sign that the essence of the country had shifted the width of a willow leaf.

"The only shock I'm preparing for is when Whelan-Jones bellows my name...like now," groaned Kate. Arnold wasn't content with hollering once and waving his disembodied hand to guide her in.

She excused herself, answered the string of technical questions Whelan-Jones shot at her and came back to Cass. The sun had set and outside the thick, small windows, the sky was a rich navy blue.

A few passengers flicked on the overhead lights but the cabin of the plane was growing darker, quieter. Arnold was going to work all night, she reported, and he wanted her on the aisle "on call" in case he hit a snag. The aisle seat beside Cass was sufficiently close, Kate had argued.

"Do you think this is a taste of what's to come?" She let Cass tuck a pillow behind her head and snuggled down under the white and red blanket. "He's doing a great petulant routine. I made tons of preliminary notes for him. What does he want me to do? Hold his hand? Be with him, under his thumb, every second?"

"He is a jealous god," intoned Cass solemnly, pulling her head down to his shoulder. He nuzzled her ear, stroked her under the cover in a way not conducive to rest. "I'm the jealous type, too, incidentally. If he plans to keep you stuck to him like a coat of paint..."

"He does. He does, Cass. There are ten pages of a regimen from dawn past dusk in my briefcase. Oh, please don't do that here...at the Princess Hotel, fine...even the back seat of a cab..."

"You're right! I'm getting crazy." He kissed her face over and over, brushing her eyelids and forehead, and made a little, low sound of discontent. "It doesn't matter. Where there's a will there's a way, and I'll find it. Because we will get together and be together whenever, wherever we can."

She muttered a sleepy, excited assent. There was a promise to dream on, nestled next to the man to dream about. All right, she should ask Cass why he was so distant before he left Riverside and why she was a "hidden thorn," but she wasn't going to. She wanted him. She wanted him too much to risk losing the comfort of his arm about her.

The dream only lasted until the plane swept in and circled the airport. She had time to repair her makeup and grab a few sips of coffee, trying to shake the groggy, cramped aftereffects of traveling. Whelan-Jones was determined to be the first one off and she found him waiting in the lounge when she and Cass filed out.

"Stop by for a drink," Arnold said to Cass. "I'm having a steady stream of get-togethers with buyers and dealers. You never know what gems of information you can mine, if you loosen these guys up with booze."

"Not before the end of the week," replied Cass. He had two days of an Expo outside of Tokyo and meetings upon meetings to follow. "I'm not going to make many of the sales. Kate and I have plans for the cherry-blossom festival." The pause he took was noticeable. "Of course, if you're interested, Arnold, you can come along."

"When I want to look at flowers, I'll buy a florist shop," Whelan-Jones advised him. "Come on, Cleary. I've got someone collecting our luggage. We're meeting him at customs."

Kate had to settle for a quick kiss goodbye and an empathetic look. There wasn't any slack in Arnold's schedule, any allowance for kicking back to enjoy or play. This was going to be a challenge. She squared her shoulders and plastered a smile on her face as she watched Cass disappear into the crush of the crowded terminal.

Whelan-Jones traveled in style. There was an eager, deferential man to whisk them through the customs lines and a black stretch limousine at the curb. Kate noted that she didn't rate an introduction, but from the two men, engrossed in talk, she picked up information on her own. When Arnold said he never missed a connection, he wasn't referring only to plains, trains, and buses.

"You stay on the case," ordered Arnold. "I know they're here and you know I want them. Call me any hour you get the word."

Kate, excluded from joining in, filed everything away for later and watched Tokyo unfold with ambivalent wonder. More and more, it resembled an endless, erratic and twisted maze.

The air was hazy with pollution and the predominant color of sky, streets and buildings was gray. At night, the gray was slashed with garish neon from some districts. She loved the quiet frenzy of Tokyo without being sure why. The sheer weight of all the people, glass, steel and concrete should have sent the city sliding into its lovely bay years ago.

The Princess Hotel, Arnold's choice, was not the newest or grandest of Tokyo's accommodations but it was a stunner to Kate. She wandered through the suite of rooms while the fresh-faced bellboys brought in her two soft-sider bags and the numberless suitcases Whelan-Jones deemed necessary. She confronted him as soon as they were alone.

"What was your thinking? Two can live as cheaply as one?" She pointed at her bedroom and bath, separated from Arnold's by a large, lovely sitting room. "It would have been cheaper and just as convenient to take standard rooms. I can sprint down the hall or into an elevator, if need be."

"You worried about me?" He smiled as if the idea pleased him very, very much. "I'm sixty-two and I've got a bad heart." He made a show of snapping the lock on her door and gave her a significant look through his aviator glasses.

"Arnold," she said, using his first name for the first time, "I think we'd better sit down and talk. Before we unpack. Before we start thumbing catalogs."

While she waited for him to respond, Kate eased off her shoes and spread the separated sheets of her schedule on the oiled slab of teak in front of her. She sank down on the fat, green silk cushions of a couch that would bankrupt her, and hoped she wouldn't snag it with her nails. She tucked her legs under her and wondered why a simple request, amiably made, slowed him down so abruptly.

"I don't care how things look; I care how things *are*," she said when he kept staring at her. "And certain things like this arrangement," she said waving her hand around, "and this," indicating the schedule, "and your cryptic conversation with Mr. Tanaka on the way here, look like they need explanation."

Arnold Whelan-Jones pushed away from the wall and began to wander toward her. Kate was pleased to see the smile of cutesy condescension was gone and a trace of admiration—not for her chest or legs, for a change—in his pale eyes.

"You are a clever girl, after all." He noticed her reaction to the word "girl" but didn't retract it.

"In other words, I worry you, not vice versa."

He sat down. "I trust no one but I respect you. You have a good, firm reputation. You just be useful to me and the more useful you are, the happier you'll be when our partnership is over. Questions?"

She glanced at the list of art dealers she was supposed to contact, beginning the following morning. Both of them were aware that there were stated times to view auction pieces and yet, Whelan-Jones wanted her to travel all over the city for private peeks, endless hours of verification and authentication.

"Sure, sure. A hundred people looking all at once in the gallery and you're liable to miss a flaw, a tear. I don't want inferior editions or a substitution on the block. I'm not saying I never made a mistake but every dealer on this list is above reproach. Not one of them would chance ruining a family name for a higher profit margin. If you suggested that possibility on your previous visits, you insulted them."

He dismissed her objection. "You handle it as delicately as you want to. That's why I brought you. You are going to hostess and grease the skids . . . but not at my expense . . ."

Kate interrupted him, following her own train of thought. "Unless, of course, you have a line on masterpieces outside of the regular dealers, the ordinary channels . . . Then, you'd have a lot to worry about, Arnold. Frauds, fakes, bad copies . . . but beautifully done. Legal ownership, legal exportation . . ."

Bingo! She saw his pupils react as if she'd shone a flashlight on them. He didn't utter a peep.

She cleared her throat. "Okay, you're going to keep a tight rein on me. You want to know what I say and to whom. But it might help if I knew what the forbidden topic is, wouldn't it?''

"When you need to know, you'll know."

"And you need to know this: if it's shady or dirty, forget it." She shocked herself but kept her voice as calm and matter-of-fact as Arnold looked. "My career's worth more to me..."

At least, he didn't have to think at length before he answered. Whelan-Jones just shook his head and leaned back with a Mona Lisa smile. "One hundred percent legitimate and legal, Dr. Cleary. There's no use going into this further now. The art in question hasn't been located yet. When it is, I'll make sure you're satisfied that it is... untainted. You will assure me that it's authentic."

Kate stood up and gathered the schedules, squaring the pages neatly. Three hours into this expedition and she was wishing for a cigarette, regretting she'd given them up a year ago. What else hadn't he told her? Why wasn't his high-priced consultant consulted?

"Well, there's food for thought," she said, starting for her room. "Both of us should keep in mind that when things seem too good to be true, they probably are. I don't want to regret my hasty eight-minute decision, Arnold. I hope I don't."

He took a cigar out of his breast pocket and nibbled at the end. "Relax. And don't get on your high horse and preach. This trip is going to be the best thing that ever happened... to us. You just have to look good, translate well and do exactly as I say. When it's over, you'll walk away healthy, wealthy and wise and you don't even have to thank me."

She closed the door, shutting out his face and shutting off his words. She had the distinct feeling that Mt. Fuji would be leveled to make a shopping center before she thanked him.

CHAPTER FIVE

KATE BRUSHED HER HAIR OUT with long, contemplative strokes. It soothed her, took her mind off the noise and laughter coming through the door from Arnold's domain. She could hear the rise and fall of voices, their words mostly indistinct, but the tone was jocular. Her attendance was not required; these were other buyers, not dealers. In fact, Whelan-Jones seemed happier that she stayed away from this particular crowd.

She loosened the tie of the putty-colored silk robe embroidered with red dragons and pushed some hair forward until it fell over one eye. Flaring her nostrils and narrowing her eyes, Kate tried on a come-hither look and laughed at her reflection in the mirror.

Not the Mata Hari type, she decided. After only two days, Arnold was reaching the same conclusion. He couldn't fault her on her dutiful approach to the dealers, the hours of tea and talk she had put in so far and her scrupulous report on every visit, every print. She just wasn't telling him what he wanted to know.

Arnold's bellow came through her bedroom door like thunder. "What was the quote on the winter-scape at Yamoto's, Kate?"

"Thirty-seven two," she bawled back.

That was his bottom line, the price per pound, she'd discovered. Her whole morning had been spent enacting a very exacting ritual with the senior Yamoto. They drank the palest green tea and discussed topics completely unrelated to the print in question. After they were both sure they were dealing with honorable and intelligent people, Yamoto brought out a handstitched envelope of mulberry paper. Kate slipped out the treasure and both of them looked at it in respectful silence.

Kate had been thrilled by the precise and awesome depiction of a scene painted over two hundred years ago. The print was a find, a delight—but not a rarity.

"Worth it, you said, but will he go lower?" Arnold demanded.

She didn't respond fast enough. The question was repeated with a smack of his fist on her door. "I don't think so," she yelled. What did Arnold care, anyway? He wasn't going to bid on it. Not the kind of investment value Arnold was looking for.

She almost missed the knock at her hall door in the swell of sound from the party. It wasn't the maid. Reiko scratched at doors, a throwback from the times when doors and walls were paper *fusuma* and a knock tore fragile dividers.

"Who is it?"

"A not-so-secret admirer," called Cass.

Laughing, her hair flying, Kate ran to open the door and beckon him in. Maybe because he wasn't expected or because her last two days were so crazy, she was suddenly giddy. But she didn't think so. It was him. Definitely him.

"Oh, this is great...wanted to see you," Kate gasped, fitting the words to an equal number of quick kisses. She hugged Cass hard, then, harder to tell him how good and solid he felt.

"A wild woman," Cass murmured, trying to pull away to look at her. "And, God, beautiful...beautiful."

"Kiss me," she whispered before she lost the wildness.

He wove his fingers through the soft web of her hair and held her face steady in the gentle vise of his hands. His mouth fell on hers with the firmness and quickness of her demand. She felt a jolt of electricity run through her, waking up her whole body, and dimly heard glass breaking next door.

Her arms tightened around him as if she was afraid he would stop. Her hands moved up and over the broad sweep of his back, kneading the muscles hidden under his suit. A tiny bubble of excitement broke free inside her and rose into her throat, escaping with the soft hum of a cat's purr.

She could taste him, citrus and smoke, a salty, rich flavor she kept remembering, thinking about. Cass laughed against her open, hungry mouth and his hands released her head, only to follow the lengths of her hair to her shoulders, to grip her hard and pull her closer.

"Two days, too long," he said raggedly.

Their bodies met and momentarily parted, sought each other and fused together. Kate lost count of the kisses, some weightless and sweet, others deep and endless. Just the heat rising from their welded bodies made her head swim and her legs get heavy.

She hadn't the least doubt or hesitation about loving him. It seemed as if the thought was there from the first night she saw him. Maybe it was.

"Expo over?" She nibbled his throat and liked the taste of him. "Do you have tonight off? I have a reprieve..."

"Don't I wish," Cass said too loudly and she had to put her fingers to his mouth.

She replaced them with her lips, whispering against his. "If Arnold hears you, he'll be hammering and bawling to know who's here."

His hands stroked a path down her back, slipping on the silk. He stopped at the arch of her spine and pressed her hips against him. "A few hours and I have to meet with someone flying in from Berlin. Do you want to get out of here? Even for a few hours?"

"Yes," murmured Kate. He kissed her again and moved against her, a tantalizing promise. "No."

"Yes, you want to leave?" Cass's hand found its way to her breast, teased at the hard peak he discovered. "Or no, you want to stay and whisper?"

She was trying to keep the laughter, the desire, the excitement under control and failing miserably. His teeth nicked the fleshy lobe of her ear. Just then, Arnold's voice boomed through the door.

"Kate, the Utamaro is going on sale Friday, isn't it?"

"Yes," she yelled back.

Arnold's strident query made her decision for her. The soft, almost sleepy invitation in her eyes vanished.

Cass concurred. "Let's get the hell out of here," he said in a raspy voice—but softly. "Put anything on. It doesn't matter."

She grabbed a pair of jeans and a sweatshirt embla-zoned with CAL TECH, sneakers without socks, and threw it all on in the bathroom. She left her hair down, jabbing in two tortoise shell combs to hold it back, and did without makeup by avoiding the temptation of peeking into the mirror on their way out.

"You won't believe what's been happening," she said, racing toward the elevators.

"I'll believe it," Cass promised. "Try me!"

On the way down, she gave him a capsulated ver-sion of the last two days. Arnold was throwing money around like mad, entertaining in the most lavish fash-ion imaginable. Generally, his philanthropy only ex-tended to dealers but tonight, he was wining and dining four buyers.

"LeClerc from France, Watanabe, Otari and an Englishman. I didn't catch his name." She ticked each one off on her fingers. "I wasn't commanded to play *geisha* tonight because Arnold's been keeping me off buyers, on dealers. You see, I mustn't let something slip, inadvertently."

"Like what? Nuclear secrets?"

The elevator doors glided open onto the Princess lobby. She wasn't going to talk with strangers around, Kate said, turning up the collar of an imaginary trench coat and skulking through the room. Cass laughed at her antics. "We'll go down into Shinjuku," he said, hailing a cab outside. "With all the foreigners and the tacky bars, you'll fit right in."

Kate grinned and bobbed her head like an idiot. The Shinjuku district was fine with her. About half the area was crammed full of cheap restaurants and little bars devoted to nocturnal prowlers.

"Let's hope we don't run into AWJ and guests," she said, climbing into the back seat of a cab. "I drew him a map this morning and had the man at the front desk write out the location of the raunchiest strip show. When the booze runs out upstairs, he had plans to... rough it with the boys, let's say."

"Don't get paranoid," Cass warned, putting his arm around her. "With over twelve million people around, he won't spot you. And he wouldn't recognize you if he did. Now, tell me what's cooking."

"That reminds me. I want to eat," she said nibbling happily at his chin. "Tell the driver to stop the second he sees one of those *oden* and *sopa* carts on the street."

"Kate, I can afford to buy you something fancier than noodles and stew if you're hungry," Cass chuckled. "Unless that's what you want."

She nodded vigorously. During the days, she'd had no time for lunch. The past two nights Arnold had laid out banquets, and Kate was sick of the bloated, piggy feeling she went to bed with after stuffing herself.

"Here's the scoop," whispered Kate. "Arnold is hunting big game, quarry unknown. Until he's ready to tell me, I'm not supposed to know what he's after. I'm just supposed to meet with the dealers and keep my ear to the ground, reporting any strange noises. However, he's in a real sweat about it."

"You don't have to whisper," said Cass. "The driver doesn't speak English."

She giggled and assumed her normal voice. "Force of habit. I swear, Arnold is getting to me. I think he listens in on the phone when I call someone. He knew how many times I talked to you yesterday and the day before."

Cass didn't look amused. He drew his dark eyebrows closer together and made a menacing noise. "I told you he was wacky. Run this by me slowly, Kate."

"Bribe me." She shrieked at the driver to stop and gestured at a vendor on the side street. While Cass paid the cabbie, Kate was already out and chatting with the noodle seller, ordering two bowls. "I lived on this stuff when I was a student," she told Cass when he wandered over. "I thought I was going to turn into a long noodle and a pickled radish."

They ate as they walked to take in the street scene. The cheapest entertainment in Tokyo was a stroll at night, watching the crowds of people out escaping the tiny apartments they lived in. Kate eyed the fashions, expensive and original creations, worn by a group of younger women—secretaries, probably—and complimented them.

Tokyo hadn't changed. The residents were still willing to spend most of their salaries on the newest fashions.

"I'm going back there and ask her what she paid for that Kenzo," grumbled Kate, looking over her shoulders.

"No, you're not," Cass said, dragging her forward. "Eat your noodles and you won't have to worry about fitting into it. Now, tell me about the rest of your mission."

She shrugged and waved a mustard pickle seductively under his nose. "Not much more to tell...from Whelan-Jones's point of view. The man must think I'm a dolt. He's confident he can keep the lid on me. But what if I tell someone else? You, for instance, or another buyer. What if I don't tell him what I find out?"

Cass stopped walking in front of a group of teenagers breakdancing to a radio that was sitting on the sidewalk. One of the boys had shaved his head on the sides and dyed the remaining strip a violent pink. "Kate," he said solemnly, "You *do* know what he's looking for, don't you?"

"I think so." She licked broth from her fingers and threw the empty plastic bowl into a wastecan. Her feet began to shuffle in time to the music blaring over the street. "I'm not as much a Sherlock Holmes as Fran is, but it doesn't take a genius to put two and two together."

It had to be graphic art Arnold was after or why would he need her? She knew bronzes and ceramics, but her specialty was woodblock prints. It couldn't be modern; there wasn't enough monetary value to interest Arnold. It had to be something spectacular, something old.

"...something new, something borrowed, something blue," chanted Kate as she clapped for the dancers.

"Okay, I give up," admitted Cass. He led her quickly past a cabaret blazing with blue and pink and green neon nudes and advertising Live Sex, Real Sex in flashing Japanese characters.

"Who would pay to see dead and fake sex?" snickered Kate. "I hope that's where the deskman sent Arnold. He'll have a coronary and this madness will be over."

"Are you through?" Cass sounded exasperated but he hugged her to his side and gave her a hasty kiss. The Japanese weren't thrilled with public shows of affection. "I want to hear it all. Tell everything; leave nothing out. What's Arnold up to?"

She put her mouth up to his ear and breathed the two syllables. *"Tan-e."*

The desired result was obtained. Cass stiffened and almost stumbled before he caught himself. The initial amazement in his eyes disappeared, replaced by disbelief. "You're kidding. Those rumors have been floating around for years. *Tan-e* are like the seven lost cities of gold, Katie. A rumor, a legend. The prints that are still around are all in museums. *All.*"

She made a noncommittal gesture with her hands. In her whole education and career, she had seen three of the oldest, rarest examples of woodblock print, and those had been in museums. Scattered across the world, there might be seven or eight other pieces of the heavy, handmade paper, all owned and accounted for. There was no color, just the black outlines of a scene over three hundred years old. The paper was destructible, flammable.

It was hard to imagine how *tan-e* would survive three centuries of war and flood and insects and the carelessness of men. But every few years, someone brought up the subject and thought he was going to buy one, an undiscovered jewel that no one else knew about.

"He must believe he's got a pretty good line to a priceless relic of some sort," argued Kate. "Arnold doesn't strike me as the fanciful kind and he isn't notably free with finances, usually. He's got a man, Tanaka, working on it and he's oiling the dealers."

"And what about your deal with him?" asked Cass. "If Whelan-Jones bought one—if there is one—at auction, you would say that the *tan-e*, naturally, was your choice for the Cutler."

"Of course, but it would never come out at a public sale. He would make a private arrangement—without me—or it would be offered at one of those very hush-hush back-room sales where the seller has to select qualified buyers."

Cass took a peek at his watch and grimaced. A few hours wasn't very long. "I think you're on the right track, but it's probably going to end up being a stolen scroll or a pilfered painting. Let me find us some sake and when we're good and drunk, I'll tell you what I've been thinking about for the last two days."

"Does it have anything to do with microchips?" She smiled at the hideous leer he gave her. "No, I guess not."

They hurried past a few coffeehouses, a restaurant with plastic replicas of its menu in the window, and went into the first bar. It was a random choice but a lucky one. There were few tourists and the hostesses were older, more demurely clad women. The strong smelling curtain of smoke hung over the bar where tired executives were conferring. One of the small booths offered an illusion of privacy.

Cass sat next to her, not across from her. Kate leaned on him, put her head on his shoulder, and inhaled the clean, masculine scent he wore. A million young couples all over Tokyo were enacting the same scene, seeking out the relative seclusion of a public bar to be together without their swarms of relatives at home to see them.

The waitress who took the order for rice wine kept her eyelids lowered discreetly.

"We fit right in," Cass said, twisting a strand of Kate's black hair around his fingers. "She thinks we're courting. That's nice. I never did much courting before."

"I'll bet you didn't," murmured Kate. "What did you do? Crook your finger and wiggle it and they fell into bed?"

"Boy, women always think men have it so easy, prowling fences like tomcats..." He brushed her mouth with his, rubbing his lips lightly across its fullness, teasing the corners. When he moved back, his eyes were serious and Kate felt her heart drumming faster.

In that moment, she knew they were playing a game and yet, not playing. He was serious about her. They were both flirting with something more than infatuation. And it was new to both of them.

"I've liked some women and I've liked sleeping with them," he said flatly. "But I haven't gotten really involved with anyone recently. One-night stands aren't terrifically appealing to me but neither have long-term commitments been..."

"Marriage?" inserted Kate. "It's out?"

He nodded. "Yes. I'm not interested in marrying a very docile, passive woman like my father did and leaving her alone to raise five children while he put in sixteen hours a day. We saw him on Sundays, on holidays. We loved him but he was remote.''

"But you do work those hours," commented Kate. "You hitched your father's work ethic to the Sunco dream and you're a star."

He poured them each another cup of steaming rice wine and held the fragile piece of porcelain up for her to sip from. "And realistically, I don't expect to find anyone willing to play second fiddle to Sunco, who appeals to me. Like you."

"I can't even play the harmonica," whispered Kate, but a heaviness gathered inside her. Cass was right. Wittingly or unwittingly, work was the priority for both of them and old habits were hard to change. "I haven't found a man who hummed along with me for more than a few bars, either. I was engaged once in graduate school, I dated some of the American officers on the base...nothing worked out for the long haul."

His fingertips traced her features, the slow, sensual touch she had learned to love and expect from him. "There are people, you know, who aren't cut out to stay through a whole song. Maybe we're two of them. You want kids? Marriage?"

Could she shock him? Or would the truth bother Cass at all? Kate had searched her soul thoroughly on both matters. While she hadn't resolved either completely, she did have some very definite ideas. The only person she trusted enough to discuss them with was Fran. But, she had dropped a few hints with Eileen Cleary in mother-daughter talks, in case the subjects became more than theoretical.

Another sip of sake fortified her. She met his eyes squarely. "I want kids—or, at least, one child. Approaching thirty makes the ticking of my biological clock uncomfortably loud, sometimes. I don't want to sound like a flake, but I have considered the possibility of ending up a single mother."

"Marriage?" he asked without looking away.

"Not necessarily," Kate said very slowly but distinctly. "I've seen most of my friends marry...and most of them fail at it. I'm not desperate to marry or fail. I'm used to winning, to getting what I want, and I'm used to waiting, if that's what it takes."

"Which makes you an independent, modern female," added Cass. "I'd like to know how you control the incurable romantic streak inside. I can't. I want everything, the new and the old."

If he hadn't chosen that second to kiss Kate, she might have told Cass. Up to now, it was easy. There hadn't been many men who made marriage look attractive to her. A brief engagement had made her wary. Despite a good intellectual and physical rapport, her fiancé made it plain in the end that he was taking charge of major decisions. Kate was expected to exercise her right to agree. The "loving" Kate mourned; the "ambitious" Kate rebelled.

"Tomorrow?" Cass kept his mouth close to hers. "Our German guest will be leaving. My apartment will be mine once more." Sunco kept a time-share condominium for Cass and other visiting businessmen in his own headquarters.

"I don't know. The first auction is tomorrow evening. Arnold will bid on three or four pieces, at the most, but one of them is that famous Sharaku. If we finish early, if I can slip away before he organizes a victory party..."

"If...if...if," he parroted with a trace of annoyance. "I hate 'if.'" He tilted her head back and drank in the sweet wonder of her mouth, the sadness in leaf-green eyes. His voice became contrite. "I'll figure out something."

He was more pragmatic than poetic, but looking at Kate inspired Cass. She was the spring; the color of new leaves unfolding to be warmed and fed by the sun. Arnold had to be winter; blustery and cold, creeping in to chill the marrow. And spring was tied to winter in the natural cycle.

"I'd like to be your summer," he said and grinned sheepishly.

"What?"

"Never mind," he laughed. "I'll tell you some other time. We've got to get going. Can I put you in a cab? I'm heading in the other direction."

She nodded yes but chewed at her bottom lip. That's what she was afraid of: he was, sooner or later, striking out in a different direction. Whatever this relationship was, it was also temporary. She must not close her eyes in passion and forget that when she opened them, Cass would be gone.

REIKO'S SCRATCHING WOKE HER the next morning. Kate rolled over and sleepily called her in. The door was unlocked, of course. There wasn't any need to lock a hotel door in Japan; the national obsession with honesty and appearance made the country one of the safest, most hospitable nations in the world. Reiko would stand outside until she was asked to enter.

When Kate wasn't completely dressed and combed and presentable, Reiko pretended she didn't see her.

Too bad Arnold didn't understand. The door connecting their rooms had to be bolted or he would sashay in, unannounced, at any moment to ask her something while she was on the phone or in the bathroom.

"Good morning," Reiko said in her precise English. "For you, please." She glided in with a gift balanced carefully in both hands and smiled at the windows, not at unkempt, invisible Kate.

There was a low black table tucked beneath the sill. Reiko took the most minuscule steps to avoid spilling a drop of water from the flower arrangement. She placed it, after a pause for thought, to one side. Asymmetrically perfect. She bowed to the gift, still avoiding Kate's presence, and turned to leave.

"Reiko, who is it from?" Kate pushed herself up on her elbows to see the gift.

"Sorry, Cleary-san. No card." The maid tipped her head to one side and evidently decided she could skirt etiquette the tiniest bit. "Perhaps your husband?"

"I'm not married, Reiko," replied Kate, beginning to smile. *She's so cute, so subtle,* Kate thought.

The maid lifted her hand in front of her mouth and giggled softly. "I am a silly girl." She bowed toward the closet and left hurriedly.

The tiny, insignificant exchange made Kate rise in a good mood. What if she didn't have an inkling of what a marvelous, ordinary scene like that meant? Reiko wanted to know personal data about Kate. It was extremely bad manners to ask directly whether she was married or divorced, had children, or a million other details. The most acceptable route had been chosen: Reiko deprecated her foolish guess, elicited what she wanted to know, and hadn't run the risk of offending Kate. Her behavior was not devious, as Westerners so often characterized their confusion dealing with Orientals. It was the exact formula to keep too many people in too little space from infringing on each other, in any form.

Well, the morning might not be perfect. Arnold rattled her cage with a loud, lengthy interrogation she largely ignored. Kate was preoccupied with the flower.

There wasn't any need for a card. She had no doubt who the sender was after she studied it. The roughly hewn stone bowl stood about four inches tall, a dull gray volcanic object. It was hard to decide if someone had formed a rock into a bowl or if it was a natural shape, eroded into a well by nature. Inside, floated one pure white camellia. The flower hung suspended, its soft petals barely rubbing the pitted rim surrounding it.

A single flower protected by a rather coarse, ugly vessel.

Kate touched the bowl and then the waxy fringe of a petal, to enjoy the contrasting texture. Before she pulled her finger back, a tremor of warmth, pure joy, surged through her. She was the flower, he was the stone—they were together.

She didn't have to hear Cass say the words. The message was exciting and sexual. *This is how I see us. I want you.*

"I have to make a call," she insisted, "before I leave, Arnold. Why don't you just go...ahead?" She could have filled in her pause with much more colorful suggestions but she was in a particularly amiable mood.

Fran should have arrived last night. Kate dialed the Muratas's number, unable to look at anything but the camellia. Hearing Fran's voice was another lift.

"You sound tired. Didn't you sleep on the plane?" Kate asked after the preliminary squealing was over.

"Well, yes," Fran said, dragging out the syllables. "But I stayed up most of last night talking to my grandparents. I guess we're a bit awkward and uncomfortable with each other still. Maybe after a few days..."

"Fran," Kate said too sharply, "is there something bothering you? Besides missing David, I mean."

Fran's laughter was obviously forced. "No, don't be goofy. My grandparents' place is very small and we keep bumping into each other. I'm serious! The mice have to work in shifts, Kate. We'll adjust pretty soon."

"Good. How about meeting me for lunch...no, not today. Yeah, at Wako, the department store. There's a gorgeous shopping mall to spend your whole year's salary at and..."

They sorted out the details and Kate hung up, relieved. Having another friendly face around was very important, for some unknown reason. Kate tapped the phone with her fingernail and went to look one more time at her present. Funny, but she suddenly realized she was thinking of Fran and Cass as much more than friends. *Allies.*

There was no war going on and she wanted allies.

YOUNG GIRLS CIRCULATED through the small crowd, offering hot tea and cold drinks. Kate fanned herself with their bid number and surveyed the room once more. Cass wasn't there yet. She nodded to Jean Michel LeClerc, whose face split in an affable grin. They weren't bidding on this item; he was.

"Twelve. Twelve thousand."

Those people with earphones listened to the immediate translation into yen, dollars, Swiss francs, marks and pounds. Kate had to listen to Arnold.

"I don't give a damn if he asks you to the prom. You watch out for overly friendly people when you're in the big leagues. Like Yashima, and that grinning moron, LeClerc...they want something, Kate, for free."

"If you don't let up," she said sweetly, "I'll buy this hideous print, so help me."

He twisted in his gilt chair to glare at her. "I'd have to pay for it but you'd have to take it. The Cutler wouldn't be much improved. Peckish, aren't we?"

She laughed. "I can't speak for you. I'm not. I didn't throw an outrageous amount away to see a bunch of female impersonators dance in ribbons and feathers and get a colossal hangover. You did."

He jabbed his finger at her open catalog to distract her. "The Sharaku is next. You'd kill for it."

"Only if I get to choose the victim," she whispered dryly.

Whelan-Jones nudged her hard in the ribs. Kate thought perhaps her banter had gone too far, but when she lifted her head and followed Arnold's gaze, she saw Cass. His tall, unmistakable figure was moving slowly through the ballroom, weaving through the red velvet ropes and high-backed chairs, and he was smiling directly at her.

"For God's sake," hissed Arnold, "are you bidding on this Sharaku or not? Don't worry about Wonder Boy. He has this print."

She forced herself to look from Cass back to the print. Once again, she was amazed at the resemblance. She wanted the man; she wanted this great woodblock. Desire so strong made it vital to slip back into the controlled frenzy of the sales and to concentrate totally on the chant of the auctioneer. The print was going to be hers—not Arnold's, but hers.

The Cutler's, Kate amended mentally. She was bidding on it to win for the Cutler. The Board would applaud her choice, Holman would praise her and the collection would be infinitely richer. *And I'll have Cass's fierce, wonderful face with me every day.*

"Seventeen fifty."

The bid was to LeClerc. There were three other men still in, as well. Kate signaled the next raise with her card but in seconds, the price was over twenty thousand with no sign it was going to slack off. She rubbed her sweaty palm on the catalog as if she could erase the figure Whelan-Jones had penciled in there. There was a limit agreed on before each item came up; Arnold didn't revise his figures in the heat of battle.

Holding his figure firmly in mind, she nodded at the auctioneer.

"Thirty, we have thirty." A collective sigh came from the crowd. A high price meant high suspense and buyers rooted for other buyers, although they never admitted it.

"Thirty-seven five."

The fixed set of Arnold's jaw and the beads of perspiration on his brow meant he wanted this work as badly as she did. If they reached their limit, would he edge it up? Only she and LeClerc and a local buyer were still in. The bidding was too rich for the others.

"Forty-two." The man at the podium gave Kate the curt nod of acknowledgment. He repeated the figure and she thought it was over.

"Forty-four."

Kate shifted uneasily and touched Arnold's sleeve. She made a mute plea. Another two thousand might take it. No one else was left.

Whelan-Jones was slow to respond, drawing her hopes out to the very last second. He stared at her as if she were insane. A limit was a limit. He shook his head. No bid.

"Forty-four. Jean Michel LeClerc. Thank you."

Arnold had the nerve to put his hand on hers and pat it. "Easy, Dr. Cleary. We can't really expect to win every single one, can we? I didn't think the Frenchman had a bankroll." His other hand slid across her back and she stiffened.

She took a long, deep breath and let it out very slowly. They had purchased three other fine works. She must not take this loss personally. "I'm fine, Arnold. I'll go freshen up, if you don't mind. We aren't bidding anything else tonight."

"There's a party—" he began.

"I know," she interrupted agreeably. Her sweater was on the back of her chair and she left it there. She even left her purse.

Arnold Whelan-Jones beamed at her like a proud father. "You're taking this very well. Tonight, a couple of drinks, a couple of laughs . . ."

He had to shout the last few words because Kate was backing stealthily away from him. She turned and trotted toward Cass, catching his arm as she passed. They moved off without glancing back to see if Arnold had caught on. With luck, the sweater and purse as tokens of her return might hold him through most of the rest of the auction.

"Where to? Or don't you care?" asked Cass, seeing the expression on her face.

"Walk faster," was all Kate said.

CHAPTER SIX

THEIR GETAWAY WASN'T AS SMOOTH as they'd hoped. Outside the Hilton, site of the auction, a light rain had reduced the usual number of cabs on the street. Kate filled her lungs with the cooler, fresher air and rubbed the tense nape of her neck. The mist was beautiful and refreshing. It also ensured that the cherry blossoms would be spectacular when they opened, but her mood wouldn't let her enjoy the prospect.

"I feel wretched," she complained. "Frustrated, down in the dumps. I shouldn't inflict myself on you. I want to pick a fight with someone or throw something."

"You look lovely," Cass observed. "How about a heartfelt scream or a good cry?"

The creamy color of her simply-cut dress emphasized the translucent quality of her complexion. A few drops of windblown rain glittered in her hair under the lights of the hotel's awning. She was a living camellia. Only her eyes, like a green sea in turmoil, gave away the storminess inside.

"I hardly ever cry," Kate said. "When I get miserable and unhappy, it swells up inside me until my head is ready to explode. No tears, usually. I have my father to thank for that. My mother cries over everything: soap operas, a supermarket opening, greeting cards."

The doorman waved them into a hard-won taxi. Cass ignored the driver who turned expectantly for his instructions. Kate had sunk deep into the upholstery and was massaging her temples to stave off a headache.

"If I take you back to the Princess, what happens?" he asked her.

"Oh, Arnold will start calling the room every ten minutes. He'll make up some ridiculous story and get the hall concierge or Reiko, the maid, to ferret me out. When I realize it's less trouble to go to the victory celebration than not, he'll be as close to gracious as he gets. I'm beginning to understand how he got where he is. Wear them out, wear them down, and strike when they're weak."

Cass laughed at the accuracy of her insight and gave the driver elaborate directions. Given the haphazard numbering and naming of Tokyo streets, directions were a necessity. Everyone, native and visitor alike, had to be able to draw the proverbial picture of where he was heading to get there. Kate didn't recognize the address and asked what the destination was, not particularly caring.

"The Sunco building," Cass said. "You haven't seen the company's apartment and it might not occur immediately to Arnold that I kidnapped you. That's what I want to do—hide you, keep you all to myself...." He wiped away a trace of moisture from her cheek. It was rain, not a tear.

Kate said nothing, watching the colors from streetlights and signs dance in the puddles. At best, this was another stolen moment, a tiny time to rest from the hurry of their lives. They might have a few hours but Cass would be gone in the morning, flying in Sunco's Lear to Kyoto. She had another week, maybe two, before Arnold Whelan-Jones was a memory.

"What do you want, Kate?" he asked softly. He put his mouth against her hair. "Whatever it is, if I can, I'll give it to you. You know that, don't you?"

Yes, she did. The knowledge was lodged not in her brain but within her heart. Neither of them had said, "Look, we're falling in love," but they both knew it. She couldn't explain why she knew, or why she trusted such an ephemeral feeling, but she did. And she trusted Cass, although Arnold did not. Maybe *because* Whelan-Jones didn't?

"I want everything," Kate said with a wan smile. "I want too much." His arms settled around her, a circle of warmth and strength, and she put her ear to his chest to hear the steady beat of his heart. With the reality of his pulse thundering in her head, she could say even more. "I want you."

He was silent but her words made his heart go faster. His hand closed around her shoulder and followed the curve of her arm down to her hand. A line of sparks should have followed in the wake of that motion; she felt them. When Kate raised her chin slightly for a kiss, she tasted a very different sweetness, a darker wine of passion, more potent and filling.

Cass was thirsty, too. He drank her in, sipped at the open, hungry mouth she offered in deeper and deeper draughts.

"Are you sure?" he moaned, even as his hands on her body worked to remove any doubt and any thought.

The cab stopped before she could give him any answer other than the one she already had. And there was no need on the ride up to his apartment to fill the space between them with talk. A curtain of tension and excitement was all around them, everything else was hazy.

It was dark in the apartment but Cass didn't switch on any lights. There was enough light from the panoramic view to see. The glow of Tokyo crept through the thinly curtained windows and surrounded them. Kate stood there, holding back the fabric a little to look outside before she turned.

Cass reached for her, held her. But his embrace was not the overwhelming kind; it was loose and tender. "I'm afraid I'm going to burst into flames," he said, half-teasing, half-apologetic.

"Would that be so awful?" asked Kate.

He put his forehead next to hers. "Yes, it would be," he said seriously. "I told you once—it seems like a long time ago now—I didn't have quick lovemaking and an easy affair in mind. I don't want it to be over before I really make you happy. Why don't we both relax and let whatever happens . . . just happen."

She was keyed up, strung as tight and fine as wire. She was almost angry that he was right and had such control over himself. But all her jumpiness and trembling was not desire alone. The auction and her loss had left her badly shaken.

"If you have basketball or gin rummy in mind, forget it," she said and laughed weakly.

"What I have in mind is criminal," he said. "Why don't you go in there and take a hot shower, wash all that pentup frustration down the drain? There are clean *yukatas* behind the door. And then..."

There was a pause while he kissed her, leaving no doubt his intentions were anything but honorable.

"Go on," said Kate thickly when he had to break for breath.

"With the kiss?"

"And then..." she prompted.

Another kiss and her knees threatened to buckle. "And then, you can stretch out on my bed, thinking beautiful thoughts. Which means, you have to stop plotting ingenious ways to kill Arnold. I would hate for you to confuse me with him and knock me off, purely by accident, of course."

"Can I bite you? A little?" She nuzzled his throat but didn't carry out her threat.

He groaned quietly, a very deep and sexy sound, and held her so tightly for a minute, she couldn't breathe at all. "God, don't push your luck, Kate. You start a fire in me very, very easily. I'd like to put it out very, very slowly...so please don't make me crazy. Not yet."

Playing with fire had never sounded as appealing before. She moved seductively against him to be tormentor as well as prisoner in his embrace. His body began to signal her success.

"What do you plan to do while I'm relaxing? Chill the wine, fluff pillows?"

"Crochet a doily," he growled. "Go on, Kate, before I give you carpet burns."

"You brute! You beast!" Laughingly she went where he had pointed.

From time to time, while the shower beat down on her and the cloud of steam rose, she had to lean on the tile wall and laugh. There were new rules or twists she didn't know to this thrilling game they were playing. There were, obviously, risks and obstacles but she didn't see how either of them could lose.

The heat of the shower melted the evening's disappointment away and colored her a vivid pink. Somewhere between a shrimp and a newborn, she thought, looking at herself in the huge expanse of mirror before it fogged up. She took down her hair and it clung to her like black seaweed while she rubbed herself dry. Cass's suggestion worked. She had a clearer head and a cleaner spirit as she slipped one of his blue-and-white cotton kimonos on. A pleasant, appreciative awareness of her own body added to her well-being. And thoughts of Arnold or tomorrow seemed the furthest thing from her mind.

His bedroom was cooler, darker. Kate shivered and held the thin robe closed with one hand, looking around. She heard Cass talking in the next room and realized he must be on the phone. Arnold? Who cared?

She padded silently across thick, dark-blue carpet and stretched out on the huge, low bed, lying on her stomach and pillowing her head on her hands. No more thinking tonight. No more worry about vaguely strange feelings. Something about tonight's bidding and the Sharaku nagged at her, but she closed her eyes and listened to the slow, calm beat of her heart until the feeling went away.

The Buddhists claimed, "Let your mind know nothing and you will experience everything." She slipped her arms out of the voluminous sleeves and eased back down, turning her head so she could see the dim shimmer of the city through the window.

"Feel better?"

The low sound of his inquiry caught her drifting between sleep and wakefulness. It might have been five minutes or five hours since she lay down. Kate wasn't sure.

"Much improved, thanks." She started to raise her head and Cass told her to stay put in that gentle but forceful way she was coming to recognize. He was used to making requests and having them followed, no matter how politely or casually he made them.

She didn't hear any sound but she knew he was standing by the bed. She was beginning to develop a supersensitivity to his presence. Then Cass sat down on the edge of his bed and lightly ran one practiced hand over her body from the crown of her head to the tip of her toes. This was, she knew, the technique of the skilled masseur who checked a client's position, height and weight in one sweep.

Kate raised her arm to reach back and pull the heavy mass of her hair out of the way. Cass tapped the back of her hand impatiently until she relented, letting him drag its damp weight to one side.

"Well, you do know the ritual," she said softly, "but are you any good at this ancient and honored profession?"

"We'll see," he replied. "The range of my talents might surprise you."

"I doubt it," mumbled Kate.

Cass took the *yukata* collar, deftly rolling it down to her waist and arranging it in a graceful drape over the curve of her buttocks and legs. He didn't touch her torso but began with her scalp, exactly the right procedure for a trained "flesh pounder."

Gradually, the small overlapping circles his fingers were describing moved downward. Cass found each of the last hidden knots of tension in her neck and shoulders and untied them. What great hands he had, she noted. The pressure of his touch was firm but not punishing, pressing into her hard enough to relax but not to hurt. She sighed her appreciation.

"I know why the best Japanese masseurs are blind, now," Cass said quietly.

"Why?" she said, sighing deeply.

"Because they can keep their minds on their work," he rasped.

Kate chuckled.

His kneading went on, searching out muscles deep under the satin skin over her shoulder blades, along the arch of her spine and lightly around the ribs.

"Good hands," she said in Japanese. The soft slide of his fingertips eased and found another spot for attention immediately.

The top of her kimono was replaced gently and Cass folded and tucked up the lower portion, allowing him to begin on her legs. "They're too long," he muttered. "This will cost you extra, Cleary-san."

She laughed and he grabbed her toes to give them his attention. Each toe was rolled delicately in his fingers and released; it tickled. With both thumbs, Cass rubbed the sole and top of her foot, caressing each curved instep. She felt a kinship with Tomadachi, the cat, as she purred contentedly.

Ankles and calves got equal, patient care. There was a lighter brushing sensation on the back of her knees, a kiss and not a touch. His fingers were ten instruments of pure sensual pleasure playing up her thighs, sending a message to her body. Each sweep of his hand was more and more leisurely until she was floating in a languorous sea. Longer, slower strokes moved his hands over the firm, rounded lines of her behind, and then she waited while he hesitated.

"Is that all?" she asked quietly and looked over her shoulder.

He was sitting there, motionless, looking down at her. The kimono he had changed to was plain and dark, a rough fabric that contrasted with the smooth, broad expanse of bare chest showing. There was a sheen on his skin, a rapid, shallow rhythm to his breathing and a look of desire so sweeping, so immense that she gasped involuntarily.

"Kate..." he said in a voice choked with need. "I'm sorry...I had to...I have to..."

She felt it, too. Caught in the grip of a blazing, terrible yearning, she rolled over and sat up, extending her arms to hold him, to touch him. There was nothing in the universe but the sharp ache of wanting.

"Oh, yes...yes, please," she moaned the instant his arms closed around her, pulling her roughly to himself. Her hands were trapped between the softness of her own breasts, the unyielding wall of his chest.

The heat of his skin was exciting. The heat of his mouth against hers warned her of his hunger and of the feast he intended to have. Kate felt Cass's arms tremble in an attempt to control this madness, but control was the last thing she wanted. Her body was greedy tonight, ready for more of him, almost screaming for release.

"Touch me. Love me," she pleaded. She slipped her hands into the folds of his robe, wanting him to be as naked, as accessible as she was.

"I will. Every way there is," Cass said hoarsely. "I have. Oh, Kate, I have...a million times in my mind since I met you."

Kate fell back, her eyes wide and wild, and reached out, but he needed no urging. His kisses were making a frantic journey down the pale column of her neck to reach the places his hands discovered first: the ripe fullness of her breasts, the impossibly taut knot of a nipple.

And lower. She heard herself making throaty cries when his mouth moved lazily over the sensitive, white flesh of her stomach and thighs to find her ready, damp. And to leave her writhing.

He slid his body upward to fit on hers, but not to fill it. Not until she begged him, not until she was clutching at him. She arched to push into the length of his body, to feel the heavy pulse of his need fully.

His first thrust rocked her whole body. She was no longer certain who was moving, who was crying out because the waves of sensation were too strong, too fast to discern. Each rippling wave surged and broke over her. This one...the next one would wash her away, pull her under as she moved toward completion, welcoming and hurrying it. She drowned in Cass and pleasure.

His mouth closed over hers, echoing the sound of satisfaction she made. Kate clung to him, dazed by not only the wild freedom she was feeling but how closely bound to Cass she felt. She was held by more than his arms and sweet weight of his body, dazzled by more than the intimacy they had shared.

She loved him. The knowledge filled her, even as his body had filled her. Her arms stayed twined around him, unwilling to let go of her lover or this precious moment.

He took some of his weight onto his forearms, raising himself enough to see her. "You always manage to surprise me," he whispered, taking a strand of hair from her mouth. "I think I know you and then, wow! Something happens and I see another side. You're like one of those puzzles . . . a thousand beautifully carved circles inside one another."

"You touched the center tonight," she admitted. "You reached the core. There shouldn't be any more surprises."

Most of his weight slid from her but he stayed close. His legs and hers remained wound together, and his hands couldn't seem to stop touching her. He laughed softly in the darkness.

"I hope not. So much passion under such a lady-like exterior almost did me in . . . you're wonderful, Kate."

"You're not so bad yourself," she teased, to cover her embarrassment. Her fingers ran lazily up and down his chest, tickled his ribs to distract him. If the talk turned too serious, she'd say too much, admit that if this relationship was a game for him, it wasn't for her. It was everything . . . or it could be.

They were laughing, whispering the nonsense to each other that new lovers enjoy so much, when she heard the noise. It was a dull buzzing in the other room. Cass kissed the end of her nose and rolled over to pick up the bedside phone.

"Damn," he said before he answered. Kate, too, had a fair idea of who was calling at one in the morning. She pulled the sheet over her face and chuckled wickedly.

"Yes, she is." There was a long wait before Cass said anything else. "No, you can't." He hung up quickly but Kate heard the garbled squawking before he broke the connection.

"Her master's voice," she said, pulling Cass back down next to her. "I should have talked to him. I'm not afraid of Arnold."

"He's the one who sounds frightened," Cass remarked. "I wonder why...." His hands began to skim down her body and Kate would have been happy if he didn't say another word. "Will you stay here?"

"Tonight? Of course." She was touching him back, finding abundant evidence that the night wasn't over. Her tongue drew a circle on his skin and she savored the slightly salty taste. When he reciprocated, an exquisite sensation rocketed through her.

"No, not just tonight," he panted. "Stay here as long as you're here in Tokyo...please, Kate."

She shook her head from side to side slowly, her hair rustling on the pillow. Before she lost all capacity for rational thought, she had to refuse. It was a touching, kind offer but it wasn't a good idea.

"I don't need a place to hide or your protection. I can be here whenever you are...if you want me."

"Is there any doubt?" Cass growled in her ear, almost angrily.

None, she wanted to answer as his hips started to mesh with hers. None, her heart pounded. But that was feeling, not fact. They both had business to conduct, not merely an affair. They both had separate lives, and it was too soon—too fragile a union they shared—to mix business with pleasure.

"Tonight," she sighed. "And when you're back from Kyoto..."

When they were both caught up in a whirlwind they themselves were creating, there wasn't any more time to talk or think. Her eyes never closed as they made love again and never left his face, storing him up, gathering memories and images to help her through the next few days while he was gone. She didn't need to say the words poised on her lips, roaring in her blood. She didn't need to hear them from him.

The silence seemed more eloquent to her than any reckless declaration, and she wanted to believe the quiet in her soul.

THE NEXT DAY, her concentration was lagging badly by noon. Picking out details to hold and relive, her mind wandered over and over the night, that morning. Kate shifted uneasily and heaped another courtesy onto Mr. Kuzihara. He retaliated, a smile overlapping another smile.

"Imprudent," Arnold had screamed from next door while she was showering and changing from last night's clothes. "Impulsive and stupid. Yashima would like to get what I'm looking for and he thinks you'll deliver it." And then, blessed silence, as if she were being punished. Maybe it would last.

"We are greatly honored by your interest in our poor offering," Mr. Kuzihara insisted, bowing as he escorted Kate to the door.

She really had to exert herself to swoop a little bit lower than he did. There were a few sore and tender spots to ignore. She loved every one of them. "I am so very grateful for your patience and kindness to me. Thank you for showing me such remarkable works."

The handwriting in her pocket notebook held all the information she accrued, scrawled in disorderly but accurate fashion. Kuzihara Galleries had nothing available that Arnold would sink money into, but he would pay handsomely for the gossip the owner had shared. The *tan-e* were real and they were in Tokyo somewhere. It was her first confirmation of Whelan-Jones's pipedream, not substantiated but trustworthy.

She left the gallery in a buoyant mood. Her crazy theory of treasure had been right. Friday, Cass would be back. She had so much to tell Fran at lunch, she wanted to scribble an agenda and make sure they didn't miss a single item.

The shopping mall they had agreed to meet at was thronged with shoppers and tourists. Fran gave her a big hug and a wobbly smile, putting a few packages aside to let Kate squeeze into the space next to her at a coffee-shop counter.

"Who goes first?" asked Kate, trying to read Fran's expression and failing. "I've got a lot of ground to cover. Big doings, public and private."

Fran folded a paper napkin in half, in quarters, in eighths, and again until it was a tiny, hard wad. "You go ahead. I'm listening."

There was a blandness, a flatness in her voice Kate didn't recognize, but she couldn't contain herself. She needed to talk about feelings too big and urgent to hold back. Without being gory about Arnold or graphic about Cass, she told Fran what the past week had brought.

"It's like a game of cat and mouse," she summed up. "It happens every time Arnold and I are together. I haven't wholly figured out what's happening yet. But I will, Fran."

"Love and hate," muttered Fran. She spilled out a miniature Mt. Fuji of salt and moved a mountain with the tip of one finger. "You got more than you bargained for on this trip. Well, so did I."

Her lack of enthusiasm came through loud and clear. This sad-eyed, impassive woman was not the go-for-it girl Kate knew.

"Your turn," said Kate. "Something's terribly wrong, isn't it? If a budding romance and the hint of a mystery doesn't get you excited, that's a sure sign something's wrong. It isn't traveler's tummy or a run in your hose, is it? Your grandparents? David?"

"Both." Fran crushed the peak of the little mountain flat and swept it off the formica with the side of her hand. Her head came up and Kate was stunned by the bleakness in her face. "First, a bit of advice for whatever it's worth. Don't care too much and everything will work out fine. You can hate with impunity, it seems. You can hate Arnold and try to outwit him, outguess him and there's no price to pay. But if you love..."

Her voice almost broke and Kate reached over and took Fran's arm. Fran actually twisted away, a violent reaction to a comforting touch.

"If you love," Fran continued, looking off into the mall, "you'll end up paying."

In a colorless monotone, she described her troubles at the Muratas. Her grandparents were delighted to see her, happy to pull out every picture and clipping and letter and discuss the family and how proud they were of Fran. They had not so much as looked at Fran's snapshots of David Townsend; they would not allow her to discuss her marriage plans.

"It's like a door slamming in my face," said Fran with bitterness. "They talk about Mom and me, Riverside and my job. They even like to tell me about my father. My memories of him are so vague, you know. And, although it hurts me, I talk to them about Jack."

Jack was Fran's older brother. His tragic death from leukemia was a deep and recent wound that Fran and her mother were still recovering from. Jack had been Fran's idol, her substitute father figure while she was growing up.

Reaching into her purse, Kate handed Fran a tissue and felt a suspicious welling in her own eyes. She couldn't cry for herself easily but she had no problem getting teary eyed for others in anguish. "There's more to this, Fran. You're leaving pieces out... or not telling me what you think is wrong."

Fran crumpled the tissue and let the tears roll down her face, making no attempt to cover them up or dry them. "Maybe if I had the good taste to fall for Cass Yashima, they'd be willing to talk about him. Or if I had the sense to marry the skinny dry-goods clerk who lives next door to them, they might be willing to listen."

Her head sagged forward and her whole body shook with barely repressed sobs. Other customers were beginning to notice and do the correct thing in such situations: they pretended there was nothing untoward happening. Kate put her arm around Fran, leaning close and hugging her tight.

"Because David is a *gajin*, a foreigner?" whispered Kate, in a shocked tone of voice. "Do you think your grandfather and Obasan are shutting him out because he's not Japanese or Japanese-American? Fran, you were born in Stockton, California. You're more a *gajin* than . . . than I am, for God's sake!"

"I don't know what to think," screamed Fran, startling people close to them. She glared around, daring someone to remark on her show of emotion, and then looked at Kate in helpless misery. She lowered her voice with a great deal of effort. "They said one thing. *One* thing in four days. 'You must not get married, Francine.' Period. End of subject."

"I don't believe it," said Kate, struggling to understand and make sense of the situation. "You told them David is going to be a fine, well-respected doctor . . . a good, respectful husband, just like we discussed?"

Fran nodded and cried harder at every phrase.

"He's kind . . . he and your mother get along splendidly. . . ."

"Yes, yes," whimpered Fran. "I'm going insane. Those two old people are my father's only living relatives; they're frail and alone and sweet...no, I mean it, Katie. They're like two brown sparrows most of the time and I can't hurt them. But...but..." She couldn't finish.

"But you couldn't give up David," supplied Kate softly.

Fran stood up fast, knocking over her coffee cup and sending a plate careening onto the floor. She ran out into the crowded mall.

"Fran! Oh, my God . . . *Fran!*"

Throwing a wad of yen on the counter, Kate raced after her, hoping Fran wouldn't lose herself in the constant stream of shoppers. She jostled people aside, apologizing abjectly and incoherently, until she saw her. She grabbed and tugged at Fran's sleeve. The simple physical contact stopped Fran and she swung around, seizing Kate as though she was sinking in the Pacific Ocean and was desperate to be saved.

"Help me," she sobbed, oblivious to the stares they were attracting. "No, you can't . . . just hug me!"

Kate did, smoothing Fran's hair, crooning to her until she was almost calm. "Maybe I can help. Let me try. Don't do anything rash when you're this upset, Fran. Don't call David or promise your grandparents anything about marrying or not marrying. Let it go and let me try to approach them."

"All right," gasped Fran, "what do I have to lose? David's or my grandparents' love, that's all. My mind? It's gone." She straightened to a full sixty inches and thrust her chin out. "Okay, I'm fine. I needed to let it out and I did and I'm sorry I dumped it on you, Kate."

"Well, I'm not sorry," said Kate truthfully. "You are my best friend, Francine Ann Murata, and my shortest. You are a fabulous, funny person who has mopped my nose when I've come boo-hooing to you..."

Fran managed a weak grin. "Even when I had to stand on the desk to do it..."

"Right! And between the two of us, there's more determination and grit than common sense. We don't quit, do we?"

"No," Fran replied dubiously. "We're the Dynamic Duo, the Giggle Sisters..." She gulped hard. "And now we're both in love."

"And we're going to go for it," finished Kate with confidence she did not feel. She put Fran in a cab with a solemn promise she'd call the Muratas as soon as she got back to her hotel.

The rest of her day was a blur—the hectic hustle from one gallery to the next that was becoming the pattern of her life. Seeing Fran had only added another pressure to a mental list growing longer every time she had a minute to check it.

Fran's warning about the price of caring too much came too late. She cared. She cared with every fiber of her being about her friends, her career, and Cass. There was no order to her love; she seemed to throw herself into everything—and everyone—that was important to her without any reservation.

Last night, she mused. *I looked into those damned blackwater pools, your wonderful, scary eyes, and I jumped in. I don't know how deep it is, I don't know if there's a bottom to those depths. I don't even know if I can swim. And, oh, how I wish you were here.*

She called the Muratas and persisted until they agreed to meet her. Her luck didn't hold when she tried to reach Cass in Kyoto or contact Yoshio Sabusawa through his secretary. Her old teacher was too ill to take any calls and the secretary was adamant that he was not allowed any visitors. Cass was touring plant facilities and being entertained by local bigwigs, she was curtly informed, and was entirely unavailable.

The pounding on her door was not as loud as usual, if there was such a thing as subdued pounding.

Kate stopped transcribing her notes from the day and opened it a crack, peering at Arnold and giving him a guarded smile. "Yes? Are you having trouble reading my scribble?"

"Your notes are fine," Arnold said cheerfully, throwing her for a loop. "They always are, as a matter of fact. If you're almost finished with the rest of them, why don't you get dressed up and come along to a party Kuzihara is throwing at some fancy Ja...local restaurant?"

A request and not a command? A compliment? Kate hoped her jaw hadn't dropped to her chest in sheer astonishment. "This is a bash for dealers, I take it. You think I should follow up and make sure he told me all he knows about the *tan-e*, right?"

"No," Arnold said offhandedly, "you thought he was square with you at the shop and hadn't seen 'em, just heard from someone who had. There's going to be a bunch of folks—dealers, buyers, a few government men from National Treasures. Some you know, some you don't. You want to come along and get out for a while?"

A venomous snake does not turn into the Easter Bunny without a pretty good reason. And she would love to know his reason, Kate decided. If there were lots of people, there was a better chance she'd uncover the source of Arnold's sudden graciousness and which brightly decorated egg was really poisoned.

"How nice of you," she said. "Why, thank you, Arnold. I'd like that very much."

IN JAPANESE Ichi meant "number one." The tiny restaurant was *ichi* in food, service and atmosphere. Kuzihara had spared no expense in arranging the evening and bringing together an *ichi* guest list.

Kate looked at the tray a waiter slid under her nose. It was a feast for the eye, a montage of sculpted raw vegetables and paper-thin slices of tuna and sea bass made into flowers and tiny animals.

"Poison," pronounced Arnold at her elbow. "What else does 'Itchy's' serve?"

"Nothing of interest for someone with plebian taste buds," interjected a distinguished-looking Englishman strolling by. He stopped to introduce himself to Kate with a few asides for Arnold.

"Alan Kempe, my dear. Surely you aren't with this troll?"

Kate laughed. There was no answer that came easier to her lips than "Yes." Arnold growled amiably and on cue, telling her about Kempe's purchases for him last year in an estate sale.

"You made a pretty penny, so smile when you're insulting me," cautioned Whelan-Jones.

"In that case I'd be wearing a permanent smile," suggested Kempe. He either had a droopy eyelid or he winked at Kate, whetting her interest. "I've bought you some pretty pictures, Arnold, but this one is three-dimensional, eager for my pearls of wisdom and too young for either of us. Allow me to enlighten her without you."

"I'll be good," grinned Kate. "I won't take notes." She helped herself to several pieces of pickled radish and crunched them with greater relish when Arnold shuddered.

Kempe knew Arnold. Knew his tactics. She mined a few semiprecious details in as many minutes. Had Kate heard that Tanaka was a former employee of Japan's National Treasures until it was discovered he was doing part-time investigations for Whelan-Jones? This involved scouting out the private collections of elderly or financially distressed patrons and giving this information to Arnold before releasing it to the National Treasures. Kempe also added that Tanaka had agreed to get this information for a nominal fee—Kempe was reluctant to call it a bribe, but Kate wasn't.

She walked on, digesting every delicious morsel.

Another tray passed by and with each sip of a delicately seasoned soup, Kate took in more spicy gossip. Art was no different from any other human endeavor; it had politics and scandals and revolutions, skeletons to uncover and rituals to follow.

Arnold flew by, a raptor on the scent of prey. He trailed the most respected of the Japanese buyers currently in evidence. "Having a good time?" he shot at Kate without slowing down.

"An educational experience," she answered.

The man she was sharing salmon with nodded approval. "You are fortunate to be working with Mr.

Whelan-Jones, Cleary-san. I was privileged to view his collection on my last trip to San Francisco. If he does not have a print, it must not be worth having. I admit even I could not attempt to estimate his worth."

"I'm beginning to think I can," said Kate under her breath. "The taste is his, the task is mine, the technique is Captain Kidd's."

Her companion's command of English was, thankfully, less than perfect. "Yes," he agreed vehemently, "he is remarkably youthful. I did not applaud when he physically struck a competitor a few years ago, but I admire such vigor, such passion. Will you have a glass of wine?"

"I will have two for the gory details," muttered Kate with a wicked glint in her green eyes. "White, please, Minato-san."

She drank like a hummingbird and listened like a hawk. She felt a bit like a vulture. This is business, Kate reminded herself, and big business at that. Half a million dollars was not chicken feed.

There was little else to gather but the crumbs of rumors, the sly seeds of Arnold's colorful personal history. Kate already knew how fascinated her educated, cultured fellows were by Whelan-Jones, a maverick in their midst.

He was self-taught, self-made in real estate and art. His late wife had only given him more wealth to work with and a greater hunger for acceptance and recognition as a social lion. His expertise in wheeling and dealing, in the gamesmanship of land and buildings, was history bordering on legend.

Arnold's newfound charm extended only so far. He snagged Kate before long, pulling her down to his table and his side. With his legs dangling comfortably in the *Kotatsu*—the well under the table provided for Westerners— Arnold was sufficiently at ease to be himself.

"Are you planning to write a paper or a biography on me or what?" he inquired. "I've got news for you. My life's an open book."

"It'll be a best-seller from the advance reviews," commented Kate. She tried to shift the subject. "Everyone knows about *tan-e* but nobody says where they are. I get the feeling there is a special twist to this print from the way they hold their breath whenever the subject comes up."

He kept his voice slightly lower than usual, confirming her suspicion. "Never been on the market before. Stay on the *tan-e* and off me." Arnold straightened the frame of his glasses and pinned her with a hard look. "Unless, of course, you're taking a personal interest in me, hunting a man to help your career."

Kate wasn't sure whether to stab him with a chopstick or not. She settled for a puckish grin. "I've got a beau," she simpered deliberately. "So sorry, Mr. Jones."

"We'd be an unbeatable team," Arnold said gruffly.

"Attila and his Hun-ee," quipped Kate.

The man across from Arnold nearly strangled but he managed not to laugh out loud. Whelan-Jones smirked, not at all offended.

"Consider this," he suggested loudly and cruelly. "You're chasing prints for me and someone's chasing you. He's bold, cool and clever and maybe he wants exactly what I do. You're the way, kid, not the prize. Ever think of that?"

"Not once," snarled Kate. *Not Cass,* she thought. Arnold would auction off his grandmother for a great print; Cass would never use her.

But she hated Arnold at that moment. He was not content to be his own man, she learned, without the added fillip of ruining others.

CHAPTER SEVEN

IT WAS THE RICHEST of the sales so far, with only seven buyers. No one was admitted without a special pass and a discreet credit check. The conference room in the Princess was exceptionally serene; a study colored in peaches and cream, with the comfortable leather couches of a living room. The atmosphere was subdued.

A gentleman on loan from Sotheby's conducted the afternoon portion of the sale. He spoke in hushed tones and accepted bids made by people who tugged at an earlobe, raised one finger or scratched a nose to indicate their willingness to spend a fortune.

Kate checked her watch for the third time in five minutes. After a break for dinner, the sales would resume in a larger, noisier setting here in the hotel, with more competitors, more offerings of less value and the curious public. She had already bid and bought four works; Arnold would be writing a bank draft for over one hundred thousand dollars without batting an eye.

She couldn't even bring herself to look at him.

"You'll bid it," Arnold instructed her as the next print was being placed on the easel.

"I'd rather you fire me," Kate said softly.

If her services were no longer needed, she was adequately covered by the terms of his letter. Her expenses to today were paid, her honorarium would be prorated, and she would have her choice of whatever Arnold had amassed to date.

"I told you, this is a joke," hissed Arnold. "My money, my sense of humor."

"My reputation," Kate shot back.

"You did your job. You told me what I needed to know. I want it anyway. Bid it!"

"Gentlemen," said the Sotheby man, "and Madame," with a nod to Kate, "this is the second Utamaro being offered this afternoon. *Blue-Veiled Geisha*, circa 1788, and one of the famous erotic women series..."

Kate checked her watch again and pinched the bridge of her nose hard. She had wanted this print, too, not so very long ago. Well, not this particular print. Her notes to Arnold had been very specific, unmistakably clear. It was neither fake nor forgery but the print had less than perfect register; the lines of the gauze veiling were blurred in spots and the color appeared slightly off to her.

She set the value at twenty-seven hundred dollars, writing that, most likely, it was a later print from the original block. When the woodblocks were badly worn at the time of printing, the results were less than perfect.

"Opening bids?"

"Twenty-seven hundred," Kate said quietly but distinctly. Her glance flicked down to the slip of paper Arnold had placed in her hand. He was willing to go to six thousand for a rather tasteless and expensive joke he hadn't divulged to her.

There were other bidders. She saw the young German bob his head and decided he was more taken with the erotic nature of the picture than its intrinsic worth. One of the Japanese buyers was reputed to have the largest collection of Utamaro's in the world; he would buy anything by the master from letters to leftovers.

"Thirty eight," she signaled reluctantly.

Great quality or not, the print was lovely, she thought for consolation. A man had to know and love women to portray them so sensuously, so invitingly revealed in private, unguarded moments. When she won this one for Arnold, knowledgeable buyers and dealers might think she was a fool for overlooking its flaws. Or worse, a shill trying to drive up the price of a lesser work to raise the value of other Utamaro masterpieces.

"Bid," whispered Arnold harshly. The German seemed determined to win it. "Or quit!"

Kate did turn her head, then. She gave Arnold the coldest, thinnest smile she could muster. If he did not willingly let her go and she quit, she would have nothing. He had seen to that. She would have to pay him back her expenses and forego her bonus. "Four," she indicated to the front of the room.

What kind of warped, sick person plays jokes with great art? What kind of man dares you to cut your own throat?

"Sold, thank you. Arnold Whelan-Jones."

The first half of the sale was over. People stood up and milled around the room, congratulating each other on purchases, trading a word here and there. Arnold levered himself off the couch and patted his breast pocket, preparing to pay out what Kate would have liked her annual budget to be.

"We did very well," he said to her.

"Yes, *you* did," she murmured. "I'm going upstairs to rest until seven." If he insisted on dinner together to plan strategy for the second half, she had ten wonderful excuses all ready, ranging from terminal cramps to chronic hangnail.

He walked to the bank of elevators and she thought she was going to break out in nervous hives. "Too bad Wonder Boy missed this one," Arnold grinned. "He would have wanted that Kato. They all did. But it's mine now."

"So is the *Blue-Veiled Geisha*," Kate couldn't resist saying.

He looked even happier, which was not her intention. "I owe this guy in San Francisco a favor and I don't like to owe anyone anything. Especially a tax accountant who has it all and never worked a full day in his life to get it . . ."

She realized she didn't want to know what Arnold's idea of a joke was. If the elevator wasn't there in five seconds, she'd take the stairs. She'd fly by flapping her arms. The break was only an hour and a half. What was she saying? Time and tide wait for no man.

"He'll put a frame on it worth more than the damned print itself..." Arnold was chuckling. "He'll probably insure it for a half a million dollars..."

"I won't write the insurance appraisal," said Kate with finality. She almost bowled someone over in her anxiety to get on the elevator. "It's not in our agreement."

"Don't be late," growled Arnold, having the last word. He mouthed another word as the door began to close and Kate smiled to herself, a genuine smile.

"Bitch" was a real tribute, considering the source.

"CASS!"

He was off her bed and in her arms the instant Kate slammed the door to her room.

"I'm not here," he told her between one frantic kiss and the next. His mouth fastened on hers hard and his hips pinned her easily to the wood at her back.

There was evidence to the contrary, she wanted to tell him but didn't get the chance. They were too busy punishing each other in very exciting ways for the loneliness of the last two days. She felt him begin to move against her with a tantalizing urgency while his hands traced the paths he'd taken the night before he left.

"Standing up?" she asked breathlessly. Her fingers curled and dug into his back, anchoring her to him. Her eyelids closed and there were a million pastel fireflies swarming behind them.

"Sounds good to me." Cass slid her skirt up, rocking gently on her and laughing softly against her throat. "How long do we have?"

"How long can it take?" she teased back, squirming and twisting. If she believed the hard flesh she could feel and the wild, damp heat of her own excitement, it would be one crazy, earth-shaking second. "An hour...a little more than an hour."

He shuddered and stepped back, his fingers still transmitting sparks along her thighs and stomach. He swore softly under his breath and then shook his head at Kate, giving her a lopsided, sheepish grin.

"We better wait until later. It wouldn't do to send you downstairs with ripped pantyhose while I hobble back across town with my back out of whack and a dislocated knee."

"Where did you come from?" she asked huskily.

"I'm hosting a cocktail party at my apartment." Cass took a deep, ragged breath and shook his head once more, regretfully. "What you do to me, Kate...I thought a man grew greater than some of his parts after adolescence, but I feel about sixteen years old right now."

They laughed and kissed with somewhat more restraint. Cass went to sit in one of the chairs by her window while Kate wiped off what remained of her lipstick.

"You look tired," Cass said. "I'll bet some jerk was keeping you up with long, late phone calls from Kyoto."

"Keeping me sane," amended Kate. She looked up in the mirror and smiled at his reflection, watching her. "It hasn't gone very well. I told you about my meeting with the Muratas, Fran's grandparents, didn't I?"

"The bare bones of it. You met, you liked them, you drew a blank."

She slipped off her shoes and went over to sit on his lap, letting Cass wind his arms around her. Some time was better than no time. Any touching was good. She had never felt this way, not even at sixteen.

"I struck out," she said. "Grandpa is one of those stern, overbearing patriarchs who can scare the stuff out of you with a look, but we got along. By the end of the evening, I heard all about how he and the colonel went fishing together.''

"And her grandmother?'' Cass played with the buttons on her blouse, opened two and put his mouth on the white triangle of flesh he exposed. He opened another button and his mouth dipped lower.

"Lovely lady,'' breathed Kate. "If you don't want to hear the rest, that's okay with me.''

"Oh, I do, I do,'' he muttered, lips moving along the lace of her bra. "I'm all ears.''

"Not from where I'm sitting,'' moaned Kate, making him laugh and raise his head. "And don't look at me like that. It's indecent...and we don't have enough time, besides.''

"You're right! Go ahead. You liked them, they liked you but they didn't tell you why Fran can't marry David.''

It went beyond a simple refusal, Kate told him. She followed, in general, the procedure any matchmaker worth her salt in Japan would use. There was a small gift, beautifully wrapped, for each of the Muratas. Kate had introduced the topic of David Townsend after there was plenty of good feeling all around. They had shared a meal, traded anecdotes and Kate had made the older couple laugh. Kate had progressed further than Fran; she was listened to when she described David Townsend in glowing terms, vouching for his sincerity and character and glorious future as Riverside's newest obstetrician.

"Thwack!'' said Kate, chopping the edge of one hand into the palm of the other. "The ax fell and the curtain descended. Mr. Murata turned into a block of stone and Mrs. Murata slipped out of the room. The old man thanked me for my concern and friendship, asked me to give his deepest regards to my father and he said...wait, I want to get this verbatim...'We have only Francine, our last grandchild. She will remain a Murata out of respect to our wishes and to the memory of her father and her brother. She must not marry.'"

Kate repeated the old man's words in Japanese so that Cass would not miss any of the force, any of the precision of his statement. It was an oath, a vow of finality.

"That's very heavy," Cass said. "I don't know your friend, Katie, but I feel..." He stopped talking and looked away from Kate. After a moment, he continued. "What do you suppose they have against David?"

"Not just David. Anyone," mumbled Kate to herself. "They are telling her flat out she must not marry anyone. It's swell to find out that racial prejudice has nothing to do with it. They don't care if Fran loves David Townsend! They are asking her to give up the whole idea of marriage."

Cass ran his hand lightly up and down her back, trying to soothe her. "This is Japan, after all. Her family can demand the unreasonable and expect compliance without explanation. Respect, honor, memory...those are the big guns. Will she agree, though?"

"She might," Kate admitted sadly. "Fran lost a lot of her fighting spirit when Jack died. She wants her family, what's left of it, to be peaceful. It's not fair!

And it doesn't make sense unless there's a really good reason..."

She put her arms around Cass's neck and ran her fingers into his hair, loving the texture of it, remembering how it tickled along her body when they were making love. She ran her tongue lightly around the rim of his ear and got a scowl from him.

"That doesn't make sense, either," he said in a mock-serious voice. "You want to start something that can't be finished, Dr. Cleary?" But he was the one who pulled her forward for a very deep, passionate kiss.

There was no really good reason why she should respond so enthusiastically. She was going to have to leave any minute. They'd steal time later, juggling appointments, disappearing for a few hours. But she did respond and kiss him as if this minute was never going to end.

Maybe that was what she was trying to tell him. Don't let it end. Make it last forever. Maybe Cass held her this tightly because he didn't want her to go. She heard the door open when it was much too late.

"I thought you were sleeping. My mistake!"

She jumped guiltily and laughed instantly, remembering a similar reaction a long time ago when she was caught necking on the couch. Arnold didn't even have the common decency to look contrite. Her father had said, "Whoops," and left it at that. She got off Cass's lap without hurrying or bothering to pull her blouse closed.

"Your mistake and mine," she said nastily. "I forgot they invented locks for a reason."

"It starts in ten minutes." Arnold didn't appear in the least disconcerted, not even as Cass stood up slowly and walked toward him.

Cass put his hand on Kate's shoulder. "Don't you get it?" he asked her. "This is part of his play, a bedroom farce. You protest you weren't sleeping. He asks what were you doing, passing along trade secrets? Next, I say that you're not his wife. Then, I punch him."

"And I quit? I always hated bedroom farce," Kate said. "Please don't hit him. He's twice your age, half your size and he has a bad heart."

"He has none," corrected Cass, and he took another step.

The older man wasn't backing off or bowing out. His tan was very gradually becoming suffused with a dark red. Anger to meet anger head-on and over what? Kate seized Cass, pushed herself into his side and the edge of panic in her grew. She could smell and taste a real confrontation brewing as if an electrical storm were gathering on the ceiling of the room.

There was iron in Cass's grip on her. There was undisguised loathing in Arnold's expression.

"Who the hell do you think you are?" Arnold snapped.

She opened her mouth and then realized she was not being addressed.

"I know who I am," replied Cass. "I'm still trying to figure you out. If I follow my instincts, I'll behave like an animal and get slapped with a law suit. Don't push me, Arnold. It might be worth it."

The red was bordering on the rich purple of apoplexy in Arnold's face. If he wasn't scared, Kate was.

Cass wasn't kidding. Seeing him like this was a revelation. The little hints she had had of the depth and complexity of his emotions didn't quite prepare her for this.

"Cass, he blundered in here...not for the first time, but I'm sure it will be the last." Her voice was no steadier than her legs. "Don't overreact, please."

"I don't blunder," said Arnold, a clear challenge ringing in his voice. "I came up here to protect my interests. He's right."

Kate put one hand flat on Cass's chest, expecting to feel the hammering of an agitated heart to match the nervous flutter of her own. It was scarier when she felt the slow, regular pulse and saw the grim expression on his face. His skin was stretched taut across the bones of his face, giving him all the cruelty, determination and ferocity that his ancestors had needed Kabuki makeup to achieve.

Only his eyes were alive, glittering and cold.

"Your interests are safe," Kate forced herself to say. "Get out, Arnold. Before I quit, preferably. You won't have an easy time finding a better appraiser for your *tan-e*, if and when you find them. I want what I contracted for, but not if someone's going to get hurt."

She'd said the magic word. Arnold made a half turn, ready to leave.

"No," was Cass's order. It came out in a guttural bark and the sheer weight and authority of one syllable worked. Even on Arnold Whelan-Jones. "Tell her," he demanded.

"Tell her *what*?" asked Arnold. "She knows what my interests are. She just said it."

"Tell Kate what she doesn't know: how you are using her. And tell me what I don't know, how else you plan to use her." Cass spat out the words.

"Somebody better tell me," said Kate, "and fast!"

She kept a lid on her Irish temper, as a rule. The few times she'd let it loose, she had wreaked havoc in her own life. It was a terrible, awesome force and safer the deeper she buried it. Right now, she could feel her temper like molten lava struggling to rise to the surface. It wouldn't discriminate between Arnold and Cass; it would burn everyone in this room to the ground.

And Cass must have picked up on her plight. He put his arm around her and relaxed his expression, but couldn't manage a smile.

"So far, it's nothing big," Cass said evenly. "But you won't like it."

Arnold grinned, apparently unaware that he was taking his life in his hands. "She won't like it but she'll live with it. Kate came here to get her share of the pot of gold at the end of my rainbow. Not just to see it and go home."

"Shut the hell up," screamed Kate before she could get a grip on herself as strong as the one Cass had. "Tell me!"

Cass began to talk faster than was normal for him but kept his voice low, calm. "Small, slimy moves are Whelan-Jones's stock in trade. He's made a real point of feeding rumors about the two of you to buyers. Maybe some dealers, too."

Arnold's smile disappeared. "You're guessing, Yashima. You've been to one sale for ten minutes. You've been off hither, thither and yon."

"I have connections, too," Cass said very simply. "A lot of buyers believe there's a May-December romance in full swing. I wonder where they got that idea? Arnold speaks more than highly of you, Kate. He's downright affectionate out of earshot."

She was taken so aback, she choked down a laugh. "To what purpose? Oh, Cass, who cares? An old geezer finds his ego, so what? No one with two neurons to rub together can seriously think—"

"You have friends," Cass interrupted before she collapsed with laughter. "Arnold has enemies. If a little of the good feeling for you rubs off on him, it's just another fringe benefit he gets for bringing 'his little professor' along..."

The way Cass said the words she knew it was a quote. She shot a baleful glare at Arnold. He smiled. She said she didn't care about appearances as much as reality. She lied.

And Cass didn't let up. "Some of the buyers are also under the impression that you don't bid only for Arnold. Sometimes, you are acting for the Cutler on the more modestly priced items."

Her face froze, all giddiness gone.

Nearly every print under six thousand dollars had gone to her in the past week. It wasn't only luck or skillful bidding, she realized with a sickening sensation. How many of those wins could be attributed to a friendly buyer who dropped out or eased off to let Kate, as a friend and the representative of the tiny Cutler Museum, take a prize he was lukewarm about? One? Three?

"How could they think that, Arnold...except through you?" She didn't recognize her own voice.

"My contacts are my friends. You can trade on my name, but not my friendships, not the relationships I built up over the years...."

"What are friends for?" asked Arnold in perfect seriousness. His blandness made her want to kill him. "Grow up, Dr. Cleary. Join the real world, for a change. I don't have to lie. Ask Wonder Boy how the deed's done. Vague answers, veiled allusions, a joking reference to a rich Pasadena widow's bequest, men kidding around with other men.... Business is hardball, not a ladies' luncheon in the Cutler's garden."

She went numb, trying to digest it all, trying not to throw up and disgrace herself. Arnold tapped the crystal of his big gold wristwatch.

"Five minutes and they start. Be there before the Matsuri goes up. It's high on your list of priorities, if I'm not mistaken."

"You bastard," she said with real enthusiasm, but it was too late. He was out and gone, leaving her with a very bad taste in her mouth, a dull pain somewhere behind her eyes.

Stalking to the bathroom, she ran cold water on her wrists and drank a glass too, but the taste in her mouth didn't wash away that easily. When she came out, Cass was sitting on the edge of her bed, flipping idly through a magazine.

"Are you ready to go like that," he asked, after a quick glance, "or do you want to throw a few things together to take with you?"

Kate picked up her purse and checked her blouse to make sure she hadn't missed doing up any buttons. "Shotgun, cattle prod...nope, I got all I need, Lefty."

He didn't laugh. "I want you to come back to my apartment with me. Not later, Kate. Now! I'm not above saying 'I told you so.'"

"So I see," she muttered, heading for the door. "Well, you were above telling me some vital information until push came to shove, it seems. We can talk about it later."

Sadness and fury were a curious combination. Her throat was tight, as if there were tears clogging it. Or was it a hard, indigestible lump that couldn't be swallowed? Her pride?

The fury was hot. She couldn't trust herself to speak now. She wasn't sure she could separate her annoyance with Cass from her utter contempt of Arnold Whelan-Jones.

Cass rode the elevator down with her, hardly speaking. His quiet disbelief was evident. Kate speculated on what he might have expected of her. Tears and hysterical self-recriminations, perhaps. She had underestimated Arnold after she'd been warned and should be ready to capitulate—*quit*—and flee to safety.

Not me, thought Kate. She might lose face even more but it wasn't going to be for lack of trying. She had her own code of ethics as stringent and strong as Cass's belief in *bushido*, the warrior's rules.

"I'm not weak and I'm not helpless," she said emphatically when they reached the lobby. He didn't offer any argument, so Kate went on. "I have to handle this...this mess...my way, not your way...and certainly not Arnold's way. I'm going to make it clear to every buyer I can get to that I'm bidding solely for Arnold Whelan-Jones, not the Cutler."

"You do that." Cass lifted her hand to his mouth and relinquished it after a very brief kiss. "You repair what you can, Kate."

As moral support and encouragement went, it wasn't much. The small tendrils of doubt Kate was experiencing threatened to spread and grow. She admitted to herself that she had misjudged the extent of Arnold's greed, but he, in turn, was misjudging her determination. It might help if Cass wasn't guilty of underestimating her. But he didn't sound or look very optimistic.

She saw a knot of people break at the far end of the lobby and move toward the room where the sales were starting. "The auction will be over around midnight. Is that too late for me to come over there?" she asked.

"Too late?" Cass repeated with a quizzical smile. "No, Kate. It's never too late, they say."

He stood there for a few minutes just to watch her walk across the lobby and disappear. Silently he nurtured the hope that she would change her mind and quit Whelan-Jones. Of course he knew the chances of this happening were very slim.

"Maybe it's too late, after all," Cass said aloud and left the Princess.

THE RIDE BACK to his party was too short. The ride back ten years in Cass's mind took time. He had to remember what he was like at twenty-five, how things had been different, and it was growing difficult to recall. He had less trouble when he imagined Kate at nineteen; she was probably not a young nineteen, just a bright, ambitious young woman with big plans and big dreams and less of a notion of how to achieve them.

He was convinced they would have had a chance—more of a chance then. The patterns of their lives weren't worn deep like grooves into rock; there was the ability to shift and change, the limitless possibilities, the endless vistas and a stronger belief that love conquered everything.

"Cass, I've been looking for you." His distraught assistant didn't wait for him to get his bearings. "About the Kyoto contracts—"

"Not now," Cass said gently, pushing his way past into the living room. "We'll talk before you telex L.A. with the details." He was visualizing a younger Kate, a younger Cass, and how it might have been.

"I wish you had told me we were settling at fourteen thirty-eight a unit. I thought the lowest figure we were going to sign at was fourteen forty-two. This means a significant loss, you know."

"A loss doesn't scare me," Cass said. "It never has." But he was afraid for Kate, a feeling he never had for himself. Intellectually, he knew she could take care of herself. She was his equal, a perfect match. At the hotel, Cass had seen her mind, body and will join forces to go back and do battle with Arnold Whelan-Jones.

The assistant couldn't leave well enough alone. "How do I explain it? For a tax write-off, it might work."

"Then, call it a write-off," replied Cass tartly. "It isn't. It's bait. I take the loss and they take our business from the Koreans in the video cassette market. But I tied to it the new personal computer programs for next year and when they take off, we'll do better in the long run."

"You got *that* in writing?" The man's incredulity was poorly disguised.

"No. Lose a battle, win the war. It's a risk but I took it."

Cass stalked away before he fought with another person tonight. He went through the motions of playing host, doing it well, aware of how effortlessly he did it. With practice, a man could play any part and not betray the fullness of his emotions. Kate was doing much the same thing, he felt sure, at her evening sales and it bothered him. Soon, she would have the practice, the combat experience, and lose—as he had—the option of not playing; she would be harder, ruthless if necessary. Finally, at times, heartless.

We stand alone. We act so strong. God help him, he had wanted to shake her like a rag doll and scream at her, not Arnold. Arnold was a hopeless cause, beneath Cass's notice. The man fought dirty for thrills and liked the chaos he left in his wake. But Kate? Kate might have heard him before it was too late.

He wanted to tell her that when you give your all, there's nothing left. Before she committed herself, she had to be sure her cause was worth it, even if she lost. *We don't surrender. We die for what we fight for.*

He collared another member of the Tokyo team and drew the man aside. "I want everyone out of here by eleven-thirty. Will you please take care of it?"

"Don't you want to meet the labor representatives from Nara and check the union problems they've been having? Those two . . . over there."

"Eleven-thirty," Cass repeated in a monotone. "Thanks."

She would have made a great samurai, Cass thought. He had seen her face confronting Arnold, shocked and sickened and thrown off balance. But she didn't falter for a second. The very traits he had hungered for and found in Kate could destroy her.

No, Cass hadn't wanted to tell her what he had learned, unless she would listen and reconsider. There was no question in his mind what Kate's reaction to the gossip would have been. His was identical. The moral indignation, the seething anger, the firm resolution not to back down, were strengths.

He was sure, now. He loved her. Ten years ago, he would have committed himself to her with all the energy and will he had used up for Sunco. He might not be as successful today but he would be happier. Much happier. A good general didn't have much time to be a good husband and father.

Someone was pumping his hand. George Breyer. He had to focus harder, Cass told himself.

"I'm not sorry you're keeping Woodruff on," George was saying. "I can work with him in Berlin. I know he screwed up but I liked his plan, too."

"That's why I won't fire him," Cass said, "and you tell Drucker when you get there. It was a brilliant plan; it just didn't work. I can't see sacrificing his brains because he made it uncomfortable for us for a while. Good night, George."

There was no way he was going to let Kate sacrifice herself in a war she couldn't win. She was fearless despite overwhelming odds, unswerving in the face of what she saw as her duty, and determined even when she glimpsed the shadow of defeat.

When he asked himself what frightened him, what had made the past few weeks a nightmare of indecision and uncertainty, Cass had an answer. Love. It was the right answer but a bad weapon. What else could he use? What else did he have?

CHAPTER EIGHT

THE PALE SHEETS were warm and rumpled, smelling of lemons and starch. Kate couldn't move. Her arms and legs were weighted beyond belief and she sighed, a sound of deep contentment. Enhancing her feeling of well-being, was the warmth of Cass's body next to hers. Her eyelids fluttered at the sound of his voice.

"Asleep?"

She slid a leaden hand along his length. It was the best she could do until the trembling aftershocks passed completely.

"Does the light bother you?" Cass propped himself up on one elbow so his body blocked most of the lamp's glow. "I can turn it off." He smiled down at her. "I don't want to but..."

There were two slight scratches on his chest, marring the smooth sculpture of his pectoral. She covered them up quickly with her hand, gave a soft, embarrassed laugh.

"I'm sorry...not that it wasn't your fault, too. Am I blushing?"

Cass lifted the corner of the sheet. "All over," he confirmed, chuckling. "It's a very becoming color."

She groaned and shut her eyes tightly. Then, she opened them wide, unwilling to lose another second of seeing him.

"It's been ages since I've blushed," she whispered. "Or had a reason to." And she raised herself just enough to kiss him lightly on the cheek.

Cass wreathed her tightly in his arms and rolled back, pulling her on top of him. She shivered, not from cold but from the lazy smile he gave her and the terrible pleasure it gave her to feel every inch of him. She crossed her hands on his chest and pillowed her cheek there.

The digital clock clicked and the numbers changed, flashing like a malevolent red eye. She turned her head away, switching to her other cheek.

"Cass," she said dreamily, "would you do me a tremendous favor? I hate to even ask..."

"I thought I already did," he teased and got a playful pinch for his efforts. "No, anything. I told you. Let me guess. Columbian emeralds to match your eyes, the name of a reliable hit man to bump off Arnold?"

Wriggling her behind slightly shut him up more effectively than a gag. Kate lifted her head and balanced her chin on the back of her hands, meeting his gaze directly. She had his full attention, among other things.

"You have a lot of government and police contacts here, don't you? Well, I've been thinking..."

"Heaven help us," he murmured.

This time, a gentle punch to his upper arm sufficed. "I think there may be a good but secret reason the Muratas won't budge an inch for Fran. If I tell you what I know about her family, will you have someone check it out?" She looked deep into the darkness of his eyes and hesitated only for a second before she began to sketch soothing little circles on his chest.

The desire in his eyes gave way to instant understanding. "You might be right," Cass said slowly. "No wonder they never told her. It's not easy to check. Most of the old records were burned during the bombing raids on Tokyo."

"Try," pleaded Kate, inching up to kiss his chin. "Okay?"

"You keep doing what you're doing," Cass said a few minutes later," and I'll be able to leap tall buildings in a single bound."

"Animal!" Kate accused happily. "We have important things to discuss and I have—" she checked the bedside clock "—five hours before my first appointment."

He started to laugh. "I'm not the real Superman. This won't take me five hours, sorry."

But the laughter died and he did not make love to her again. After a few lingering, tender kisses, Cass put his arms down at his sides and shook his head imperceptibly from side to side.

"No, we better talk. I may have to go to Nara the day after tomorrow about some snag with the union." Kate's disappointment was obvious. "Oh, Kate," Cass said, opening his arms. "Come on...come here. I know...it stinks."

She nestled back against him and burrowed her face into the welcoming curve of his arm. "I hate this...I'm beginning to hate this..." she whispered without censoring herself. Hadn't she solemnly sworn to herself she wouldn't demand or promise more than Cass did?

He couldn't keep his hands off her. He couldn't help her, either. "Go ahead. Say it . . . for both of us."

"Stolen moments are very exciting. Part-time lovers . . . makes every moment so intense. But . . ." She caressed his chest and fell silent.

He said he'd give her anything. Anything but what she really wanted. More of him and more time. This was a game and she was playing it for real, in earnest. She couldn't quite bring herself to say she would not settle for these frenzied, white-hot moments and be left without seeing him at all.

"Kate, I can put the work off but I can't put it down," he said softly. "Not entirely. You could go with me. Listen, I'm trying to set up a week or ten days off when all the contracts are concluded. We could stay right here. Or Paris? You've never been there, and here it is, spring." His mouth slipped down her body, more persuasive than words. "Say yes. Nod. Please, Kate."

Her mouth quivered. So easy. One word before she became incoherent with passion, a wonderfully happy, stupid state.

"No," Kate managed to gasp through clenched teeth. He wasn't listening. "No, I can't go to Nara with you. I'm working, too. And Paris . . ." Paris was a dream, a fantasy he was spinning out to bind her tighter and tighter to him. Something would happen— the new offices in Germany, the contracts in Washington.

For one heart-stopping second, when Cass looked at her, she thought she was going to burst into tears. It was so much easier to fight with someone whose face didn't fill her with happiness, whose eyes weren't filled with such love.

"You could quit," Cass said gently, "and go with me. Make Arnold fire you; overbid like a maniac during the next sale and he'll fire you in front of the whole room. Witnesses galore..."

"Would *you* do it?" Kate asked, knowing the answer. She stroked his cheek and the tense line of his jaw. "Can you really read my mind?"

"Our first fight. You're furious with me; you want to cry but you're not going to. What a lot of goddamned nerve I have. No, you made a deal and a bad bargain is still a bargain—"

"Stop it!" ordered Kate angrily. She shouldn't have asked. It was horrible to find out how much he knew about her, more than any man on earth. She started to move out from beneath him.

Cass pushed himself harder on her, pinning her with his weight and caught both her hands in his, leaning on his elbows. "What about the rest? Don't you want to get it all out in the open?" His voice was as taut as his body.

"Okay," she rasped. "You can't set what you do aside. You *are* what you do but that's all right! You're a man, an important man. And I'm the woman, the junior five-figure curator of some rinky-dink museum...hardly what you call important."

It was no gift to discover she could read his mind, too. They could have everything if she wasn't stubborn. They could be together more if she was less convinced that her career, her obligations were as important and necessary as his. All it would take, she went on, was for her to give in to her feelings and sacrifice her life's work.

"That's the old way," she finished, pained. There was also pain in his expression, but incredible power in his hands, ceaselessly roaming her body. "The fairy tale . . . he takes her away to his castle and they live happily ever after, except that she gets bored cleaning house and he's always off slaying dragons."

He stopped her from saying more with his kiss, sapping the strength from her again, reaching into her soul. His lips hovered over hers.

"That's right. It's a traditional, outmoded love story and we both once wanted it. You can feel what's happening to me, how much I want you. You want me, too. Right now. This minute."

She squeezed her eyes closed as hard as possible but one tear welled out and trickled back into her hair. It was true. She could hate her own body, her own heart, but it wouldn't do any good. Her longing betrayed her.

Making love would not resolve the problem but it would comfort them both.

As she kissed him back, her tongue finding his, Cass entered her and she was conscious of only him, finally understanding why he made their lovemaking last as long as he could.

It was the space and time where they were both completely free, not caught between any two worlds, any two conflicts. There was no country to belong to; they belonged to each other. There were no borders to cross beyond those of their senses. They were ageless, forgetting what was right or wrong, modern or past. When she lost herself in Cass, Kate realized fleetingly that she had somehow found herself.

Afterward, they were closer and quieter.

"It's amazing," Kate said, "how much alike we are. But you're just as trapped as I am. Our souls may be free but we paid the price. We live our lives according to *Business World* and the Equal Rights Amendment."

"We're in Tokyo. Think about a Japanese love story," suggested Cass. He closed his eyes. "No, don't think at all."

"That's not funny. All Japanese love stories end tragically...beautifully sad."

He didn't say anything and he didn't have to, really. Kate knew a realistic prediction when she heard one. They felt fated to be together, though the same signs were there leading to an inevitable end. No, don't think at all.

Go to sleep, Kate commanded her body, not believing it would obey. The descent was so swift that she whimpered and didn't feel Cass touch her for reassurance; hers and his own. She didn't hear him whisper the three words he found so difficult to say aloud but meant with his whole being.

KATE'S MOTHER HAD a pet theory she liked to expound on at meetings of military wives. Eileen Cleary held with lots of crazy theories, according to Kate and her father, the colonel. But they thought the one that explained why the Irish and the Japanese were the most compatible people, took the cake.

Kate had nearly forgotten about Eileen's Shamrock and Rising Sun connection; it was an old family joke to haul out every once in a while and kid about. This morning, running a half hour late, breaking a heel in a sidewalk grating, shredding her stockings and frantically heading back to the Princess to repair the damage, Kate thought suddenly of the Cleary Theory.

Simply put, it hinged on how living on islands thousands of miles apart made two cultures "kin under the skin." The Irish were moody and melancholy with a fatalistic streak, a reverence for nature, the love of gambling and—most importantly—the unshakable belief that unseen forces were all around at work in this world, every minute. So were the Japanese, according to Kate's mother. Eileen Cleary rested her case and refused to listen to the suggestion that *perhaps* she was oversimplifying.

Maybe she wasn't. Kate never believed, or thought, much about fate. Until last night, until this morning...no, until she met Cass. Accident or fate?

"Ah, good morning, Dr. Cleary." Jean Michel LeClerc halted Kate's progress through the lobby by grabbing her hand and shaking it until she returned his greeting.

"I'm sorry, Mr. LeClerc, I can't stop to talk. As you can see, I'm a mess." She offered her shoe for evidence. Her hose spoke for themselves. "I'm late for an appointment and I have to dash upstairs and change. Nice to see you!"

He fell into step with her as Kate headed for the elevator. It was easy; she was limping. "No rush! Mr. Whelan-Jones is still in his suite. I was just now up there with him."

"Grand," said Kate dryly. She was counting on Arnold's being out bright and early as usual. The morning would not be improved by seeing him.

"You are distressed," Jean Michel said sadly. "You don't wish to see him?"

"You have the gift of understatement."

He shrugged and smiled at her. "I'm French."

Kate laughed. "And the gift of stating the obvious."

LeClerc beamed at her and swept his arm toward the hotel's coffee shop, suggesting she take refuge there. "Only for a few minutes, some coffee or tea? I have wanted to talk with you. Ah, and I have purchased several *netsukes* I would like to show you."

Kate's professional opinion of *netsukes*, the small carved wood or bone ornaments worn centuries before, wasn't worth a sweet roll, she said, but she took his offer impulsively. Any port in a storm. Her opinion of the French buyer was rising rapidly. He seemed companionable, amiable, and enthusiastic about his first trip to Japan.

LeClerc had been one of the people Arnold didn't seem eager for her to mix and mingle with. That was reason enough to share a silver pot of coffee and admire the three ivory finds LeClerc wanted her to see.

She fondled the most intricate piece, making polite conversation, and finally handing the miniature horseman back. LeClerc looked pleased as he carefully rewrapped it in a purple flannel square and tucked it into his pocket.

"Oriental art is not my specialty," he confided. "I am fluent in four languages but Japanese is not one of them. My father and I have an excellent collection of antique French ceramics and many, many French and Swiss clients."

"You're a little far afield, then," commented Kate. She kept checking through the shop's windows to see when Arnold passed. "How and why did you end up buying Eastern treasure?"

"A couple of our regular clients wanted 'exotics,' something different. Then, too, I appreciated the experience of these sales, the commission and counsel of your Mr. Whelan-Jones."

"He's not *my* Whelan-Jones," said Kate before the full import of LeClerc's words sunk in. Commission? Counsel, yes. Arnold gave advice like it was going out of style, but commission?

She leaned forward and wanted to bat her eyelashes at Jean Michel LeClerc. He was French and he was doing a nice appraisal on her. She settled for softening her tone. Her eyes felt squinty from lack of sleep.

"But Arnold is very generous with his counsel," she went on. "I'm sure he showed you the ropes and pointed out the real buys."

She got a noncommittal nod and an offer to buy her a drink tonight. *Down, boy,* she thought and tried to think of another opening. Espionage and politics were foreign languages to her, obviously. She let the offer of drinks slide.

"Of course, we're none of us infallible." Kate prayed Yoshio Sabusawa knew what he was talking about when he had cautioned his students not to approach any problem with a superior attitude. Her old teacher argued that brilliance cloaked in deference and humility produced fine art and fine solutions. "Were you at the sale where AWJ bought *Blue-Veiled Geisha*? I bid it but I think he made a big mistake. I'm upset when I remember how much money he threw away on that print when there's so much of real value to buy."

"I wasn't there, unfortunately. My personal finances did not gain me entrance, Dr. Cleary. It was, as I understood it, a bargain. Whelan-Jones would have gone to six thousand, no? Had I been there, I could have jumped in and forced Mueller out sooner for Mr. Whelan-Jones. Well, no matter. One way or the other, he got the print."

He knew the price. He knew too much. Kate strove for composure and neutrality and looked into her coffee cup for answers. "I see. So you have bid, I assume, on occasion for Arnold."

"Oh, yes. Like you. His commission is most generous."

"I'm *always* bidding for Arnold," Kate said, wanting to scream. "Despite what you may have heard, I am *never* bidding for the Cutler."

"Truly?" Jean Michel looked completely baffled, stared off into space and then, back to Kate. "But, at the first large auction..."

"You bought a Sharaku print, a very expensive and beautiful print," Kate reminded him. "Or rather, you bid against me so Arnold could have it. Am I right? Let's see, at commission..."

He understood and LeClerc's mouth twisted. "I told him that whenever you had a conflict of interests between bidding for him and for the Cutler, I would be delighted to act as his agent. The Sharaku is on its way to San Francisco now."

She said, "I see," again and she did.

"I am so very sorry," Jean Michel LeClerc said. "I have made an error. It would not be my intention to cross-bid with you or take your commission."

"That's all right. There was no error on your part," Kate said quickly. If Mr. LeClerc was a crook like Arnold, he would never have said a word. "Cross-bidding by using several designated agents at one sale isn't exactly illegal, Jean. Not nice, not ethical, but not a hanging offense."

Silently, Kate debated whether she would rather shoot Arnold or set him on fire. His plan was a stroke of genius, if she considered that master criminals were often regarded as geniuses.

She jumped up from the table, feeling more fibers give way down her leg, and shook LeClerc's hand, thanking him as graciously as she could for the coffee and chat.

He was bewildered once more. "Shall I speak to him, Dr. Cleary? Should I refuse to allow this to go on? It's dirty business."

"Oh, no, I'll speak to him," Kate assured him. "As for accepting commissions, you'll have to do what you think best. Now, please excuse me. I have to go upstairs and sit with a friend who I hope is going to be extremely sick."

"Pardon?" Jean Michel rose to his feet as Kate shot out of the coffeeshop like a rocket.

It hurt. It hurt her to think about being made a fool and being wrong. Arnold's arrangement was so simple and subtle at the same time, Kate would have admitted it had a certain greatness to it. Her commission was her promised "pick of the litter." If Arnold didn't want a particular work included in the litter, he simply got someone like LeClerc to bid against her with a different price limit. Maybe the Sharaku was the only one he had held out on. Maybe not.

The most reliable, reputable buyers used agents and there was nothing wrong with the practice. She was a designated agent. She and how many others? How many others here thought she was bidding for the Cutler and bid *for* Arnold at a sale. "Some of the buyers," Cass had said.

Thinking of Cass stung, too. Facing Arnold and calling him every dirty name in the book had a certain appeal to her. Facing Cass and telling him what a complete, trusting jerk she evidently was...oh, that would be even harder. Kate had been naked and vulnerable in Cass's bed but she had never felt as totally naked, totally vulnerable as when she pictured herself admitting her monumental weakness and lack of foresight.

She did not knock. She pounded as Arnold had taught her.

He swept open the door and looked her up and down, smiled and replaced his cigar in his mouth. "Must have been some party! You missed your eight o'clock with Nishi. He called here."

Kate marched into the room, stiff-legged. "I was conferring with Jean Michel LeClerc. A fabulously interesting conversation. I thought I might share it with you."

She almost pitched on her face, forgetting that she had one leg slightly shorter than the other. She sat down and pulled off her shoes, brandishing them at Arnold.

"LeClerc? Wouldn't have pegged him as your type," Arnold said, flicking an ash and missing the ashtray. "Yashima, the fast operator, to a Gallic charity case? You know art, Cleary. You don't know beans about men."

"But I'm learning. I'm a real fast study," Kate retorted. "I learned how you could take the loss of an *ukiyo-e* with an air of good grace and sportsmanship. You didn't lose it! LeClerc got a cash commission, you got the Sharaku, I got cut out. Cross-bidding is a nasty little scare tactic to drive up prices and frighten other bidders off. You refined it a bit."

Arnold went over to his desk and riffled through papers, keeping her in his line of sight. If he was worried about her going berserk and acting violent, Kate felt she had accomplished something.

"Do you hear me?" she shouted. "I know! You hired me to bid, appraise, buy, walk all over God's creation...sole agent and aide, and there're people out there bidding for you whenever something comes up that you would not give away. I get to pick one! How many did you feel it was necessary to eliminate from my possible choices?"

He produced the letter of agreement between them, flourishing the single sheet of paper like a shield. "Sit down. Cool off. You'll live longer."

She took the contract with numbed fingers and forced herself to read it very carefully. She studied it as a lawyer would, not the delighted curator of a small graphics collection. Salary, expenses and "a gift from the works collected, to be selected by Dr. Katherine Cleary of the Cutler Museum" didn't give her any sense of triumph, now.

"You're in there as 'designated agent solely for...blah, blah, blah,'" explained Arnold, although there was no necessity to rub salt into the wound. "I never signed you on as 'sole agent,' and if you got the wrong impression—"

"My tough luck," said Kate calmly. "And if I quit, I don't even get to choose from what there is."

"Yes, indeed."

"And you won't fire me if I tell you that you are an unmitigated bastard and I will spread the word."

"No," he chuckled. "I've been called worse."

"Not without justification, I'm sure. Well," she said on a long exhalation, "I believe I will give this some thought. I wouldn't want to do anything rash, would I? Not twice."

"Hey, don't whine," Arnold suggested. "The pieces we have bought, you and me, they aren't exactly five and dime works. You'll have a dandy bonus. Just not my Hiroshiges..."

"Or your Sharaku." Kate went to the door and put her hand on the knob, looking back at him ruefully. Losing, she thought, is bad. Losing to a cheap, slick chiseler is intolerable. "Arnold, as we are fond of saying back in California, have a real nice day!"

She slammed his door behind her as hard as she could but it wasn't much satisfaction. Truthfully, it wasn't any satisfaction.

Taking a shower and changing helped. It helped to call Nishi's office and apologize profusely and cancel the appointment. Crying for twenty solid minutes like an inconsolable child was, undoubtedly, the greatest help.

Kate made up her mind she was going to waste the entire day, shopping, reading, and feeling sorry for herself. She would enjoy frittering away a month's salary on a dress, even knowing it was her equivalent of stamping her foot. If Arnold didn't like it . . . he could fire her.

She dialed Cass's office, prepared to deliver her elaborately concocted alibi to beg off tonight's dinner. It wasn't so much a question of whether she told him or not, Kate rationalized. She was bound to be honest but there wasn't any particular rush. Whenever she told Cass, they would most likely quarrel about what she should do. Crow was a better meal eaten alone.

"Hello, this is Dr. Katherine Cleary. I'd like to leave a . . . hello?"

Cass was on the line before she could get her bearings. "Kate, honey, what is it? Besides telepathy, I mean. I was planning on calling the Princess later to tell you some good news and some bad news. I'm going to Nara—bad—but I'm going tonight—good. The sooner I get there, the quicker I'll get back. We aren't going to miss one petal of the Cherry Blossom Festival."

"Oh," was the measure of her eloquence at the moment.

"Kate? Kate? Are you there?"

"Not all there," she said weakly. "Well, okay. You're in a meeting. I didn't mean for your secretary to put me through. I can hear people in the background so I'll . . ."

"No, you won't," retorted Cass. "Kate, I gave the secretaries standing orders that if you called, they were to get me. Now, what's the scoop?'' He lowered his voice. ''You wanted an afternoon rerun of last night?''

''Ah...oh, I called about the dinner.'' She smiled faintly, knowing she was a miserable, transparent liar. ''It doesn't matter now. I'm taking the day off and I was planning on bolstering the Japanese economy. Call me tonight before you leave, darling, to say goodbye.''

''Don't you want to see me?''

She bit her lip. Damn the man! He either could read minds or hear things in her voice she didn't say. ''Of course, but you had a big day planned. When can you fit—''

''I'll send the company limo over to pick you up now. I can walk to the Tokyo Tower and meet you there. We can have lunch, pretend we're in Paris on the Eiffel. Kate, you are very quiet!''

And you're very perceptive. Very smart, very tough. ''You are in conference. I feel kind of guilty, making you walk out.''

His softest voice again, the one that made her feel as if he were right there, touching her. ''It's shocking what you can make me do, Dr. Cleary. And it's good. I need to change. You seemed to think so last night, anyway.''

''All right,'' she said weakly and sat down on the edge of the bed. There were new wrinkles every day to deal with, but she was also contending with the oldest feeling in the world and it was brand-new to her. ''Cass, I wanted to tell you something else. It could wait. Or I can tell you again when I see you. But I want to say it . . . just because I want to. I love you."

"I know, Kate," he said very soberly, "and that's what's making me feel alive."

CHAPTER NINE

IT WAS THE STUFF of a young girl's dreams—although not hers—brown Mercedes, tan leather upholstery, a liveried chauffeur who glanced at her once or twice in the rear-view mirror. Kate studied a tiny stylized gold sun, the Sunco crest, on the plastic barrier that separated her from the driver, and ran her hand over the luxurious seat.

The car slid close to the curb at the base of the imposing tower. Cass was already there, waiting for her. It was only a matter of hours since she'd left his arms and his bed but the little start she felt whenever they met was still there, too.

He had chosen this place to meet. Accident or another nudge from fate, Kate wondered as she got out. The Tokyo Tower was tall, free-standing and made of steel. So was Cass. She could not allow herself to be less, a Leaning Tower of Pisa who needed a prop.

"Long time, no see," she said with a kiss.

Cass waved the driver away. "Hey, I figured if you could get a day off, so could I. Well, an hour or two, anyway. Are you out on pass or absent without leave?"

They bypassed the tower's complex of shops and restaurants, recording and television facilities and headed for the observation platform.

"I haven't decided yet," Kate said as they were rising the full thousand feet. "Fran always told me that when the going gets tough, the tough go shopping. When you go back to work, I'll try it out. I've been here almost two weeks and haven't bought so much as a postcard for myself."

From the circular viewing platform, nothing was hidden. There was Tokyo Bay, ships riding at anchor and moving in and out of harbor. The sprawling city was completely exposed for the crazy-quilt snarl it was, made uglier by the distant farms and forests, glimpses of Japan's rural tranquility. It was the sight of Mt. Fuji, though, and the volcano's foothills that always took Kate's breath away.

"I climbed it one year," she said. "Nine hours up, five hours down, just to see the sunrise. Sometimes I take the walking stick out of my closet at home and look at the wood-burned signs of the ten stations and I can't believe I did it." She turned her back on the magnificent, sacred mountain which symbolized the whole country. "It seems like it was a hundred years ago, like I was a different person then."

"I've never climbed it," Cass said. "In more than thirty trips here, I haven't taken one step on the slopes. My grandmother thinks it's a very important thing to do and I . . . never mind."

"Tell her you will and do it."

Their eyes met. Cass put his arm around her waist and they resumed their walk. "If I do," he said, "I'd like to go with you. That is, if we can find the time."

Every square inch of the city below them was priceless in real estate terms. The winding trails of narrow streets would never be widened because of that fact, and yet there were plenty of green blotches in the city's patchwork. Parks and gardens were not amenities; homage to Nature and space to honor her were necessities.

Kate gestured at Ueno Park. The recent rains had done their work, swelling the acres of cherry blossoms into a soft green mist, almost ready to burst and open into white and pink fragrant clouds. The display this year would be spectacular but even if it wasn't, she would enjoy it. Seeing and sharing the festival with Cass would make it particularly memorable.

"I'll be back in plenty of time for the Cherry Blossom Festival," he promised. "By then, my sources should have turned up the information you wanted on the Muratas, I'll know how long I can get away for, and you may have decided to tell me what's bugging you."

She kept leaning on the railing with him, gazing off at the promise of the trees. "You know. I'm concerned about Fran and I'm still mulling over our disagreement last night."

"We made up this morning...or else, it was the next best thing to making up. And I just said there's someone on the case for Fran. Now, does it still call for a day skipping school?"

A lie or a clever evasion might forestall more trouble but it wouldn't solve it. Kate turned her head slightly to see his profile, sharply cut against the sky, and couldn't lie.

"Yes. I don't want to sit in the hotel room, wearing a dunce cap. I am getting an education I never expected from Arnold. I want to tell you about it. I want to talk about it and ask for advice." She paused and he smiled, knowing what was coming. "But I don't need you to laugh or say, 'I told you so,' or, worst of all, tell me to do what I know you would not do yourself—not in a hundred years."

"And what would that be?" His smile faded, his eyes stayed fixed on the organized madness of the city.

"Give up. Cut and run," Kate said. "If I quit, this trip is a complete loss so far. I'll go back empty-handed, the empty-headed, double-crossed dolly. A bimbo."

She was warming up and as Kate went along, telling him about her morning coffee klatch with Le-Clerc, she didn't spare herself. Arnold Whelan-Jones had planned the arrangement and written the contract, a foolproof scheme. But he had only nominated her as the fool; she had willingly elected herself to the post.

Cass listened intently and asked a question or two. He didn't laugh.

"He knows I won't quit," she said loudly. "Half a loaf is better than none. I might have, if I had caught on sooner. Before the first sales, say. But he was right. I've put in my time and I want to collect. There are two more auctions; he might use Watanabe to bid another print or two he doesn't want included in the spoils. Okay, I'll have to live with it."

"You mentioned advice. What kind of advice, Kate?"

Glancing down at her fingers curled around the railing, Kate saw that her knuckles had gone white. There was no feeling in her hand, but a strange feeling was inside her, one she was unfamiliar with. It was almost as sharp as desire but not as sweet. It was powerful enough to make her head swim for a second, something akin to stepping too close to the edge of a cliff and looking down—half thrill and half fear.

"He shouldn't get away with it," she blurted out. "He's got the letter of the law on his side but not the spirit of the law. There are ways to beat men like Arnold at their own game. You do it! You do it all the time, dealing with him or others just like him. And so could I."

"Yes, you could," Cass agreed. "And you might, seeing how cold your eyes have gone, how cold your fingers feel." He pried her hand off the railing and held it. "Please don't ask me to give you tips on how to take Arnold down, because I would squash him like a bug if he crossed me, but I won't coach you."

"Why not?" Kate demanded. "Why is it all right for you and not for me?"

Cass hit the steel bar in front of them with his free hand so hard she felt the impact run from him through her. It must have hurt but he didn't appear to notice. He looked so sad, it was painful to see.

The sunlight caught on the gold pin on the lapel of his black suit. She dropped her gaze to the metallic flash and saw it was the company's emblem.

"It's not all right for me," Cass grated. "I have to pay, like everyone else, for what I do. The costs are heavy and hard to calculate because it isn't usually in dollars and cents. I have to pay in feelings. I have to care less."

There was a new note in his voice, a raw timbre that made her look up and see a different sheen to his eyes, the moist glint of unshed tears. If he had argued or screamed or ordered her to forget this nonsense, Kate would have been capable of taking him on.

She put her arms around him and her head on his chest, not as much to comfort him as to hide from the terrible grief in his eyes.

To a casual observer on the tower, they were a loving couple, nothing more. But much more was going on. Even Kate could not put into words what was happening, a desperate hold, a struggle to reach each other, a longing that went far beyond physical need.

"Think about it," Cass said after a few minutes. "Oh, Kate, Kate, Kate...I don't want to go. It's all so simple when I'm with you. I care and I feel and things make sense."

They walked some more, around and around the platform, oblivious to the views they passed. As lunchtime approached, there were more tourists and a group of shrill, chattering school girls to avoid. Kate had to smile when she noticed that she and Cass were as much a curiosity, the object of quick glances and whispers from the middy-clad girls, as the panorama of Tokyo.

"We have an audience," she warned him when Cass brushed her cheek with a light kiss. "And I think they're forming a fan club for you. See the cute chunky one with pigtails? She's dying to come over here and get a good, close look at you and find out why a movie star is with a beanpole *gajin* like me."

Cass disagreed, shaking his head and laughing softly at her. "You don't understand what happens when you walk into a room. Some of the men are scared that you'll talk to them, the others are afraid you won't. I'm only guessing, but I imagine most of the women sit there and hope you won't talk to their husbands at all.''

"And which group of men did you fall into when we met?''

"Neither,'' Cass said with a grin, his old grin. "I didn't want to just talk. You brought out the primitive, basic man in me. I didn't believe the veneer of civilization was so thin until that night at the gallery; I was seriously considering what would happen if I made a grab for you, dragged you off and did every unspeakable act to you I've read about. Then, we were going to have a nice, long chat.''

"About unspeakable acts, I hope,'' said Kate, starting to laugh. "Hail, the conquering hero! Well, it is a simple, direct approach.'' Kate sobered instantly when she remembered the approach Cass had used when Whelan-Jones had walked in on them. He had gone from tender lover to formidable adversary without blinking an eye.

"Talk about conquering heroes,'' she said. "You never let up, do you? You never just relax and forget about work. Work is your arena. It's where you shine, where you conquer the world. But the world is full of people like Arnold who don't play by the rules and you don't like to play dirty.''

He agreed wholeheartedly. "And what about you?'' Cass asked. "I'm not the only one born out of this century. I don't want to leave here with us fighting but it should be said, Kate. You can't relax and forget your work because it allows you to hide from a world you don't particularly like. The pace, the technology, the deceits. You could have lived so happily in the Japan of the woodblocks, a place that doesn't exist anymore.''

Kate gave Tokyo a final glance and wondered if he had hit her problem on the nose. When it was Edo, built on swampy lands, the city was simplicity itself. The people lived simpler, harder lives with clearer goals; bad taste and bad manners were moral offenses. Warriors with the most rigid discipline were the most highly exalted class, not because they took lives at their discretion but because they were required to throw their own away without a second's hesitation.

''I've got to go,'' Cass said for the third time before it registered. ''I'll call you from Nara every chance I get. In the meantime... I'll leave a key to my apartment with my secretary. Kate, don't argue with me. I'll leave it, that's all. You are going to do what you want to do, I know that. I'm entitled to hope whatever you decide doesn't drive a wedge between us, isn't going to destroy you.''

''What entitles you?'' Kate asked, wanting to hear him say it. *I love you.*

If the words emerged in a passionate confession made while his hands and mouth were driving her wild, they would be wonderful. But she longed to hear him admit it without the drug of desire. Why couldn't he say it? She had.

''This does,'' Cass whispered and he kissed her with such abandon that they had to stop when the school girls' chorus of squeals made them both laugh.

DESPITE THE FACT that Cass had not given her any advice, Kate decided to take Arnold Whelan-Jones on. She had a plan. First, her logic dictated that she dress herself for battle. Her mouth went dry when she looked at the price tags on designer dresses—the modern woman's answer to armor. Live a little, she urged herself, and found it didn't take that much urging, after all.

Fran was on to something. After the first dress, it began to feel good, trying on the most outrageously priced and extravagantly beautiful clothes, and saying, "This one…and this one." The shoes were easy; she always had a weakness for elegant shoes. The silk—ah, real silk—underwear was pure self-indulgence. Any woman would feel invincible with silk underneath it all.

Kate had no doubt about the black linen outfit with a long brocaded paisley jacket. She wasn't as sure she would have the nerve to wear a perfectly simple, immensely revealing dark-green dress. It screamed, "Eat your heart out" in every language known to man and it was so gorgeous Kate didn't want to take it off. Impulsively, she bought. Where she would ever wear it, she didn't know.

The second step in her plan was to arm herself and plot her campaign. There was ample opportunity during the rest of the day and that night to see and talk casually with many of the same men she and Arnold had done business with. There was plenty of evidence freely offered when she turned on the charm. By the time she was finished, she'd have enough on Arnold to hang him with.

What was she waiting for? Kate touched the stiff fabric of the brocade jacket before she hung it up in the closet. She had gathered enough not-so-tasty tidbits at tonight's dinner to choke Arnold Whelan-

Jones. There was no corner he hadn't cut, no toes he had missed stepping on at one time or another.

One bite at a time, it wasn't much, but a buffet of those tidbits would probably sicken him, make it incredibly difficult for him to move with ease in the more respectable art circles. Setting the table and exposing him for the monster he was looked almost easy.

Kate knew it could be done, and now she knew how to do it. She had lots of influential friends here and across the Pacific. They trusted and valued her opinion on art works. They weren't likely to dismiss her appraisal of Whelan-Jones, and all the money in the bank of California couldn't buy a decent reputation. He could be exposed, humiliated and ridiculed.

What was she waiting for? She couldn't ruin Arnold or bankrupt him, but she was holding the power to hurt him with this same hand that touched a fine work of art with reverence or stroked the body of her lover with delight.

And when Cass called her that night, she said, "I'm basically weak, I guess. I never genuinely hated anyone before. I hurt people but I never did it deliberately.

Cass replied wearily, "He's not worth your hatred, Kate. You pick your friends so carefully, and like Fran they're probably good friends, good people. Even allowing for a certain bias, I think you have only considered decent men worthy of loving and damn few of those. Arnold's not your equal as a foe. Don't waste yourself on him."

They fought without raising their voices but it was fighting just the same. Kate hung up, feeling empty, feeling hollow and miserable, hearing the same feelings echoed in Cass's voice. As she took down her hair from the elaborately braided crown she'd tortured it into, there wasn't the usual sensation of relief, the small but real pleasure when its weight came off her head.

Tomorrow. She had to make a decision and do whatever she was going to do by tomorrow. The end of the sales was in sight. Arnold was making noises as if the *tan-e* were about to appear any minute and she would be required, by the contract, to evaluate them for him.

Tired beyond feeling, drained past the point of caring, her last conscious thought was of Cass, though, not Arnold. Not the *tan-e* she didn't want to see in the hands of a clever, nasty old man.

Dreams are a way to hide from a world that is unpleasant or unlikable. Kate found solace in one, an often repeated one. It was a different Japan, the place she had seen so often hanging in the galleries—the feudal glory restored in crisp, realistic detail, all the colors more vivid than in the woodblocks, all the silenced voices speaking to her.

Cass had only guessed that she longed for it, but no one knew she had been there. It was a comforting dream, if not a comforting world. Populated with beautiful, graceful women and fierce, proud men, her dream world came to life, but it was always manageable. The men didn't have to fight the bloody battles, but pose at the ready, eyes flashing and voices raised.

The women swayed and moved in the flowing, flowered silks that whispered. There were crickets calling and the time to stop and listen to them. She was there, knowing it was a world of danger and beauty, but there was no confusion over which was which. There was compromise and sacrifice but the stakes were higher—love, war, life and death.

Cass was there. She had her warrior in a silk-laced and metal-plated shirt armed with two finely crafted and tempered swords. He fit into such a world easily, but was the lady with the green eyes only watching or was she there, too?

Kate surrendered to the dream and sank deeper into a quiet sleep. Her cheek pressed the pillow, warmed like flesh, and her mouth formed a name and relaxed into serenity.

The next day she walked into Arnold's suite with no plan, no thought of how to proceed. She felt composed, calm and blank.

Arnold paced the carpet and clipped off the end of his cigar with a vengeance. "We have a sale tonight. You are planning to attend, I assume."

"No," Kate said coolly, "I wasn't. Before you wear a path in the rug, why don't you mix us both a drink and we'll swear to be civil with each other?"

He raised his eyebrows, wrinkling his brow, but proceeded to fix two glasses. Kate got hers handed to her with a wide, triumphant smile.

"It doesn't really matter if you go to the auctions or not," he said. "You did all the notes I need. There's only one job left for you to take care of..."

"The *tan-e*? Or using my dealer-buyer grapevine to let everyone know how slickly you operate?"

Arnold sat down, blew a smoke ring and watched it disintegrate. "Don't get cute," he said. "You've got a lot at stake, Katherine. I don't have to enumerate."

"My reputation, my self-respect." Until that second, she wasn't sure what she was prepared to do or say. The words wanted to come out of their own volition and she let them. Whatever happened, she was going to be strong.

"A warehouse of fine works, a lot of money," countered Arnold. He reminded her of *Jaws* when he flashed his perfect dental work. "You're not able to fox me, little girl."

A twinkle of real amusement crept into her eyes. "You think I'm trying to cut myself a better deal? Drive up my price? Yes, you would. Nothing. I'm doing nothing for you or to you. I'm quitting."

He didn't believe her. The wheels in his head were spinning so fast, Kate could have sworn she heard a whirring noise. The ice-blue eyes opened and narrowed in suspicion.

"Where's the catch? What's the sting?" he demanded with a quiet menace. "You quit, you get nothing."

"I'm cutting my losses." Her explanation was clear and firm but soft. "I remembered why I chose my field, Arnold. It was out of love, a very pure love, and it wasn't muddied with greed or blind ambition or hatred. Now, it is."

"Spare me," he growled, thrusting his head forward. "Write me a check for your expenses and I'll believe it. Walk out of here without your precious bonus print and I'll be impressed."

Kate opened her purse and extracted her personal checkbook. She could feel his eyes on her as she filled it out, the pen moving in smooth, confident swoops.

"What do you want?" he asked in a snide tone. "Did the work cut into your love life too much? Okay, you're off the hook until the *tan-e* pop up. I was young and foolish once."

She glanced up with green marble eyes, betraying not a hint of feeling. "Here's young-and-foolish Kate's tuition. I've learned a great deal from you, Arnold, but I'm willing to fail the course. I don't like your course of study. If I do what I was planning and smear you, I pass with honors—your honors."

"By God, you're serious," he said, getting up and striding over to the couch. "Why? Why?"

His face was a sickly oatmeal color and he pulled the check from her fingers, staring at it with a dull, uncomprehending look. When Kate stood up to leave, he backed away as if the piece of paper was proof that she was a lunatic.

"Don't try to make sense of it," suggested Kate, seeing his confusion. "I wanted to do the right thing, not the sensible thing."

When she took a deep breath, there was a stab of pain behind her breastbone because it *did* hurt to lose. But not as much as she had anticipated. She wasn't crushed, ground into powder, only humbled.

"I'll pack now and be out late this afternoon," she said on her way to the door. She thought about Arnold's prediction that she would thank him and smiled faintly.

Arnold followed her, recovering his usual wit, charm and style as he bore down on Kate. He yanked at her wrist, gripping her hard. She tried to shake him off but he clung to her as he evidently was clinging to another strange idea.

"It is the *tan-e*," he roared. "You have seen them. What is it? They're fakes and you want me to be taken? Or they're great and someone offered you the right price to work for him.... There's an angle. There always is."

Without screaming back at him, Kate insisted that Arnold had three seconds to take his paw off her. She didn't color or pull against him but she meant it. After he let go, she smiled again, ignoring the red marks marring the whiteness of her wrist.

"I didn't even threaten you with anything," she said, talking more to herself than him. "I'm the loser and you're the one that's scared.... How very interesting!"

She was down the hall with her hand on the door-knob. Arnold blistered her back with a string of short, inelegant phrases and Kate was aware of relief and a quiet sense of happiness. She was free. Poorer by a hefty sum, sadder but wiser, and free.

"You screw me and see what happens. All hell will break loose...you and Holman will both be janitors."

"Have a real nice day, Arnold," Kate said. She was sure he was planning who the next innocent would be. Whom could he bend to his will next?

The snags in acting on feelings, on impulse, presented themselves immediately. She hadn't done her normally organized thing and planned step two. The deskman downstairs practically wept in apology, but he was booked solid on single rooms for the next few days. He called the Plaza, the Hilton and the Kiyo for her and kept calling Kate back, moaning, until she was busy reassuring him that all was well. She was beginning to believe he was going to ask her to his own home to spend the night.

All right, she thought with resignation, snapping the locks on her suitcases closed. She didn't want to take Cass up on his offer, but it was another case of pride above anything else. Tonight, when all the implications of what she'd done hit her, it might be uncomfortable to be in the bed where this was all foretold, but having no bed was worse.

Swallowing pride and eating humble pie in one day was a new diet. Well, a lot of new things were happening, she decided philosophically, and went, bag and baggage, to Cass's apartment.

The expected case of the blahs struck her and Kate curled up in a bed too long, too wide, too lonely for one person. She was dry-eyed but wide awake, restless when the phone finally rang.

"My, what big eyes you have! Who's sleeping in my bed?"

The clock clicked and it was just past midnight. Kate sank back on the bed. "I'm not sleeping. I was wishing you were here."

"If I were there, you wouldn't be sleeping, either," Cass said softly. "Nara is dull. It doesn't offer much for the weary traveler. Tokyo has everything I want right now."

She laughed but her heart was racing fast enough to reach Nara and back in the pause. She was with him, magically. He was with her, whispering in her ear.

"I'm fine," she said. There was a sanctuary in his throaty baritone. "I left not only the Princess but the King. It was the right move."

Without warning, she felt tears begin to slide down her face. Her voice was still steady, but the tears were hot and burned her skin.

"Are you hurting, Kate?"

"My pride. My pocketbook. I'll heal," she replied slowly, gathering control of herself.

"Did he hurt you? In any way. Kate, I've seen him get violent. Tell me the truth." He had gone steel and stone. A cold wind swept all the way from Nara. "Did he hurt you?"

Arnold, count your blessings, thought Kate. "No. I don't want to talk about it because it was . . . unpleasant. I've got some time alone, peaceful time to think and I need it. I finally got through to Yoshio's secretary and I can see him late Monday— maybe!"

"Good, a weekend off. And I'll be there sometime tomorrow." He chuckled. "I know this fellow who is able to work miracles with a massage. Would you be interested?"

Kate rolled onto her side and relaxed her hand, letting the pillow hold him next to her ear. The thought alone could excite her. "Do you know him? Where I can reach him?"

"I taught him everything he knows," Cass responded with unmistakable huskiness. "And, Katie, you reach him . . . more than anyone else . . . so easily, it's indecent. He doesn't even have to see you or touch you."

"Cass . . ." she sighed with longing. Tonight, another day, any waiting was too much. She said his name again, hoping it made him feel the way she felt when he said her name.

His breathing quickened. "You can say my name and get me aroused. Have you wondered what power feels like? Say it once more, Kate, and hang up and you'll know. Wait for me tomorrow."

"Cass. Oh. Cass." She put the receiver down quickly and lay there, staring at the ceiling. Her whole body was pulsing like a heart.

After all these years, she was learning how little she knew about herself. She had always supposed, as a winner, that she would be a good and gracious loser and she wasn't. There was still resentment and a craving for revenge inside.

She had always supposed, as a grown woman, she had explored the limits of her own sensuality and she hadn't. The need in her for Cass was overpowering, frightening in its persistence and strength. They made love and he satisfied her physically and she wanted more than the wild release, the instant of calling his name. More of him. All of him.

Kate, she told herself sternly, you are going to get hurt very badly. You've tasted failure today and you're hungering, begging, setting yourself up for more. No marriage, no long-term commitment and his words, "I have to care less."

More of him, all of him, insisted a voice within. And she knew she was going to listen to that voice.

Her internal whispers were even louder by the time Cass was due back from Nara. Kate was at the small airfield Sunco maintained to greet him. She couldn't have waited at the apartment when the desire to see him was too much to ignore.

His face seeing her was reward enough. His hug was as fierce as her silent voice, the look they exchanged as wild.

"You didn't have to meet me..." Cass began but he clutched her tighter. "Yes, yes, you did...and I'm glad."

They walked, arms linked, across the tarmac.

"No brass band would do. How about me?" asked Kate. "I can hum on key."

"You sure can. All the time I was away, there was a little buzzing sound in my head. 'Katie's waiting, Katie's waiting.' You believe in mental telepathy?"

Yes, she did. Love was a new wavelength, a clear channel to him. When would he say it? Could he?

"I've really moved in on you," Kate said with two meanings clearly in her mind. "My nylons in your bathroom, my toothbrush leaning on yours. You might have to shoo me away before I start rearranging the furniture."

Cass tweaked her nose. "Not likely. My house is your house, as the Spanish say. What'll we start with? Pictures on the wall, Ito and I grunting and groaning with the couches?"

"You mean it," said Kate quietly.

He tapped on the limousine's glass and the chauffeur drove them away without a backward glance.

"I mean every word I've told you," Cass confirmed. "And I haven't told you half of what I want to. It's a Yashima tradition and good business to be tight-lipped and keep 'em guessing. The last few days in Nara I went nuts thinking you might move out. 'I should have told her how badly I wanted her to stay,' I kept thinking. I should have."

"You just did," breathed Kate. "It's nice to hear. The lines are open. Call in your requests. I believe in mental telepathy but there's a lot to be said for direct quotes, too."

"I didn't want to go. I don't want you to leave." Cass half turned toward her and touched her cheek. There was a plea in his eyes Kate was being permitted to see—what he wanted, what he didn't want to say.

She had to push herself to her limits to know the best and worst about herself. She couldn't back off now. "Why? Is the taste of domesticity so sweet or so new? Are we living together as an appetizer or a dessert?"

He spread his hands, palms up, and put them on his thighs, studying the intricate pattern of lines and whorls. "This affair was started for the life of the product. I want to reach in my briefcase and hand you a lifetime guarantee, Kate, but I know there isn't one in it. I wanted to bring you back something from Nara that would show you how much I care."

"You did. You came back."

"And you were there," Cass said. "Minute to minute, I don't want anything else but you. Stay with me as long as you can, as long as you want. I don't know what else to say or offer."

She put her hands over his, felt his fingers begin to curl and hold her. "You could tell the driver to speed up a little, I guess. I've missed you an awful lot."

CHAPTER TEN

KATE SAT PROPPED UP in bed, balancing the manilla file folder on her knees. Taking off her reading glasses, she chewed one earpiece and watched Cass adjusting the knot of his tie.

"Ito's in the kitchen, fixing your breakfast," he cautioned her and came over, draping her bathrobe over the foot of the bed.

She put the glasses back on and scanned the photocopied sheets in front of her. The police prefecture files were, and always had been, meticulously kept. Every Japanese citizen all over Japan was on file. There were records on births, deaths, and registration upon moving from one place to another.

Knowing Japanese red tape, these had been very difficult to obtain. Cass had gone to a lot of trouble and expense for her and for Fran.

Cass walked over to her, dropping a kiss on the top of her head. "You are too smart for your own good, aren't you? I might have come up with a good reason in...oh, two or three tries. You got it on the first try."

"Unlucky guess," said Kate. She reached for and held his hand. "I'm glad you didn't get this sooner. We wouldn't have enjoyed the night out with Fran as much. I would have blabbed."

"What are you going to do? You are planning to tell Fran, aren't you?"

They could hear Ito singing a rock and roll ballad in Japanese through the closed bedroom door. Cass would be late for his meeting on discretionary funds if he didn't hurry. Kate glanced down at herself, naked to the waist, reading glasses perched on her nose, and thought about what a strange domestic scene it was.

"I'll call David this morning before I go see Yoshio Sabusawa," she said finally. "David should be told before Fran, I think. I have to know where he stands."

Cass just stood there, rubbing her bare shoulder and looking down.

"I was starting to believe that the Muratas were set against her marrying an American, a Caucasian. But it wasn't him, at all. It's her."

Cass put into words what she didn't want to say aloud. "You're going to give David the opportunity to bow out before you tell Fran. Kate, if he loves her..."

"He does," said Kate with certainty.

"Then, he'll want to be here with her. Alone and unsupported, Fran will crumple and agree to anything. And unless he's right here, David will never understand completely the depth of the Muratas' feeling." Cass bent down to kiss her goodbye.

She held him there a little too long, a little too tightly for a simple goodbye kiss. She couldn't bring herself to thank him for his efforts and she knew he understood why.

Cass was almost out of the bedroom when something occurred to him. "David Townsend will need a plane ticket. Have my secretary—"

God, she loved this man. "No, that's okay," said Kate softly. "He's my friend. I'll get his ticket ... but thank you."

"Will you call me at the office if you think of anything else?"

"Yes," promised Kate, lying outright. She must not rely on him so much, depend on his help and quick understanding. Soon, Cass would be leaving and she would still be here in Tokyo—but not in his bed, not in his apartment.

She got up and got dressed as soon as Cass left. The contents of the manilla file had killed her appetite but Ito would be hurt if she ignored his breakfast. So, she ate eggs Benedict and drank her fresh orange juice, swallowing the lump in her throat. And she praised Ito which set off a fresh burst of vocalizing while he did the dishes and she made her long-distance phone call to Riverside Hospital.

Her lack of doubt and trepidation about David was rewarded immediately. He would be there, if he had to do the Australian Crawl across the Pacific. Kate assured him she would be glad to pay for a round-trip ticket, but David insisted he would foot the bill. Even if it meant breaking into the honeymoon coffer to do so. Interns may be poor but they were proud. They were also virtual slaves. David didn't know how soon he could arrange time off.

"I'll get back to you as soon as I see my chief," he swore, stumbling over his words. "Kate, I...geez, I'm really...thank you and...I love you, Kate."

"I love you, too. I'll see you soon." She felt better when she hung up. Talking to David was like having her faith in mankind confirmed. He would always be there for Fran, no matter what.

ON HER WAY TO Yoshio Sabusawa's, Kate mentally prepared herself for bad news at her old professor's home. It wasn't like him to be difficult to reach or keep visitors at bay. During her days at the university he was never in robust health, and yet there were always swarms of students—"my family," he called them—around. He must be very ill to curtail his activities and need a full-time secretary to guard him.

He lived in the heart of the city on a lane too narrow to drive on. Kate walked the familiar twisting path, waving at children playing baseball and stopped to chat with a wrinkled crone who remembered her from her student days.

Nothing had changed. This was the Tokyo visitors rarely saw with tiny houses and smaller gardens, outdated plumbing and the appearance of another century. Yoshio's wooden house was more dilapidated than ever, worn to a lovely silver gray. There were roof tiles missing and the weathered gate hung drunkenly at the entrance on two of three leather hinges.

She revised her opinion as soon as she went into the courtyard and saw his pocket-sized garden. There was a change; the garden was far lovelier than her memories of it, with freshly swept walks, carefully pruned and cared-for plantings. Through the slatting of a checkerboard fence, a skinny flowering vine wove its way and Kate stopped to admire it. The fragrance was unbelievably sweet.

"Ah, a friend of the humble," a male voice said happily in English. "Perhaps it's not the prettiest but it is tenacious and brave."

He was a perfectly round little man with the suggestion of a mustache. His work clothes and the tightly held broom proclaimed him as a gardener but Yoshio had no gardener, as far as she knew. The professor's pride and joy was this tiny plot of ground and caring for it himself.

"Please," said Kate with a small bow for the sake of politeness, "what plant is this? I like it very much."

The man stared at her quizzically and set his broom aside with great care, propping it against the fence. "Why?" he asked.

The question struck her as ridiculous. Why does anyone like a flower? Kate reached up and unwound a long tendril, broke it off and practically stuck it under the little man's nose. Her presentation proved too enthusiastic; he began to sneeze violently and regularly.

Each sneeze was preceded with a gasp, a startled look, before he bent double with his explosive efforts.

Kate had no intention of being rude, but she became weaker and weaker with laughter watching him bob up and down. All she could think of was one of those ridiculous toy birds that sit on the rim of a glass of water and peck uselessly and endlessly away.

His wild string of sneezes ended and the man recovered quickly, watching her with quiet, undisguised interest. Kate was completely helpless, holding the stitch in her side and wiping her streaming eyes in a futile attempt to amend this unseemly behavior. When she wheezed to a stop, he smiled broadly and dropped her a bow that matched any she would give the honored professor himself.

"Hello and welcome, Dr. Cleary," he said. "I was told to expect you and the unusual."

"Well, I wasn't expecting you," chuckled Kate. "Oh, I am sorry about this inexcusable..." She went off into a long peal of laughter, just thinking of how he had looked.

Her appearance and reactions did not disturb the man in the least. If anything, he seemed delighted and his small dark eyes were alive with unasked questions. When Kate had to sit on a nearby stone bench to recover, he joined her, unwilling to leave her to her undignified, solitary giggling fit.

She tried offering an explanation. There had been lots of pressures and anxieties lately, she was excited and edgy about seeing her teacher again. The gardener shook his head, dismissing her excuses.

"I'm Hiroko Kishi, Yoshio's friend." He shook hands with her as if they were meeting at a cocktail party. His English was very clear, unaccented and cultured. "Secretary, gardener, nurse, scold and friend."

She complimented him on the garden but looked slyly at the unpainted, splintered house. It needed a friend's hand.

"The house will soon be empty. The new owners can deal with it as they wish," announced Kishi flatly.

Those simple words confirmed what Kate felt all along. Yoshio's letters skipped over his condition as if it were an inconvenience, but she knew. No fuss, no false shows of emotion. Death was natural, inevitable and treated as such.

She started to get up from the bench but Kishi restrained her gently. "Sit here a while longer and we'll talk. The visiting nurse is giving him his treatment and when she leaves, he'll be able to see you."

"How long?" asked Kate, staring straight ahead.

Kishi shrugged expressively. "Not long but long enough, he says. He works every day on his manuscript—his long overdue textbook. His strength is limited, so it is best that he sees very few people. When he is restless, he works or sits out here."

Yoshio's dream of writing the definitive study of Japanese art had occupied him, on and off, for thirty years. His students used to tease him about the cardboard boxes of collected writings strewn around his house. He could never seem to organize, to finish his dream.

"That's good news, at least," said Kate sincerely. "Is there anything he needs, anything I can do to help?"

"Of course!" Kishi shook his balding head in amazement. "You can be here and make him laugh, tell him the gossip he so loves to hear. More, perhaps. Ask him."

He glanced at the house and a nurse in trim uniform appeared in the doorway and waved a message to Kishi. She disappeared around the house, turning over the care of her patient to this jolly, strange little man.

Kishi took Kate's arm as if he were escorting her to a formal dance and led her up the rickety stairs.

"Look what good medicine I found for you in our garden," he crowed as they entered the cramped living room.

Amid an incredible clutter of his books and papers, Yoshio Sabusawa was enthroned on his bed, propped up by pillows. The warmth of his smile was unchanged, and his eyes were as penetrating and bright as ever. Kate went to take his slender hand, feeling fragile bones under the papery skin and kissed him.

"Sensei," she whispered, putting her whole heart into the respectful title of "master."

"Scarecrow," he countered and laughed. "Wasn't that what I used to call you when I was angry with you? Now, look at me...I can frighten off the crows."

"You look very thin and very tired," Kate said honestly. "Shall I wait for a better time another day?"

He grinned. "There are no better times and fewer days left. I will have all the rest I need very soon. Hiroko, shall we all have tea?"

His lack of anger and self-pity made it easy to fall back into old patterns. Yoshio pushed aside a pile of books with a skeletal arm and Kate sat down with him, scolding him for misleading her in his letters about his illness.

"It was pointless for you to worry and it will be equally stupid to waste a visit being chided," her teacher snapped. "You should tell me all about your work and this trip. Then, I can share my own happiness with you."

It made for an unusual tea party. Kishi, a gardener who spoke a nearly Oxfordian English, sat cross-legged on the floor. Yoshio kept his eyes closed but nodded or murmured quietly while Kate spoke more freely and frankly than she had really intended.

The major story was the state of the Cutler, her bargain with Arnold Whelan-Jones and an account of the subsequent troubles. She worked herself over for being such a naive, trusting idiot and mentioned, as she went along, the added complications with Fran and falling in love with Cass. Once started, she didn't want to stop, and by the time she finished, her tea was ice cold.

"Every thread of my life has become knotted and tangled," Kate said. "Thoughts seem very clear one minute and vanish the next, leaving me with my mouth hanging open. And I've talked way too much. *Sensei,* you used to tell me that was a good sign of bad character."

Yoshio's eyelids fluttered open. "Not always. Some very interesting things are occurring to you. And you have changed, Katherine. Very much changed."

"For better or worse?" asked Kate.

"Both," Yoshio answered quickly. "You have wasted energy on a man beneath your notice and persist in agonizing over what is finished. Casually, you tell us about another man who, I think, means everything to you and you expect a few words to suffice about him."

Kate thought it over for a minute. "Love, for Cass and me, is an impossible dream we're living for a short while. Arnold and his schemes are a cruel reality I have to deal with in my life and work."

"So smart, so enlightened a student and a foolish woman, all the same." Yoshio took the medication Hiroko passed him and asked to be lifted up on his pillows. "I can save my breath and show you my good news. When I get long-winded, it is painful."

Hiroko brought three large boxes over to them and Kate thumbed through the nearly completed manuscript. It was hopelessly jumbled, his writing as messy and disordered as his house, but brilliant. She was reminded of his lectures; he was never able to stay on one topic long enough to exhaust it. He wandered erratically and the students were forced to organize his genius and insights for themselves later.

"Twenty-seven years' worth," Kate said, awed.

"The book and I were waiting for you. How much time can you give us?"

Hiroko Kishi smiled at her, an I-told-you-so smile, and silently left the room. Kate didn't have to ask what help she could offer the professor; he was telling her.

"Four or five weeks for the final rewrite and organization," said Kate without hesitation. "If it isn't enough, I'd ask Holman to extend my stay. Could we do it that quickly?"

Yoshio nodded his head "yes" which set off a paroxysm of coughing. "Consider it carefully. Perhaps it will be too much to take on."

"What else can I give you?" asked Kate. "There is nothing else you want or need. And at that, I'm giving you a minnow for the whale you gave me in education and friendship."

Time would not clear her debt to this man. Without his support and encouragement, Kate knew she would not have persisted and achieved as much. She used the Japanese concept of *on*, the traditional obligation one person took on when he received a gift.

Repaying a debt was a matter of honor and in this case, something she wanted desperately to do.

"I wasn't *that* good a teacher," protested Yoshio with a faint laugh. "I am getting tired. Go hunt up Hiroko and tell him I want him to show you the other piece of good news."

The shadows and lines of his face had deepened. A momentary sadness swamped Kate and she wanted to refuse to leave him alone, doubting whatever he had to show her was as important as being with him. But she gave in, seeing his eagerness and realizing he wanted to avoid dwelling on himself.

Hiroko Kishi was back in the garden, pruning a tree to within an inch of its life. He asked Kate to allow him to finish before they complied with Yoshio's wishes. She was content to ask a few questions of her own. Kishi interested her. How long had he been here, tending to Yoshio?

"A little more than a year." He worked slowly with the most meticulous care she had ever seen. Every tiny scrap he cut off was painstakingly collected, every motion was perfect. "I will return to my temple in Kyoto when I am no longer needed here."

She must be truly befuddled or have been asleep these last two hours. Of course! Kyoto was the center of Zen Buddhist followers and Hiroko Kishi was a Zen monk. If she'd been sharper, she could have guessed it by his amused acceptance of their strange meeting. Zen masters found immense humor in the ordinary events of life and they liked to use humor in ways that shocked people out of complacency or ignorance. And he labored like a monk, devoted and intent on whatever he did, finding the simplest task worthy of every ounce of his effort.

He confirmed it. "I came here from Ryusenji with my abbot's permission to stay while I can be useful. Yoshio and I have been close since we were boys growing up together."

"I'm going to stay for a while, too. I'm glad there's some gift I can offer him."

Kishi stood up, brushing off his dirty knees, and looked at her with open delight. "There is no gift but the one of self," he said with an impish smile. "Come with me and I'll show you what Yoshio was talking about. He was afraid it would be gone before you got the chance to see it."

Kate assumed Kishi meant a special flower arrangement or a sapling budding out. Yoshio would think of those things as good news and treasures. They followed the stone path along the battered house to Kishi's room, stark and austere, devoid of any comforts but overlooking the garden and right for contemplation.

Kate obliged him by taking his one floor cushion. He brought out a burlap sack, opened it and produced an ornate brocaded case of the type fine prints were carefully preserved in. The richness of the fabric alone alerted her.

The case looked totally out of place in the calloused hands of a gardener. Kishi delicately slipped open the intricate system of silk loops and ivory pins locking it.

"They will be sold shortly but you should see them."

He started to open the stiff outer binding and stopped, inviting Kate to go ahead.

She was speechless, almost scared. Before she looked, she asked Kishi how her old professor who lived like a mouse, gave away most of his salary to help his students eat and buy winter coats, came to own genuine treasure.

"It was mine," said Hiroko. "I put them away for this specific purpose long ago. There will be a gift made to my temple and Yoshio's university from the sale's proceeds."

She sat, struck dumb, blinking at him.

He went on, happily. "Yoshio told me that he knew the Cutler could not afford such works but you would be glad simply to see them. The money they bring will endow scholarships for new students and Yoshio would like a small brass bell cast in his memory to hang in the temple at Ryusenji. Look! Why do you sit there?"

Kate's hands were shaking with excitement as she reached for the print case. Her heart rate shot up when she realized there was more than one print. A single print would be rare. She found there were four *tan-e*, an incredibly priceless set.

She studied each one, long and lovingly. The *tan-e* were as complete and perfect as the day they had been carefully peeled free from an intricately carved block of wood. Four sheets of slightly ivoried, heavy, hand-made paper were printed with crisp black lines more than three hundred years old. She couldn't even believe she was holding them in her hands.

They were as vivid and powerful as the day they were made. Kate smiled at the artist's special touches, the facial expressions painstakingly recorded on the minute faces of workers, merchants, prostitutes and nobles of a forgotten time. One picture, in particular, was such a tender portrayal of parting lovers that tears formed in her eyes, comparing her dread of losing Cass to the legacy of pain from the past.

Finishing the examination, Kate reluctantly lifted darkened green eyes to a thoughtful Kishi. "How did you ever come to possess these marvels? I know you own nothing as a monk."

"I entered the monastery ten years ago, liquidating my business, giving my wealth away, but these *tan-e* were set aside and stored until such time as I could make a gift, a memorial gift, to Yoshio."

Hiroko Kishi was a wealthy industrialist, it turned out. He had achieved the pinnacle of material success while his best childhood friend had pursued the heights of academic achievement.

"This," said Kishi, gesturing at the case between them, "is paper, ink, cloth and thread. It is beautiful only as long as the material endures. Yoshio wishes to transform it into another kind of beauty. The deep, booming sound of a bell calling monks to meditation will shatter the air and shake the lazy swallows out of their nests. His scholarships will plant seeds in minds and, in time, they will bloom into other flowers."

"And others will finally have the *tan-e* to look at until they crumble into dust," added Kate. "A lovely plan, a fine prospect, and I hope it happens."

The sobering thought of Arnold intruded. She asked about the arrangements for the sale and Kishi began to tell her, casually picking up the case and shoving it back into the sacklike protector. His hands owned nothing and wanted nothing, Kate realized.

She felt a twinge of chagrin and shame. She was more like Arnold right now, wanting it all—Cass's love, the Sharaku, the *tan-e*, praise and approval from the board, and Whelan-Jones's defeat. Cold-hearted? No, but greedy. Kate sighed. Yoshio was right; she had changed drastically.

"You will, I hope, be at the sale as an observer," invited Kishi. "The man you worked for will be there. I was fascinated to hear about him; I know the other interested parties but not Whelan-Jones."

They returned to where Yoshio was napping and the sound of footsteps was enough to waken him.

"When you are ready to begin helping me, call and Hiroko will make a place for you here," suggested Yoshio. "We can discuss the *tan-e* another day. You are looking at me with expectation, Katherine. What is it?"

Revenge, she thought. "I would like you and Hiroko to invite another bidder to the sale, *sensei*. Cass is also a collector of great art. He is here on business but I'm sure he would be willing to give you a sealed bid, if he won't be here for the sale."

"Done," they both said together.

She wanted to call Cass instantly but there was no phone in the house. Both of the older men were eager to meet him personally if she could arrange it.

THE SMALL MOM-AND-POP grocery at the end of the alley had a telephone. She could not wait longer, Kate decided, and stopped in to dial the phone with icy fingers.

"Are you able to talk?" said Kate without preamble when Cass came on the line. "Are you alone?"

There was a variety of strange, garbled sounds. He must have cupped his hand over the receiver and spoken to people in his office.

"Now," he said clearly. "This must be pretty good or pretty bad to get you to call me. Which is it?"

Kate laughed, not wanting to keep him in suspense much longer. "I hope you got your allowance this week. Better yet, tell me your piggy bank is full, you are in a shopping mood, and the soft-voiced, steely-eyed Miss Yamaguchi will not make you eat your lunch today in the office."

"Aha...you're going back for the dark-green dress," Cass speculated. "You don't need me along for that shopping trip, Kate. I told you I'd like it if you bought one of those in every color of the rainbow, charged it to me, and we'd call it my contribution to making the world a better, more beautiful place. Go ahead!"

Kate snorted derisively. "And I told you that was absurd. Think big! The biggest!"

Her barely concealed excitement really tickled him. "You're going to buy the whole Shinbashi store, including the designer...Kate, *this* from the woman who wouldn't let me give her a little computerized doll that bowed and danced and played the harmonica?"

"It wasn't a doll, it was a monkey and he reminded me too much of Arnold," she howled. "I don't want you to buy me anything! This is something I want you to get for you!"

"Can I have three guesses and a clue?"

"Four pieces of paper, about ten by fourteen inches. Not a water spot, a blemish on them. Early seventeenth century."

Silence. A long silence from his end. Then, a low whistling sound. "Wheeeew."

"Fate," said Kate with the sound of a believer. "It had to be. Of all places, of all times, and there they were. Not to be bought up and hidden away for another ten or fifteen years—by AWJ or anyone else like him. Do you want to see them? I can arrange it; if the owner lets you bid, you can leave a sealed envelope with him or me."

More silence. What was there to ponder, wondered Kate, twisting the telephone cord around her hand and cutting off her own circulation. Come on!

"High six figure? Low?" asked Cass in an almost cold voice. "You will, obviously, vouch for the owner's legality of sale or you wouldn't have called."

She calmed herself, understanding his changed tone. This was business; this was his Cass-doing-business manner. She had nearly forgotten. It had been a while since he'd used that brusque technique in her hearing.

This was not business to her. This was a thrill, a professional joy bound up inextricably with personal matters. She wasn't so foolish and slaphappy to imagine the Cutler would ever have a chance at acquiring such works. That financial impossibility left her free to want the next best thing—someone who would appreciate and love the *tan-e* combined with the surety that the prints would be seen, made available to more than a handful of people. If the buyer could be an American and not the Silas Marner type, she'd be in heaven. Who else was there? Who else had fate plunked down?

She fought the attack of silliness and excitement to a standoff. "Here's my best, short sight appraisal. Given the national pricing on similar works, any figure below four hundred thousand dollars would startle me. Practically speaking, six hundred thousand wouldn't be out of line. I couldn't be completely objective if I were bidding; they're priceless."

"Good enough," said Cass. "Where are you and how do I get there?"

She was standing dazed in the crowded store, when the whole situation really struck her. Cass was on his way already. Just like that! There were individuals, not only foundations and museums, who could decide on spending—or attempting to spend—half a million dollars faster than she had purchased two dresses.

It wasn't necessary to excuse Arnold's behavior, but in a brief second of insight, Kate saw how easily it might be to grow selfish, self-centered, self-indulgent on a grand scale. Her few weeks of playing "If I had all the money in the world" with Arnold's money was a minor brush with the feeling.

She watched herself bid and buy prints, any one of which would have caused her to faint dead away if someone had contributed it to the Cutler. But she was unable to forget the loss of a few works or forgive Whelan-Jones for his duplicity and greed. The *tan-e* and their disposition was important, but it was crucial to her that Arnold did not succeed, that his bankroll and bankrupt behavior didn't pay off.

CHAPTER ELEVEN

THEY LEFT YOSHIO'S arm in arm, with Kate babbling happily. She was exuberant, talking about how well things had gone, how much Yoshio and Hiroko seemed to like Cass, how excited she would be at the sale just knowing Cass's sealed bid was there.

A thousand things bubbled inside her, all good. The bitter was tempered with the sweet. Arnold wouldn't stand unopposed for the *tan-e*, there was something in the works for Fran—a ray of hope—and Kate had a mission, a purpose.

"After all these years," she exuberated, "his book is almost done. And to be able to help and play some part in finishing it . . . I'm so happy!"

"I never could have guessed," he teased. "The limo is just down the next street, waiting, but if you need to get rid of your excess energy, we can run through the city. Or you can do an Irish jig."

"Or we could take a very long, executive lunch." She gave him an unmistakable look. "Jogging and jigging aren't the only outlets for energy."

"Wicked, wicked woman," Cass said with enthusiasm.

He appeared to mull it over, as they got into the car. He settled for a kiss and a quick negative shake of his head. "No, let's drive over to Ueno Park. I'd rather celebrate at leisure tonight."

"Okay, an afternoon with the early cherry blossoms," Kate agreed amiably. "We'll be Fred and Lil from Menlo Park, California, with a camera and a basket of fried chicken."

He laughed. "All tourist, all American. I want a shot of me feeding the ducks with the Buddha in the background."

Kate read his eyes, not his smile. "No, you want to talk about something."

There was new grass on the small hills near Ueno. For Tokyo, the sky was remarkably sunny and clear. Many of the city's residents had taken the same notion to check out the blossoms on such a glorious day. Flocks of families, visitors with cameras, students in uniform, and casual lunch-time strollers inched by in procession.

Cass and Kate fell in with the parade of admirers and watched the ducks paddle through a lake sprinkled with fallen petals. The trees overhanging the water were heavy with masses of flowers, slowly opening.

The chauffeur had thoughtfully supplied a lap robe. Cass spread it for them on a relatively undisturbed patch of ground and they took in the scene, sitting silently.

"Are you really going to stay with Sabusawa?" Cass plucked at the fragile blades of grass. "No chance that you'd change your mind?"

"No reason, no chance," Kate said softly. "I want this. Nothing I did would begin to repay that man."

There was only a trace of perfume from the cherry trees on the wind. The smells of Tokyo were too

strong, overpowering. Ueno was lovely but there was
the feeling of the city encroaching, not one of peaceful contemplation. Kate concealed her disappointment; the ancient festival did not hold up very well
under the pressure and conditions of urban sprawl.

"I can't take off ten days," Cass said suddenly. "I
tried, Kate, but my juggling skills let me down."

He touched her hand and the surge of energy between them was very real. But so was his news. There
wasn't going to be extra time, a vacation for two.
Hadn't she known it all along?

"Where to? And when?" Kate focused on a family
coming toward them. A young couple, an elderly
woman in kimono, and a child approached and sat
close by.

"Berlin. I'm opening the branch office. Then, to
Washington for the rest of the government contracts.
A few more days . . . I'll push it to a week more."

Every time she was away from him, she felt as if a
piece of her heart were missing. This separation would
be the final one, the goodbye without the hello in a day
or two. Knowing the inevitable did not bring resignation. It wasn't fair, it wasn't right, it didn't make
sense.

"I took the next few days off," Cass said. "I'd like
to go away with you. We'll be back before the sale,
before David arrives."

"You'll miss the festival. *Hanimi*. But the cherry
blossoms are still beautiful," Kate whispered, as several floated by. The little toddler was trying to catch
one. "It's not the way I remember it, though. I used
to sit for hours, all by myself, in a part near the university and stare at one cherry tree."

"Say no more, pretty lady," Cass drawled. "That's why I was aiming to take you out to the country. We can see the real thing, the old *Hanimi*."

She turned to smile at him, Lefty Yashima, her California samurai. They took as much pleasure in looking at each other as in the cloudy, pale flowers. When he left this time, she might as well pack her whole heart in his suitcase. He was going to leave and she wanted more than a few days. There should be a polite way to ask for forever.

He was staring at her too openly, trying to see hidden thoughts.

"If there's one cherry blossom in Japan without soot on it, I want to see it," said Kate. "With you."

The child was stumbling closer, waving plump hands wildly over her head, emitting the full-throated chortle of sheer joy. The grandmother smiled indulgently and the child's mother leaped to her feet to give chase to her own errant flower.

"Sachiko! Sachiko!" she giggled.

The sound of that name, Bliss Child, ran through Kate with the force of a physical blow. What bliss! A child was a piece of forever. In the time it took for the woman to hurry over, scoop up Sachiko and bow apologetically to Cass and Kate, Kate held her breath. She was struck with thoughts so secret and well hidden that she wanted to keep them even from herself.

"A weekend," sighed Cass. He raised his head and grimaced. "It won't be enough for you, Kate." He threw a pebble to the side, angrily. "It isn't enough for me but that's what I have...that and a few days afterward to finish up. I can't ever be with you long enough. When you need me, I'll never be around."

She knew what lay behind his words and wished she didn't. She could agree, admit how futile it was to go anywhere for a last memory and say it should end now. Or she could cling ferociously to him and every second, every insane hope and dream.

"Whatever we have will be enough," said Kate. "Most people haven't had nearly as much in their whole lives."

She felt the enormity of the lie choke her. It was the most important and the most difficult lie she ever told. Drawing on an inner reserve she wasn't aware of before, Kate smiled at him, calm and reserved. She could live with this lie.

The truth was that she loved him and she wouldn't have Cass for any longer than cherry blossoms lasted.

TAKE NOTHING, Cass had instructed her. She followed his directions to the letter, pausing only to buy them both tangerines from a vendor at the train station.

In the blue jeans, plaid shirt and Frye boots, he was the Cass she went riding with in One Oak Park. Kate tossed him his snack as the *Limited* to Kyoto pulled into the station. The sleek, bullet-headed train made her imagine a trip to the moon, not a suburban park.

"Hey, are you going to tell me where we're going?" she asked as he helped her on board. "I don't even have a toothbrush."

"Place your absolute trust in Yashima Tours and you will be thrilled and delighted beyond your wildest expectations," Cass intoned like a recorded message. "Ready for adventure? Your money cheerfully refunded if we do not provide every comfort, gratify every whim, fulfill every fantasy. Mint toothpicks offered after every meal."

She pelted him with her tangerine peel.

The train was crowded with others heading for similar weekend celebrations. The scenery slid by slowly and then snapped by too quickly to enjoy. The passengers, so different from the usual hordes of business commuters, were infected with a holiday air that was contagious. They laughed and ate and showered Kate and Cass with questions when they discovered she spoke Japanese.

"Okitsu," announced the conductor and Cass jerked his thumb at her to get up.

"Here?" Kate dredged up her mental map of Japan. Okitsu was a minute speck, right off the famous, old Tokaido Road. Hundreds of years ago, the artist Horoshige immortalized the place, the bay at Suruga, the seashore and an inn, ancient even then.

"We had to find our century," commented Cass as they climbed down.

Four years ago, Kate and her father had driven stretches of the Tokaido. She was searching for Hiroshige's pictures but there was little left of the rugged scenery, the vast open expanses, the twisted lovely highway he had drawn. She had seen concrete roadbeds, diesel trucks and buses, billboards and the shells of new gray apartments.

"That Japan is gone forever," she murmured, a little sadly. Cass hired a car to drive them from the station to a walled inn less than two miles away. The huge beamed wooden gate stood open as it had for four centuries.

"Let's see if you're right." He winked at her. "This is the place!"

Kate walked slowly into the neatly raked gravel of the courtyard in disbelief. The inn must have been remodeled and renovated countless times but she recognized it. In the main, it had been no different when a wandering artist had sketched it.

A maid in a brilliant sulphur-yellow and scarlet kimono came running out to greet them as she loudly alerted the staff inside of their arrival. Kate bowed back, coming face to face with her own tartan slacks. She laughed out loud. She was out of fashion by four centuries.

Cass stood patiently in the hallway entrance and helped the tiny girl who insisted on pulling off his boots. Kate wrinkled her nose at him and went on alone, her feet whispering in the soft slippers provided for guests.

"The Emperor stayed here," Kate said, awe-struck, to the older woman at the desk. "Didn't he?"

"Several of them," replied the woman with her welcoming smile. She was effusive and warm after hearing Kate's Japanese. Not one American in a thousand mastered the difficulties of the language, and very few in her recollection had stayed there.

Cass got a lower bow, Kate noted. This inn *was* a throwback.

"Your room is ready," the woman said softly. "Yuki and Fumiko will see to you. Tea and cakes will be brought and our garden awaits your pleasure."

Kate was busy peeking into several suites as they followed a maid through the low, mazelike building. Most of the rooms she saw were modernized with televisions and the supreme concession to Western comfort, innerspring mattresses. Such an old, well preserved link with the past had been adapted to the convenience of the new. But the inn was a business, Kate reasoned, and it had to change to exist.

Yuki led them around the far wing of the inn, knelt on the velvet-smooth and shiny wood to slide back a paper wall. When they stepped inside, the *fusami* was shut soundlessly.

"A time warp," Kate whispered. "My God, it doesn't seem real."

Cass put his fingers lightly on her lips. "Japanese only, please. I can use the practice and you can use the atmosphere."

"Hai," she agreed, a trifle stunned.

The enormous room was matted with woven *tatami*. The furnishings were sparse but all genuine articles. A single amethyst iris, the emblematic flower of warriors, stood in an exquisite pottery vase. Kate opened one of the paper and wood panels at the end of the room and exclaimed over a manicured, miniature private garden.

"You missed the main attraction," commented Cass. He pushed her ahead of him into the tiny area off the main quarters to display a private family bath. There was no gleam of white tile and chrome here; it was cedar wood and hand-hewed buckets.

There was a scratching noise behind them. The maid bowed and pointed at the tray of tea and cakes. "Will you take your bath before dinner?" she inquired.

There was a dark fire in Cass's eyes and he smiled lazily at Kate. Somehow, the familiar and ritualistic routine of Japanese bathing did not come to mind.

"Now," Cass said.

The maid immediately set out a folding screen and brought a stack of neatly folded fabric. She offered them plain gray kimonos and gestured prettily at Kate, indicating she would act as *sansuke*, back-scrubber, and help her dress afterwards.

"I didn't bring a toothbrush but I have my own back-scrubber," said Kate, declining politely.

Cass laughed. The maid giggled, hiding her mouth with her hand, and vanished, probably to share this silliness with Fumiko.

As they undressed and put on the cotton robes, he teased her about turning into a pumpkin at midnight. It was too much like a fairy-tale place. "And they think the circus is in town," he said. "We look like giants. I feel like Gulliver among the Lilliputians."

"If I'm dreaming, don't wake me up," cautioned Kate.

He turned to her, his bottomless black eyes embracing her as securely as his arms. "No, I won't. This is for you, all for you. Whenever you want the fantasy to end, say so."

And if I never want it to be over? She pushed the unbidden thought out of her mind. It had to end. It was nicer to think about the enormous trouble Cass had gone to to make a dream happen. It was the most beautiful, loving gesture anyone had ever made for her. Treasure it, she told herself.

"Reality is not supposed to be as wonderful as our dreams," Kate said softly. "Or as terrible, for that matter. I never lived my dream before but I'll tell you later if it was good or bad."

"Our bath is waiting," he said. "So am I."

The small room was misty with steam and heavy with the scent of herbs and minerals, a woodsy, close place. A bucket and ladle were set next to a pair of low wood stools, side by side. The antique cedar of the tub was warm to the touch, moist and still aromatic. When Kate stared into the deep, very hot waters, they were clear but dark. Still she could see the black tarred bottom of seamed planks.

Cass turned around so she could see his back, the sash wrapped and tightly knotted there. "Help me," he demanded.

"Ladies first," Kate answered in a teasing tone.

"This is old Japan," he said. "I walk first, you follow. I can call Yuki or Fumiko to untie it and scrub my back."

Her hands rested for a minute on his lean hips. Her fingers touched the knot and undid it, passing the long ends in front and back, weaving her arms around him. He shrugged and the *yukata* fell for Kate to catch and hang on the wall peg.

There was no male body she was better acquainted with but suddenly, he was different. Kate felt the tension inside her as if she was seeing him for the first time, discovering him all over. Magnificent, exciting... hers.

She took off her robe. The quick intake of his breath made her smile faintly. He sensed it, too.

Filling the bucket, Kate began to pour dippers of hot water over him as if this was the usual way to spend a Friday night. The steaming water ran in rivulets over the breadth of his shoulders, the smooth honey skin of his arms and chest. He ducked his head and Kate obediently doused his inky hair. Walking behind him as he soaped himself, she stretched up and poured dipper after dipper down his back.

She watched the silver streams run over him down his narrow waist and over the hard-muscled flesh of buttock and thigh. When he sat down to spread more lather over himself, she sluiced herself and joined him.

The only safe place to look was into each other's eyes. Custom did not condone the glances they gave each other. They rinsed off curtains of suds, helping one another, melting maps of soap off and revealing new places to explore, but custom forbid it.

The steam rose in small plumes as they gingerly lowered themselves into the tub. Simultaneous sighs of contentment broke free and they laughed for the first time. The sound rose with the heated mists and faded, taking the tension with it.

"Don't ask me to scrub," Cass ordered huskily. "Once I start, I won't stop and we'll both drown gloriously. I may look Japanese, I can speak Japanese, but I am thinking typically American right now."

Kate laughed, full, throaty and rich. She slipped completely underwater and Cass hauled her up by an elbow, sputtering and laughing.

"We would have disgraced ourselves at a community bath," she said, tucking long wet strands of hair behind her ears. "I don't usually spend so much time soaping my toes and taking peeks peripherally. I have remarkable peripheral vision."

"You have many remarkable features," Cass said, openly enjoying them. "Thanks to years of discipline, I've perfected the art of appearing calm and bored while I go crazy. I'm beginning to feel like an overwound watch spring. If you have any hope of seeing the inn's famous cherry tree, we'd better not stay in here too long."

"I'm getting dressed. Right now!" She draped her washcloth over his face and got out of the tub quickly. While she was toweling herself off, he lifted a corner of the cloth and leered at her. When Kate threw a dipper of water at him, he chuckled and dropped the edge back in place.

"Breach of manners," she scolded. "You've behaved badly and lost face. Ogling at the bath? Tsk-tsk."

"Hey," he shouted after her, "I wanted to give you your fantasy. I don't see why I can't enjoy a few of my own at the same time."

"You can...later," said Kate from the next room. She knelt before the mirrored vanity and brushed out her hair. It required Fumiko's help to dress in a pale-green kimono figured with plum blossoms over an orange underslip of silk. Yuki was offering to arrange her hair when Cass strolled in.

"No, leave it as it is," he said and was instantly obeyed, without consultation from Kate.

"It was a man's world," she said in English when Yuki placed the comb on the vanity. "A nice place to visit but I wouldn't want to live here."

"Neither would I," Cass retorted, surprising her. He slipped on his own kimono, patterned in geometric designs of brown and burgundy, and inclined his head toward the garden.

It was growing dark. The flat polished flagstones were softly illuminated by squat stone lanterns. Kate could only hear, not see, an artfully placed waterfall. Flickering candlelight barely lit the crisscrossing strips of moss tying the tiny garden together. The moon was up, moving in and out of masses of clouds.

The inn had installed lights around their prize display, but Kate asked Cass not to let the gardener turn them on. She would rather sit on the bench provided and peer through the soft darkness at the ghostly outline of the tree they had traveled so far to see.

Cooler evening air swirled around them from time to time but she was warm, insulated from the touch of night by the bath.

"Sometimes a dream is better achieved with patience." Cass smiled at her and brushed back the thin veil of her hair from her cheek.

His words seemed to set the stage. As if the players were cued, the moon made her entrance. Between the thick, black banks of clouds, she appeared.

One very old, large tree trembled with the light's caress and appeared to bloom before their eyes. The shapeless mass became a huge, stirring waterfall of flowers sweeping down along arched, drooping branches to end in a foam of fallen blossoms.

Kate made a sound of astonishment and her hand reached for his. Their fingers welded together, her hand light as the blossoms against the warm gold of his skin.

No language expressed the inexpressible. There was beauty in the tree, in every single flower, passing description. For one brief moonlit moment, it was perfection. In a day or two, it would be gone. All the beauty she was seeing was already fleeing, ready to fall and blow away until another whole cycle was completed.

Cass stood up slowly and walked closer with her. The tree seemed to fill her wholly, every sense was open to it alone. She let the sigh of wind, the blinding snow of flowers and the fragile, quiet odor surround her.

Without touching the scarred bark, she knew its texture. Without tasting the juice of yet unformed cherries, she savored their sweetness. As if she had become the tree, Kate understood it. Time was measured in the fall of petals and the ripening of fruit.

"Kate?" Cass was calling her back.

Seeing her face, his heart had slowed and strengthened. He saw the wonder of a child when the Christmas lights are switched on for the first time or when a butterfly's wings unfold, orange and black, to be dried in the sun.

The capricious breeze picked that moment to tear hundreds of blossoms free, spilling them in a shower over the two of them standing so close and still. The petals clung to their skin and hid in the folds of the kimonos. Kate's eyelashes were hung with silken flakes and her long hair caught and held the whirling specks of the cherry's snowfall.

She laughed, seeing Cass dotted in white, and reached to brush them off her own face. His free arm shot up, grabbing her fingers hard. The speed of his movement, the power of his grip made the laughter die in her throat.

"Don't shake them off," he whispered. "That's a good omen—one of the best—to be given the flowers' blessing."

It was an old superstition. When the petals fell on a child, his mother gently counted them off, one by one, or let the wind take them. Girls were counted with, "luck, love, luck, love," and boys, "honor, riches."

"You don't believe in it," Kate said. "Or do you?" Her hand dropped to her side, sending a tiny drift of flowers to her feet.

Cass touched his forefinger to his tongue and pressed it to her cheek, counting away a single petal. "Just for tonight," he answered. "It seems right. Love."

The night was a blanket around them. The moon went into hiding once more. Cass slid his arm around her waist and pulled her a step closer with flowers floating at the touch. He kissed the corner of her mouth, taking away another flake of white. "Luck," he murmured.

Her hands met behind his head, drawing his mouth to her. Kate felt the compelling hunger for all of him. She wanted to know him in the same, mystical way she had seen the tree—with every sense, with perfect openness.

"Love," she said, all reserve melting in one fiery kiss.

The heat of anticipation welded them together. When his head lifted slightly from her, Kate almost screamed with the need for so much more.

Wordlessly, Cass led her back through the quiet halls to the room. Their passage was marked by a few scattered flowers. No sound, not even a whisper of the excitement they shared, escaped them.

In the darkened room with neatly spread and waiting quilts, Cass untied the wide obi around her and unwound it. He lifted the thin layers of silk from her, each layer warmer than the next, in an unhurried gentle way.

Kate bit down on her lower lip to hold back the sharp eagerness. When she was clad only in a final long slip of blue, his hands left her. The small bows closing the garment rose and fell with her labored breathing.

He was more careless undressing, the kimono sighing and sliding into a heap on the mats. Holding his hand out to her, Cass moved to the quilt and pulled back the cover. She went to him, longing to hold that body, so proud, so unashamedly male.

"You mean so much to me," Cass whispered, pressing her downward. "Too much, maybe. You mean everything to me."

"Yes, tell me," whimpered Kate.

His fingers were as impatient as she was tonight, tugging the thin ties of the slip until he spread the silk wide enough to suit him. He told her things, things he'd never said before. Her breasts were firm, round flowers with tight, sweet centers. There was no inch of her that didn't excite him, he said.

The futons beneath her were cold compared to the blazing heat of his body, the fires his words ignited in her.

Her mouth and throat burned under the slow trail of damp kisses he covered her with. Her hands held the knotted sinews of his shoulders and twisted in the thickness of his black hair. When his lips crossed the satin of her stomach and traced the curves of waist and hip, Kate called to him.

"Cass, tell me..."

The moist glide of his tongue, cool on the heated flesh of her inner thighs, slowed. While his fingers traced the path he wanted to follow, found her ready, all but wild with desire, he lifted his head.

She could not stifle a small sound, urgent and needful, or smother it entirely with her hand. Her eyes wide and blurred with passion also pleaded, tell me, while his touch made the fires join into a single towering flame.

"I love you...love you...love you," he moaned and rose over her, his body hard and throbbing, and his fierce kiss sealed the bond.

There was only the ultimate expression of love left and Kate reached out blissfully with her heart and body. As fully as he possessed her, she felt she now held him closer than ever before.

Hope as well as trust and surrender shone out of her face. He was lit by the moonight; she was illuminated by more love than she thought possible, shattered by the ecstasy of what they were doing and what they meant to each other.

The muscles of his back bunched and trembled under her touch.

"Kate," he groaned against her mouth. "My Kate."

She held him even tighter, ever tighter, locking him within her. Floating gently, unburdened by the sweet weight of his body, there were no dreams she didn't dare dream. With the explosive release of her body, a million white petals were drifting down endlessly, soundlessly in her mind. With his strength filling her, there was nothing more to want but a forever like this, a child like him.

CHAPTER TWELVE

IN THE SUBDUED LIGHT of morning, the room was cold. Kate woke huddled deep in the quilts and found herself alone. She tucked the batting closer and listened to the rustle of activity in the halls.

A maid scratched for admittance. "A restful night?" she asked brightly, sliding the tray with morning tea, hot and fragrant, toward the bed. "It is a very lovely morning."

Kate saw some scattered flecks of white, edged with brown, on the mat near her hand. She smiled faintly. "Thank you, yes," she muttered. "Please, where is Yashima-san?"

"The gentleman is still busy at the desk with phone calls. He regrets he is kept so long. Breakfast?"

The night was over with the announcement of business as usual, but Kate could not plunge into the day's reality so easily. She woke up in the world of commuter trains, scrambled eggs and business calls after falling asleep in a world of flowering trees. This was the end of the dream.

"Coffee and rolls?" she asked the maid hopefully.

She put on her clothes, not the crumpled silk robe. If she ached slightly, it was from sleeping on the floor, not from love. Had the fantasy ended for Cass with a bad back? The idea made her chuckle sympathetically. Reality was back with a vengeance, but she had no regrets. None.

"Ready for a walk?" Cass asked from the doorway.

"Before or after?" The look crossing his face made her clarify the thought. "Breakfast!" She emphasized the word.

"Oh, *that*! After breakfast, then."

By some unspoken, mutual agreement they were speaking English again. The fantasy had been acted out and it was better to drop the costumes and trappings of a dream. But, Kate discovered, a change had been wrought by a single evening. There was a new intimacy, closer than before, though she would not have believed it possible.

During the breakfast, Cass talked not only about the phone calls but what demands were being made on him. There were massive, almost frightening complications in his world that made even a few days away seem insignificant. "Losing himself" at Okitsu was more difficult for him than for her.

Like children, they held hands and explored the black sands of Mihu Beach. The sea wind was cold despite the sunshine and they ran the beach's length to keep the chill at bay.

Kate pointed at a wind-stunted pine. "This one?"

"So far you've asked about twenty different trees," Cass scolded and hugged her for her impatience. "The angel's pine is marked. Look for the sign!"

The wind licked up small, foamy waves to inch up the dark sands and sink without a trace. Kate slowed her pace at the promised marker and intently studied the gnarled, bent pine as if she, too, might find—like a legendary fisherman—an angel's feathered robe hung on the skewed branches.

"There aren't any angels in sight today," she said, wrinkling her nose. "I was going to make my own bargain. Forget the original story about the guy stealing it and making the angel dance on the shore to get it back. I was going to hold out for a better price."

"Like what?"

"Oh, never mind," Kate answered with a secretive grin. "There's lots I want but my list is between me and the angel . . . who seems to be on break."

"I'm not so sure," Cass said, pulling her down into the dunes surrounding the tree. "I see an angel."

The wind was chilly and Kate buried her face in his sweater, moving into the curve of his body for warmth. He only smiled when she rubbed her cold nose on him and he covered her face with light, tender kisses. When Kate began to reciprocate, he caught her chin firmly and tipped her head back to look at her.

"I wanted to barter with this angel, too. I wanted her to come with me to Berlin. I even booked another ticket—"

Kate raised a finger of warning to his lips. "That's not fair," she said, quickly and thoroughly subdued. "You told me I had the power to end this dream when I wanted to, but you're going to do it. Don't ask . . . I can't . . . and I want to."

"I know. I know," he said sadly. "But I had to ask."

The pine above them groaned in the wind and Kate's heart mimicked the sound. It was not the cold around them creeping into her brain and bones, but the full realization of how soon the end was, how inevitable.

"You, of all people," she said with the edge of pain in her voice, "know better. We're so much the same, you said. I couldn't live with myself if I let Yoshio down."

She kissed him gently, hoping to erase the lines of strain near his mouth, but his expression did not change. He was withdrawing from her, going into himself. She could see it happening, feel it and was helpless to stop it. The strong fit of his arms was still around her but they were already moving away from each other. She could feel it.

"There's one big difference," Cass said, unable to meet her eyes. "Your world turns on detail, Kate. A perfectly executed line on a print, the absolute match of a color. I can only see the whole, the big picture. I run Sunco and the company runs me, as well. I married that shrew I created and—"

"You can't be unfaithful to her too long, too much," finished Kate.

No matter how sharp the pain within her grew, she would not yield to tears. The price of caring was steep but her decision, her choice. She was the other woman in his life. The old saw about no one being able to serve two mistresses was true.

"I've given you so little," Cass said miserably. "So damned little."

"You've given me everything," Kate said quietly. "It just won't last for as long as I want."

She conjured up a vision of cherry blossoms and let them fill her mind. They lasted such a brief time but they bloomed, at least. And so had she. When Cass kissed her, she made herself stop thinking entirely.

"And you're as headstrong as I am." He smiled at her and helped her up. "Reckless and headstrong. Let's go back to the inn and get warm."

She wanted to protest. She wasn't headstrong, but he wouldn't understand the term she coined for it. Heartstrong.

"Ah, you had me pegged for a helpless, bookish female," she teased.

"There's nothing weak or helpless about you," Cass told her with the suggestion of a smile. "But you are one hundred and ten percent female. Perhaps I can hope for a demonstration of that fact a few more times before we leave."

"I thought you'd never ask." Her grin was real this time. "Lead the way."

They made love recklessly, spurred on by the knowledge that today would end too soon. Desperately, they strove to give each other not pleasure alone, but to find the hold that separation could not break, to make the joy too complete to fade when memory was all they had. When there was no future, they found the only way there was to make time stand still.

The train back to Tokyo was mercifully crowded and the trip brutally quick. It was easier to return to the reality with strangers surrounding them. It was business as usual, but Kate knew there was an imaginary line, one perfectly executed line, to mark everything in her life before Cass from whatever would happen after him.

DAVID TOWNSEND INCHED his way through the customs line at Haneida Airport. Kate wished momentarily for some of Arnold's power to scoot him through the formalities more quickly. He spotted her waiting outside the barriers and threw her a kiss, finally getting the okay from the inspector.

"You look like you've got the jet lag, not me."

Kate hugged him tight in welcome. "I was worried sick that you wouldn't get here before Fran had to leave. I had a devil of a time getting the Muratas to agree to see me again. The cab's outside and the Muratas are waiting, I hope. Did you have a chance to check everything out you wanted to before you left?"

"I didn't have time to change my socks," joked David, but seeing her worried expression, he unzipped his airline bag and gave Kate a sneak peek at a sheaf of papers. "Hey, don't get scared! I buttonholed every hotshot I could find on such short notice. Besides, I don't need a bunch of affidavits and journal reprints to settle this. There's no question in my mind."

"That's not the problem," Kate reminded him as they got into the cab. "It's the Muratas and Fran who have to be convinced, not you or me."

David nodded and ran his long fingers through his unruly mop of cinnamon hair. He succeeded in making it stick out in new directions, not taming it.

"Franny know I'm coming?"

"No," said Kate. "I thought it best if we handle everything all at once. Seeing you will get her up and excited; she'll need it. This has to work." She closed her eyes tightly. "I think this will work."

"It will," said David with more conviction than Kate felt. "Fran and I will never forget this, Kate. No matter what is said or promised or done, I'm not going to vanish quietly into the sunset or up Bedpan Alley. She and I are going to be married."

Kate waved toward the Muratas' apartment building and tried to issue one last caution. "Restraint, David, please. You don't want to alienate her grandparents, or Fran will lose them. Just make your case with a sort of kind firmness and keep thinking of what they've been through."

Although she got another nod of agreement, Kate wasn't sure he'd really heard her. David was all elbows and knees scrambling out of the taxi in his hurry to get to Fran and get it over with. The Muratas had managed to keep a secret for forty years and David could barely keep himself from bowling Kate over, racing up the narrow stairs.

Grandmother, Obasan, opened the door, ready for Kate with her fixed half smile and her torso slightly angled in a greeting bow. The tiny curve to her lips disappeared and her posture straightened instantly, distressed at a stranger's presence.

Her sharp intake of breath made Kate fearful that the door would close on them. "May we please come in?" she asked in a tone she would use to gentle a frightened animal.

More than seventy years of practical courtesy overcame the old woman's natural inclination. She stepped back and bowed. Her black eyes did not sparkle in welcome but shifted nervously toward the living room. Kate seized one of the woman's hands, felt how cold it was, and prayed the look of betrayal she was getting would vanish.

"Fran?" David's call wasn't necessary. Fran seemed to sense his presence even before he was in the apartment and came running to him.

Happiness rendered the two of them inarticulate. David lifted Fran clear off the floor to kiss her over and over. Fran clung to him, solidly anchored once more, and the strangest noises of pain and pleasure drifted from her busy lips.

The grandfather was at Fran's heels and he watched the young couple with eyes as hard as stone. His mouth formed a thin slash of disapproval, cut into his seamed face. One look sufficed for him. He stared with anger at Kate and turned to his wife for an explanation.

"You'll have to be angry with me, not Fran or Obasan or David," said Kate imploringly. "I'm responsible for bringing him here. I wanted you to listen to him. That's all, just hear him out!"

The old man glared. "This is a very grave mistake. This is a family matter and you are not a Murata."

There was authority to his voice and rigid posture. Kate was supposed to look down in shame, back down and apologize. She met his eyes and stiffened her own back.

"Out of whatever respect you have for my father, I am asking you to take this step. I am willing to risk anything for Fran's happiness. If my father, the colonel, was here, I am sure he would ask you to be fair, to listen."

"He would be shocked at your presumptuousness," retorted the man. "He would be appalled at your interference in matters that do not concern you."

Fran and David broke apart and stood there, holding hands awkwardly, waiting for the old man's verdict.

"You know him," said Kate. "You and he went fishing and talked at length, you said. He could have handled this with more diplomacy, perhaps. He might be angry at my handling, yes, but he would have asked the same favor. Wouldn't he?"

There was a pall of silence, an atmosphere of fear so thick it was palpable.

Grandfather Murata looked directly at David for the first time. "Sit down, please. We will have tea, Mariko." The order to his wife marked the end of the old man's resistance; his shoulders slumped and he took his gaze from the intruder.

The years of dreading this confrontation had taken their toll, Kate saw. When the old man walked into the minuscule living room, he looked very old and defeated, sorrow replacing his anger.

Fran saw nothing but David and her love. She kept touching David to make sure he was real. She giggled at his discomfort on a chair too small for him and the sound hung inappropriately in the air. She realized it and began to play nervously with her engagement ring.

"But how did you...Dave, the money for the ticket? Why did the hospital let you ...?" Fran's agitation grew when no one answered her timid questions.

"Calm down, hon," advised David. "You should sit next to Kate and let your grandfather and me get acquainted, I think."

"There is no need for introduction," Mr. Murata said before Kate could open her mouth. "We have seen your picture and heard about you."

"Good," responded David, ignoring the hint that his case was already decided. "I hate being rude and rushed but I don't have a couple of weeks to meet you both and talk. I have to be back in the hospital Monday morning. We'd better get right to the reason for the trip."

"We are opposed to Francine's marriage," her grandfather said tonelessly. "Time and argument will not change our position."

"I understand that." David and Kate could see Fran's lip begin to tremble at the adamant, blunt words. "If time alone could solve this problem, I would have told Fran when she got back that we would just wait until you and Obasan were gone and then we'd marry."

David's equal directness shocked Fran and she hid her face in both hands. Kate could offer only the comfort of her arm around Fran's thin shoulders. Mr. Murata, however, reacted to truth differently. His chin went up a trifle and he viewed David with more respect.

"The objection is not directed at you personally, Dr. Townsend," he clarified. "You know, I believe, why we do not wish her to consider marriage to anyone."

David took his papers out of the airline bag and shifted them from hand to hand. "Yes, I know, but Fran doesn't, and I came to make sure she does. If forty years can't change your mind, maybe the best authorities can."

Obasan slipped silently into the room to serve tea in her normal graceful manner. She moved smoothly but Kate saw traces of tears on her cheeks and damp streaks on her sleeve. She thought of Cass telling her she was as reckless and headstrong as he was. A novice at dangerous games can get hurt, can make a mess. This meeting would destroy the peace and security the Muratas had built for themselves over years. It might also mark the end of Fran and David's love, Fran's friendship with Kate.

She would feel braver if Cass were here. At this particular moment, Kate found herself longing for him more than ever. No, she thought, he wasn't going to be there when she needed him.

Murata directed his wife to bring out a family album.

"I've seen all those pictures," sputtered Fran, confused. "We've been through the albums, grandfather. It has nothing to do with me and David."

The head of the family took the volume his wife brought over and opened the cover. "*Ano-ne!* Look here." Fran went to him and dutifully looked down at more faded photos. "There we are, Mariko and I, at our wedding. We were married here in Tokyo and our first two children were born here."

"I haven't seen these," said Fran.

Mr. Murata turned the page with a slow, loving care. "Here is your father. He was born here, too— but much later. It was not the same when we had him."

"I thought my father was an only child," Fran said with a puzzled look. "Daddy didn't have brothers and sisters that I ever heard about."

To everyone's surprise, Obasan finally spoke. "He *was* an only child, my last son," she whispered. "He was our child of the dragon." She fled the room.

"Your father was born in '46," David said. "Your grandparents had moved back to Tokyo by then."

There was horror in the old man's eyes and another emotion clear in his face. Shame. When he spoke, it was in a reedy, thin voice Fran and Kate did not recognize.

"We went—Mariko and the two children—to stay with her sister. I was recovering from typhus. The air, they said, was better outside the big cities. Her sister's family had a home on the outskirts and a big vegetable garden. Food was in short supply; we had children to think of. We stayed there for just a little while but we weren't far enough away from the city."

"What city?" Fran asked in horror.

"Hiroshima. August, 1945." It was David who had to answer, seeing the truth take hold of Fran.

A handful of old photos slipped out of Fran's fingers and fluttered to the floor. She bent forward to collect them and could not bring herself to touch the grainy black and white prints. Two serious-faced children stared up at her. Until today, she hadn't known of their existence, but it was clear she would never forget their faces now.

Obasan came in without a rustle. She knelt down and gathered the photos, the faded petals of her own life, to hold them to the front of her kimono.

Fran started to cry, the short spasm of weeping passing as soon as she saw the outward poise her grandparents maintained. A scene would embarrass them and add to the burden they bore.

"Mariko and I returned to Tokyo," Mr. Murata went on. "Less than a year later, we were parents again. A fine, healthy boy. We were doubly grateful for him. He brought us the sense of family once more and by then, we had heard of the unfortunate ones whose children were not normal. We raised him knowing he was a child of the dragon. He knew and he knew why we were careful not to allow anyone else to learn it."

Fran looked helplessly from one of her grandparents to the other. "But *I* didn't know! Why didn't you—someone—tell me?" Her voice rose, high and sharp. "This thing happened forty years ago. It's not something to be ashamed of...."

"Some feelings haven't changed," Kate said softly. "Half the population today in Japan wouldn't marry a survivor, even a descendant of a survivor, of Hiroshima or Nagasaki. They're afraid of genetic risks."

"We did not know about the risks when we had your father," Mr. Murata said to Fran. "But when he was growing up, we knew, and we told him—as we told you—not to marry. Failing that, not to have children."

Fran pulled at her bangs in anguish. "His death, and Jack's leukemia...of course..." She stammered in nervousness. "Who would risk having children? It's true, David. If we marry, I could have something wrong with me genetically. Our children might..."

David ran over with his pathetic bundle of papers to wave at her. He pulled her knuckle down from her mouth.

"Stop it, Fran, and listen to me! It might be true and it might not. I went to Stanford, UCLA, half a dozen places, and I talked to three different bio-geneticists before I left. These are reprints of research work. Fran, no one knows conclusively—"

Fran screamed at him in terror. "I know! God, David, now I know. Marry you and wait and see? Would you watch me for signs of a fatal disease? Even if it turns out I'm okay, what if I got pregnant? What would you do, then? Sit and watch our baby for clues as to whether he's normal or not?"

Mr. Murata looked stricken, dying. "You see, granddaughter, it was better not to tell you. We would rather you thought it was for other reasons."

He recited dispassionately the story of her father. Fran's father was a strong-willed, defiant young man who could not accept the limitations imposed on him by an accident of birth. He went to California, fell in love and married. Fran and Jack were the results.

"No," Mr. Murata corrected himself. "Today is the result. You are the only grandchild left us, the Murata who comes after us but . . ." His voice wavered finally and Obasan came over to stand next to him, the steadying influence and presence for fifty years. "Do not marry," he concluded harshly.

"I can't accept that as a solution," said David Townsend. "None of this changes the way I feel about Fran. I refuse to believe it changes what she feels for me. We can make a decision about having children after we're married. We can have some genetic tests done in California. I'll research it further."

Fran was somewhere else, twisting her bangs into a tight little clump. "Did my mother know?" she asked plaintively. "Did she marry my father knowing what could happen, or ignorant of it?"

When David folded Fran into his embrace, she looked like a frightened child. "Your mother knew," he said. "She and I talked, too. She told me to go ahead and say whatever I had to say when I got here. I didn't get the feeling that she regrets her marriage, her decision to have kids one bit. She loved your father and Jack; she misses them very much. You could call her tonight and she'll tell you herself. She was sorry she had to keep a secret like this one for so long."

"Our doing," volunteered Obasan timidly. "We asked her to. We are ashamed of the grief we brought to a daughter-in-law and now to Francine. We are deeply ashamed that we have lived longer than our children and our grandchildren. We both have suffered knowing we must forbid Francine her happiness."

"You don't have to," objected David. He peered down at Fran. "Honey, I don't care if we're talking about ten minutes or ten years or ten lifetimes. I want to marry you. I'd risk anything to marry you. Just say you don't care about the risk, either. Doctors are notoriously bad risks as husbands but you didn't hesitate to say yes before. The first time we met, remember? I asked you to marry me. We can adopt kids."

Fran smiled up at him and her answer was clear, at least to Kate. Once the initial shock was subsiding, Fran was still Fran and able to face whatever was in store for them. Her dark eyes flashed over to her grandparents, asking for their acceptance mutely.

"I want to do what's right," David said to Mr. Murata. "Kate told me she could make arrangements for us to be married here in Tokyo by a Buddhist priest she's met. I thought you would like to see your granddaughter married, sir. We'll still have a ceremony back in Riverside as we planned at Fran's church.''

Kate took a long, slow appraisal of the old man. He was balanced on a thread, teetering over the wide abyss of his emotions and struggling not to show it. It unnerved her to see him.

"And with your permission," David continued, "and the help of Morris Yashima back home, I've applied to the California courts for a legal name change. I'm so confident of the future, Mr. Murata, I petitioned to take your family name and let our children continue the line. Townsend-Murata. Long, but it has a nice ring to it."

"Funny," whispered Kate under her breath, "you don't look Japanese! But you are, David. You are."

She had not suggested this plan. She was totally astounded at David's brilliance and daring. It was not uncommon in Japan for a husband to take his wife's name to keep her family line going, but it was considered a great sacrifice, a sign of real faith. A *yoshi*! It took Kate's breath away to hear David propose it and the expression on Mr. Murata's face mirrored her astonishment. He realized what a courageous man wanted to marry his granddaughter.

It was very quiet in the room for what seemed like an hour, to Kate. David and Fran probably felt it was a century, she thought.

"You are right," said the old man with dignity. "I would prefer to see you married in a traditional Buddhist ceremony. I am deeply honored to have you join this family."

Kate couldn't have contained her tears if she wanted to. Her display was shocking bad manners but one of total relief and joy. This was a moment for wild jubilation and unselfish happiness and she needed to cry. Maybe no situation was so hopelessly dark that love couldn't illuminate it.

Fran and David gathered her into their own embrace and garbled their thanks to her. She tried incoherently to explain their wedding to them.

They could be married in Yoshio Sabusawa's garden in two days. Her old professor was more romantically inclined than Kate had ever believed and Kishi was delighted to officiate, with aid from Shinto priests from Hata-Yuguri shrine. Yoshio had promised a small reception afterward as his contribution to a young couple.

"We were married at Hata-Yuguri," said Obasan shyly.

"I know," Kate said, laughing through her tears. "Although David will have to wear his own suit— there's no way we can find a robe big enough for him on short notice—I rented Fran's wedding kimono as my gift. We are going the full nine yards on this wedding!"

Fran alternated between hysterical giggles and sobs. "Kate, those outfits cost a fortune... with a full wig? The horn-hider?"

"What in the blue blazes is a horn-hider?" demanded David. He pushed aside Fran's black hair to check her ears out.

"Apparently all women are universal in certain emotions," said Kate dryly. "It's a headdress that covers up the bride's horns of jealousy."

David laughed and protested. "I didn't cover all this ground and come armed to the teeth with arguments to marry a woman I'm lukewarm about. If I ever fool around, Fran, I deserve to be gored."

"You will be," promised Fran with a touch of her lost spirit. "I may be small but I have secret weapons."

"Sharp elbows," David confided. "Big deal!" Fran demonstrated and he winced.

They were so happy, the feeling filled everyone vicariously. Mr. Murata brought out a bottle of whiskey and insisted a toast was made to the couple. The toast was solemn but the mood wasn't. The old man even unbent to scold Kate, mocking himself.

"You are the most unconventional go-between, but your father would have been proud of you. As I am." He gave her a respectful bow.

"You staying, David?" asked Kate when the festivities wound down. She kissed Fran and got ready to leave.

"We'll stay up and talk all night," David said. "Obasan's already said she'll keep an eye on us."

"Both eyes," amended Obasan.

"Too late for that," whispered Fran at the door. "But there's no use in trying to bring them into the twentieth century in one giant step. Thanks, Kate, for everything. For the rest of my life."

Kate tugged at Fran's bangs. "Be happy! And don't worry. It worked out like a dream, didn't it?"

"Like a dream," parroted Fran.

CASS WAS STRETCHED OUT on one of the huge couches in his living room, sprawled with his notes and papers. He was so intent on reading them, he didn't hear Kate come in. She sneaked up behind him and ruffled his hair, just to see him start with surprise.

He pulled her down on top of him, papers and all. "Kind of a switch, isn't this? Me, sitting up and burning the midnight oil to wait for you..." After his kiss, deep and searching, Cass smiled at the tell-tale happiness on her face. "So, when's the wedding?"

"Two days away. How did you know it worked? I'll bet you guessed because of the little pinwheels and rockets going off all around me."

He stroked her face, kissed her mouth very lightly. "I had complete faith in you. I know you. *Kuroneko wa mayoke ni ii*. Did I get it right?"

"Black cats keep devils away," translated Kate. "Perfect, but I'm no black cat."

He brushed a bunch of papers away, settled her on his chest and buried his face in her hair. "You are. A black-haired, green-eyed cat who brings good luck."

"That's only here in Japan. At home, black cats are bad luck. Wait until I tell you what a stroke of genius David came up with to settle the whole mess...." She was smoothing down his jet-black hair, drinking in the sight of him.

If it was possible to store someone in the ends of her fingertips, she would always have him. If it was possible to etch every detail of the way he looked, into her mind, she would never lose him.

"Cat!" He nibbled at her lower lip and ran his hands up and down her spine. "You arched your back and spit at Arnold and scared him. You hissed and clawed your way through two old people's demons and

chased most of them off. I never had any doubts you
could do it."

"Such confidence." Kate ran the tip of her tongue
along the sculpted line of his upper lip. Without getting up, she worked her shoes off and let them fall.
"Such blind faith in me. I'm flattered."

His mouth turned hungry. His hands became
greedy, less gentle. "You ought to be," he said raggedly in a few minutes. "You have a real talent for
getting what you want, if you decide to use it. In about
five seconds, you're going to get a lot more than just
flattery from me."

"Five seconds?" Kate asked archly. "You must
have had a tough day. Five . . . four . . . three . . ."

Cass made a growling sound deep in his chest and
she lost count.

CHAPTER THIRTEEN

CASS WAS ANGRIER, more on edge, than she'd ever seen him. "Look, if we're going to fight, why not forget the play and do it in comfort at the apartment?"

Kate turned to him and saw the blue and red neon splotching his smooth cheeks like garish makeup. "Are we fighting? I said they were both disappointed that you couldn't stay for the wedding. So am I. Particularly, now that I know you were the one who suggested the idea of *yoshi* to David."

The Ginza district was bustling. The people milling around the Kabukiza were hurrying not to miss the beginning of the play, while Kate tried not to think of tonight as their final act. It was impossible. This was the last time they would be together.

The violent colors made Cass's face look hard and bitter but his hand on her arm was gentle, protective. "Why did my calling David bother you? I tried to help in my own way. It did and I'm glad."

"I could have asked you to help," Kate said, "but I didn't. I can't lean on you. It's not right when you're not going to be here. You don't ask me to direct your company, solve your problems.... Don't you see? I have to manage by myself. I always have."

"I see," Cass answered gruffly. "It's okay to want me but not to need me. Then you'd have to compromise, or sacrifice your duty, and come with me tomorrow."

"All right, *now* we're fighting!" Kate glared at him and shook off his touch. "Why should it be different for you than for me? Because it isn't. I'm doing exactly what I feel I have to. I don't have to like it, any more than you do."

He quoted an old proverb to her, infuriating her. "Duty is heavier than a mountain."

"Not this one," retorted Kate quickly. "I can't pick up and take off for points unknown with Yoshio dying. You can't tell Woodruff or Woodman to take over for you in Berlin and cut the ribbon himself. So, here we are!"

He stood there for a long time, staring back angrily at her, his jaw set, his mouth taut. Finally, he looked away at the audience filing into the theater.

"No, you're right," he said almost inaudibly. "And, of course, neither of us wants to admit we're just as angry at ourselves as we are at each other. Do you want to go in or go ho...back to the apartment?"

"I'd rather see a tragic love story than live one," Kate admitted. "Does art really imitate life?"

The only purpose she could see in the lovely, lengthy performance of Kabuki tonight was to relieve her own frustration. They sat in plush seats, not the wooden benches of her student days, and watched the spectacle of traditional heroics and passions unfold.

People moved constantly, in and out of seats, during Kabuki. Most of the audience knew all the plays so well that they recognized lulls in the action. Every dry spot was a signal to run out for refreshments or to gossip in the lobby.

No one worried about missing a famous speech or an emotional high point. They were announced loudly by the hollow clapping of wooden sticks in time to allow devotees to flood back.

Bit by bit, Kate let herself get swept up in the story, forgetting reality in the unbelievably grand problems of the play. The vivid costumes and makeup, the exaggerated posturing of the actors was an escape, but when she began to cry with other spectators for the doomed lovers, she knew she would have to leave.

It was not the lovers, stark white and black in costumes, she was weeping for. It was for herself, for the man sitting next to her.

"My sentimental Irish streak is running wild," she whispered to Cass, nudging him gently. "I have to go outside for a while."

He followed her, weaving through the chattering mob. When he caught up to her, she ducked her head but not fast enough.

"Why are you looking at me like that?" She hiccuped and stared at the carpet. "My nose is bright red, isn't it?"

"Your mascara ran," Cass whispered back. "You look like a beautiful raccoon and the saddest part is yet to come."

"Says you," she snorted, mopping her face with his handkerchief. "I'm all cried out."

He dabbed at a smudge she missed. The clatter of the wooden sticks began, warning the crowd of the final stirring scenes. Cass ignored the sound, lacing his fingers through her slender ones.

"I want to miss the death of the virtuous and handsome lovers," he said.

"I can't face it, either."

He drew her closer to let others scurry past to their seats. His face suddenly looked tired and drawn. "Let's leave, Kate. I'll go anywhere you say but I want to spend the night alone with you."

Behind him, she heard the timbre of wailing rise and the volume swell. Art did imitate life. Reality did surpass any dream, any nightmare. She cupped his face with her hand and smiled. "Yes, let's go."

The door to his apartment closed and shut out the world but Kate sensed the world's presence, waiting for the night to end. She didn't want to talk about it; outside might be reality and this place only an illusion, but she was going to hold on to illusion for as long as she could.

Cass undressed her slowly, pausing to kiss her often. His fingers patiently outwitted the tiny line of pearl buttons closing her blouse and caressed the soft, perfumed skin he exposed. She was tense but she began to warm, relax.

He brushed soothing kisses along the side of her throat but when he touched her breasts, he stroked excitement into their swell, into their peaks, until she ached.

Her pulse leaped in response as he slid her hose down the length of her legs, awakening all the sensitivity of her skin. Her blood heated, coaxed by the lazy, easy way he moved, fueled by the tender sweep of his fingers.

Only after she was completely naked, her hair taken down and spread over her shoulders, did Cass reach up and loosen his tie, slide it off. Watching her all the while, he touched the top button of his shirt.

"Let me," Kate said and her hands intervened.

"I'd let you do anything," he whispered. "I'd do anything to make you want me...need me...as much as I want you."

Her fingers slipped under the open shirt, moving on the warm promise of his skin. She took as much time teasing as he had, grazing him with unspoken messages, growing bolder as she felt his body's response. She worked him free of his clothes and found the sight of his arousal stirred her own response sharply. Her hands closed around him, felt him shudder, and the more she touched him, the more her own body signaled its needs.

Cass stood perfectly still as she pressed herself tightly to the length of his hard body. Kate's mouth explored him, teased him and moved damply along his burning flesh. Her lips forayed lower, making more daring discoveries, as her fingers caressed at the dark copper coins of his nipples. He groaned, a harsh, deep sound, and it told her all she wanted to know about his need for her—a need they shared. She loved the taste of him, the dizzying exhilaration and power that made him cry out and clutch at her.

"Oh, Kate...no, no, not yet," he said hoarsely, pulling her upright, holding her close. His mouth scorched her with kisses and his eyes were bright, burning coals.

Kate leaned on him, feverish and awed that love so strong left her weak. Cass lifted her effortlessly to his chest and stretched her out on the bed. His expression told her more clearly than his muffled, whispered words how desirable she was, how much he wanted her. She believed that stirring look with her whole heart. Her body pulsed, calling for his. His name was on her lips when she reached up and drew him down to her, into her, to hold once more.

"Love me," Kate moaned, a demand and a plea. "Love me now." But "forever" throbbed in her heart.

With his mouth buried in her silken hair and his body buried in hers, he promised, "I will. I will."

Cass paused, savoring the storm of sensation building in them. He looked along the length of their bodies welded together and back to her face, eyes wide and seeking his. "God, Kate, what have you done to me? What do you want from me?"

She could not put it into words but she let him see into the wild depths of her soul and he trembled in her arms.

Even as their bodies joined and moved, it was their spirits she felt melting and flowing together tonight. There was no frenzy now, no struggle to reach release. Tonight was the thrill of giving and taking pleasure slowly, reveling in one sensation that followed another.

The closer they drew, the more inevitable the ending. Ultimately there was no more postponing the tempest that overtook them, engulfing them both in feeling and fury. Kate dimly heard Cass call to her over and over, her name said with pleasure and pain.

In the quiet following, they held on to each other convulsively and Kate gnawed her lips to hold back silent tears.

"Please don't cry," Cass begged her. His lips moved along the damp skin of her temple, her cheek, and tasted salt. "Don't make it so damned hard to leave you."

"Don't ask me to make it easier, either," whispered Kate. "Tonight is our 'enough.' I won't see you again."

"And don't say that." His hands brushed her with more feather-light caresses, reluctant to leave her. "Besides, we knew it wasn't going to be all, everything. We agreed all we wanted was here and now."

It was as though he was daring her to reproach him for what had to be. Her own words made her a liar. Whatever we have is enough. She felt a surge of bitter, burning acid inside. Was it really as easy for Cass to decide how much love was enough? Was he able to love her so completely one minute and go away the next?

The hurt spilled into her eyes but she did not cry. She lay there, sleepless and pained, and waited for him to get up and leave. His flight left early; he still had to finish packing.

She would be at Yoshio's tomorrow. It wasn't possible to stay in this apartment and know Cass wasn't coming back.

The bedside light snapped on abruptly and Cass turned, propping himself on one elbow. "I'm sorry," he rasped and Kate saw the tears unshed in his eyes. "I'm sorry."

Kate watched Tokyo's glitter blinking on and off, the lights before dawn swimming into a sea of colored stars. She could hear the sounds he made dressing, moving through the room, closing drawers. If she reached for him, he might come back to her arms. But only for another hour, and that was not enough.

"Kate, I have to go," he said, standing at the foot of the bed. "That's the problem. I always have to go. We'll both hurt more if I lie and say I'll be there for you whenever, wherever you want me."

"Go," she said in a strangled voice. She would never be able to say it if she looked at him. She kept her eyes on the city. "Goodbye, Cass," she said.

When she heard the bedroom door open, her heart threatened to stop beating altogether.

"I love you," Cass said.

She squeezed a bunched corner of the sheet as tightly as she could. "I know you do...and that's what's killing me." When the door closed behind him, Kate heard her heart grind to a halt.

FRAN WORE the full formal regalia of a traditional bride. From her elaborate headdress like a cloth ship under full sail, perched on top of a glossy black wig, down to her many-layered kimono, she was practically a model bride. It took hours for Kate and Obasan to dress her in Kishi's room.

"Walk for me," ordered Obasan, surveying their handiwork.

"I'm going to fall flat on my face," wailed Fran. She did look alarmingly unbalanced and the voluminous brocades hampered her walking down to tiny, mincing steps.

"Not if you *glide*," instructed her grandmother. "You are supposed to be shy, demure...not marching up there like a soldier. Try it again!"

Fran's second try got a nod of approval from Obasan and a peal of nervous laughter from Kate.

Fran waved away the finishing touches, the stark white makeup that was being readied to cover her entire face.

"Yech! I'm drawing the line at that. I don't mind looking like a big silk chicken on my wedding day, but I refuse to look dead!" She took an experimental glide away and achieved the proper fluid motion.

"I will go see if everything else is ready," Obasan said. "Don't move, don't do anything but stand still, Francine."

"Fat chance," murmured Fran. "I'm so trussed up I can't take a normal breath."

"You look absolutely gorgeous," said Kate.

Fran wanted to turn to her. She had to execute a tricky maneuver to keep her towering headgear in place. "Are you planning to tell me what happened between you and Cass?"

"No," Kate said flatly, smoothing down the multi-layered gown.

"He's gone, you're here. I'll bet he was part of the reason you decided to stay here with Yoshio. Well, you can't escape love by putting a few thousand miles between you. I thought more about David here than I did in Riverside."

"Don't. Please don't think aloud," asked Kate. She handed Fran a lipstick less objectionable than the blood-scarlet Obasan wanted her to use and held up a mirror. "I want to edit Yoshio's book. It's something to focus on. Work will restore my equilibrium."

"Sure, it will." Fran sounded very dubious. "If you're trying to sell yourself on that line, fine. Don't try it on me. I went out with you two. I saw the way he looked at you, the way you made up excuses to touch him.''

"It's over," Kate said. "And your happiness, your wedding, is the best painkiller ever invented. Listen to Yoshio!" She nodded toward the other end of the house and they could hear laughter. "There's a time to 'go for it' and a time to let go. Let's not talk about it anymore, okay?''

Fran opened her mouth to say something, thought better of it and closed her jaw with a little snap.

Obasan came to escort Fran out and Kate slipped off to check on Yoshio. He had elected to watch from the porch and Kate wanted to stay with him in case the festivities proved too much or too long.

He allowed her to walk him out, leaning heavily on her. Kate arranged him in a chair, making sure he would miss none of the service.

"Get off the porch," he told her sternly. "Tuck the blanket in and go down there. I'm fine. I love weddings. I have plans to get drunk and tell dirty stories at the reception." His grin stretched the skin over the prominent bones in his face.

"You are deliberately revealing your flaws to me." Kate smiled. "I should pretend I didn't hear that. I always think of you as my most distinguished, eccentric and unworldly teacher, not some tipsy, bawdy old man."

"Live and learn, sister," Yoshio said in perfect English.

There were no tears shed during the ceremony. It was lovely, so much so that it would have been spoiled by tears. David Townsend towered over the Shinto

priest but he kept his hands folded meekly and his eyes
cast down like a father being scolded by his child. Fran
looked the part of the sweet Japanese bride, except
when her glance strayed admiringly to her bride-
groom. Without the normal mask of white, the radi-
ance of her happy face dazzled everyone.

After Kishi's role in the wedding was completed, he
went to stand with his friend on the porch. Kate
checked from time to time and saw them whispering
together, enthralled by the wedding. Once or twice she
got the eeriest feeling that she was a subject for their
discussion, as well.

The high point of the wedding finally rolled around.
Fran and David each took the three ceremonial sips of
rice wine from red lacquer cups and were married.
There would be an encore performance of today at St.
Marks in Riverside, but Kate wouldn't be there. She
was elated not to miss at least one of their weddings.

Her kiss of congratulation was jubilant. There was
a special, private meaning to her fervent wish for a
long and happy life together.

"David will be good luck for health," Obasan
whispered like a conspirator to Kate. "Not because of
being a doctor. Look at him standing there!"

"The crane," giggled Kate. He did look like the
lanky bird who was supposed to ward off sickness.
Tall, thin and gangly, David even came equipped with
a crest of unmanageable red-brown hair. When she
kidded him about it at the reception, he said it fit in
with his image as Dr. Stork.

One drink and he was announcing their departure.
"A night and a day in Tokyo isn't much of a honey-

moon, guys, but it's what I've got. Actually, it's a much snazzier honeymoon than I planned."

Fran cracked, "Yeah, he had a wild picnic planned in One Oak Park and he would have brought the dumb beeper with him."

He tugged at her arm. "Doctors' wives! We're not married an hour and she's already complaining I don't spend enough time with her."

Fran minced over to hug Kate once more. "And what about you?"

"No one asked me to get married. I'd have settled for One Oak—"

"Come on!" Fran's forehead creased with worry. "I meant, are you going to be okay? Is there something I should do when I get back?"

Kate clucked her tongue. "Francine Townsend-Murata, you are an incorrigible meddler, snoop and all around friend. Write and let me know how things are going. Learn how to make a decent spaghetti sauce and fatten David up a bit . . . and don't worry."

"But Cass," began Fran.

Kate handed her best friend over to an impatient groom. "Forget it. That particular road is closed, if you follow me."

"I felt like that a week ago," shrieked Fran as David dragged her off. "Here we are zooming off into the sunset."

And here I go . . . toward what? Kate asked herself as she went back to the house to join Yoshio and Hiroko. She had sounded sure and brave, talking to Fran, very mature and reasonable about the end of an affair. But inside, she was scared, the plain, unadorned fright of being cast adrift.

Fran could not possibly understand. The truth had been the very thing to help her and David surmount their problems. Once Fran had known the whole truth, she made a decision and nothing could keep them apart. The truth was the very thing between Kate and Cass.

"I wanted today to be your wedding," sighed Yoshio from his pillow-throne. "Well, any happy event was good medicine. Your young man was unfortunate to have missed it."

"He was," Kate said disinterestedly. "Impossible to take a later flight, I guess. He certainly gave them a nice present. A honeymoon at the Imperial Hotel and a dancing, bowing monkey."

Yoshio cackled. "The doctor was more impressed with the toy than the honeymoon suite, I hear. I was glad Hiroko and I had a chance to say goodbye to Mr. Yashima."

"You did?"

Yoshio shook a bony finger at her. "You see, you don't know everything in the universe, yet. Such an important man and he took an hour yesterday afternoon to come and see two old relics."

Kate didn't say anything; she didn't have to. Yoshio Sabusawa was such an inveterate gossip, all he ever needed was an audience, not a show of interest. She pushed herself a spot on his bed and folded her arms across her middle, waiting.

Yoshio glanced at Hiroko Kishi's room and cleared his throat, trying not to cough.

"You aren't supposed to be telling me this," guessed Kate. "Hiroko told you to butt out, didn't he?"

He nodded his head in assent and looked unperturbed. "We had tea, talked politics and business in the garden. Yashima is a knowledgeable man. Polite, too. He took a long time to come to the point of his visit. You."

Kate picked at a cuticle and tried to present what Yoshio used to call "a good face," devoid of clues as to what was churning around in her stomach.

"What tact!" Yoshio crowed. "Without mentioning the terrible condition of this miserable house or how feeble its two tenants look, he wanted to make your time here as comfortable as possible. With a delicacy you might learn from, he offered, in effect, whatever he could to relieve us of any strain, any burden."

Kate could feel the heat and color rising in her face. "I hope you told him what a ridiculous, old-fashioned notion he was playing with. I'm not his responsibility, and I'm not yours. Cass owes me nothing."

Yoshio inclined forward slightly and studied her. "I was rather touched by his concern and love for you. You seem annoyed by it. Curious!"

"Makes me sound like I was a kept woman," mumbled Kate, plucking at the bedcovers.

"He said he loved you," Yoshio said seriously, all trace of his twinkling spirits gone. "But it was not so much what he said as the way he said it, that marked it as the truth for me. He said he did not feel free to offer you what he should, that you would take nothing from him, in any event."

"Did he tell you he was married to his work?" snapped Kate. "Such wives are impossible to divorce.

But he is honorable; too honorable to ask me to be only his mistress."

"Now who is being old-fashioned?" asked Yoshio evenly. "I told you to cheer you up, not to raise your hackles. He thinks of you, he cares for you. What more can you want?"

"When I know, I'll tell you," said Kate, and she excused herself to help Hiroko with the cleanup.

She told herself it was too soon to know, the memory of Cass was still too fresh and painful to think about. She could work hard and tire herself out during each day and perhaps keep from dreaming at night.

If exhaustion wouldn't hold Cass at bay, nothing would. And the fright, the scare she felt squirming inside, said it wouldn't work. But he had to leave her mind or Kate saw a future where she dreaded dreams, sunsets, the appearance of cherry blossoms.

Nothing lasts forever. There was a small measure of reassurance in the thought and she seized it. In time, Cass would fade from her life and other men replace him. The image of his face would blur until the recollections of how his eyes smiled, his mouth disapproved mutely, his eyebrow showed amusement would be gone.

That night, she rubbed body lotion on the indented place on her ankle, a childhood scar. She couldn't recall the incident, but the scar was there, slightly paler and smoother than the surrounding skin. There was no memory of the pain, either.

Cass had to be a memory like this scar. Nothing lasts forever.

In some safely distant place and time, Kate fantasized about some exhibit in Los Angeles, a cocktail party when she would see Cass again. They would smile cordially, shake hands and talk about their respective work: the Cutler was doing well; Sunco was opening another branch in some foresaken wasteland; his new subsidiary company was running like a top.

There wouldn't be any secret fire when his fingers met hers. She would have forgotten how to read the line of his mouth, the dark and exciting message of his eyes.

She would turn to someone—another man, yes, another man—and say, "This is an old friend, Cass Yashima. I don't believe I've ever mentioned him."

Kate's fingers lingered on the scar. The pain, the memory was gone but the scar was there forever. She wasn't going to be able to lie to herself. There would never be the same sudden wonderful pulse of excitement, the feeling of swooping down to touch the earth and then soaring up the sheer face of a mountain.

She would never soar over the rocky peaks and sail into the heart of a red sun. There would not be another man who made her so fully, joyously alive again. Kate Cleary was no phoenix, rising out of the fire of love to experience it over and over.

CHAPTER FOURTEEN

ARNOLD WHELAN-JONES was the last of the bidders to show up. He arrived late at the gallery Hiroko Kishi had made arrangements with, Mr. Tanaka in tow as his interpreter. He stomped in with the jovial bearing of a sure winner.

"What a surprise!" he boomed, spying Kate and rushing to wring her hand. "I thought you'd be long gone. Heard Wonder Boy left last week, so I assumed..."

"Making assumptions can get you into lots of trouble," interrupted Kate. "I wouldn't have missed this for the world."

Arnold gave the assembled group, five in all, the once-over and patted his suit lapel as if the night were in his breast pocket already. "Then, look happy. Your eyes are bloodshot, you look thinner. This is like Christmas. Afterward, I'll take you to dinner to show there's no hard feelings. Okay?"

Kate was amazed that her stomach contracted and growled its own answer. She shook her head no and went to sit behind Kishi, musing on the irony. It didn't matter if the world collapsed; life went on if you were a survivor. She cried, she got hungry, she had gone back to work.

"Gentlemen, please join me in a cup of sake," invited Hiroko.

"I do my victory drinking after the fact, usually," joked Arnold. He refused to sit on the floor with the other bidders and Tanaka dashed off to find him a chair.

Hiroko smiled patiently. "This is a ceremonial occasion. The drink is to ask the seal, the blessing of the gods, on our dealings."

Arnold had the good sense to listen to Tanaka's advice buzzed into his ear and followed the lead of the other men, listening attentively to Kishi, waiting respectfully and then, sipping—not swigging—the hot rice wine down. He couldn't resist a muffled "Confusion to the enemy" toast but no one in the room except Kate, Hiroko, and Arnold's own minion understood English.

During Kishi's showing and discussion of the *tan-e*, he grew restive and wandered over near Kate.

"We already saw them," he complained. "Right here, yesterday, when he took the bid envelopes. I thought this would be over—boom! What's the delay?"

"Business is an art in Japan," Kate whispered to him. "Keep your voice down, go sit down, and please don't light that cigar in here. Restraint, Arnold, respect, and a modicum of modesty will get more done than just the money. The hard sell isn't going to work tonight!"

He chewed on the end of the cigar thoughtfully. "No one in San Francisco will believe this scene. We're sitting around like a bunch of old ladies sucking up rice wine and tea and trading anecdotes about half a million dollars' worth of prints...who's this Japanese sandman?"

Hiroko Kishi half turned and smiled at the question.

"He's the owner of the prints, legally," said Kate. "He decides whose bid to accept. I'm sure Tanaka can explain the details again to you, if you're still confused."

The conversation was becoming more animated among the other men. Arnold was losing his golden opportunity to get the jump on every museum and collector of Oriental art, and he didn't know it. The other interested parties were demonstrating their knowledge, their taste and restraint before the actual decision by Kishi, showing how worthy they were to possess such treasures. Arnold was annoyed, raucous and rude.

He leaned forward and adjusted his glasses until he was sure of his sight, focusing on the displayed prints. "Tanaka already explained this procedure to me but it still doesn't make sense. The owner gets to decide who the winner is, who he wants to get the *tan-e*, and it isn't necessarily by the amount bid. How these people got to be a world power is beyond me, Kate. What am I supposed to do? Beg them to take my money?"

No one in the room had mentioned a figure so far. Kate shook her head in disbelief. "You're on the right track but a little late, Arnold. And put that cigar out. It's not good for your heart and it stinks."

Surprisingly, Arnold waved at Tanaka and ground the stogie out when he was brought an ashtray. "I'm touched. You must care. That's only the second nice

thing you ever said to me, Kate. Of course, I don't remember the first time."

The first time. A rush of images—of Cass, of the
inn at Okitsu—ran through her mind and settled in her
heart. She watched Arnold stroll back to his chair and
forced herself to listen to the discussion. A prominent
local art historian was making an elegant, under-
stated case for keeping the *tan-e* in the country of their
origin.

After an appropriate amount of time—and a few
gallons of tea—Kishi stood up and thanked everyone
profusely for attending and made a short, succinct
announcement.

"The bid of the Sunco Corporation has been accepted."

The Japanese bidders nodded sagely and continued
to drink tea. Arnold was thoroughly disgusted and
unable to contain himself. He came over to Kate, not
Kishi, for the satisfaction of the last word.

"I wouldn't gloat, if I were you," he said. "Yashima got what he wanted, whipped the pants off me, but
I noticed he's run out on you, too."

"He left," corrected Kate calmly. She had cried a
Dead Sea's worth of tears, since Cass left, raged
against Arnold enough to empty her of any more anger. "He said he was leaving Japan and he did."

Arnold clenched the stub of another cigar in his
teeth. "Not without the spoils . . . and you helped him
get them. Don't deny it! He didn't buy a single piece
of art on this trip before this sale. I outbid him. I know
I did. I put over half a million bucks into this and I still
lost out. How?"

She stood up slowly and smiled. "I might have greased the wheels of justice, Arnold. That's all. But you can be comforted. I don't feel as good as I thought I would about it. I'd trade those little gems in a second...I'd put a match to them myself if I—" She stopped herself.

What was the point in telling Arnold more? She'd followed through with her plan for revenge. It played out perfectly and it was over. If she thought she would be relieved and elated, she was wrong. She was drained, hollow, past caring.

If I could be with Cass, she finished mentally. *If we could be together, I'd watch them burn and never wince.*

Arnold was eyeing her suspiciously. "You're not as tough as you thought you were. It shows. But you're okay, Cleary, and you saved me from boredom on this trip. You aren't fond of me, but there's lots more to me than you know. I'm on a losing streak as of tonight...so what the hell! I might as well try to straighten things between us."

"What?" She couldn't shake the visions from her head. *Go away, Arnold. Go away, Cass.*

He gestured at Tanaka and mimicked hitching himself a ride. "Well, I'm leaving tonight on the first plane west. When you get back, you'll find a souvenir of our association waiting for you at the Cutler. Compliments of Arnold Whelan-Jones. Make damn sure they spell my name right on the brass plate at the bottom."

It sunk in almost too late. He was halfway out of the gallery before Kate scrambled after him.

"A print? That wasn't necessary, Arnold. It's very nice but it . . ."

He grinned at her. "It isn't *that* nice. Don't break your neck trying to thank me. It's the *Blue-Veiled Geisha*. Hey, something's better than nothing."

He rolled out in his usual freight-train fashion, leaving her to stare at his back. Her bewilderment dissolved into indignation and then, to laughter. How typically Arnold! Even his attempt to make a halfway decent gesture was tinged with nastiness.

The print, Arnold's little joke, would be a good reminder for her, as well as a souvenir. As lovely as the Utamaro was, it was flawed, and she'd be faced with what her own blind ambition had almost wrought. Kate shrugged, and still laughing, went to find Kishi to go home.

THE FIRST TWO WEEKS had been stressful and disorienting. Yoshio Sabusawa had never been orderly or easy to work with, but the additional burden of his physical limitations put even more strain on Kate. The professor worked for short periods only and he claimed that he thought more clearly at night. Kate adapted, feeling like a barn owl. She and he conferred during every brief burst of energy Yoshio had— regardless of the hour. By day, she compiled the finished material in a semblance of order.

Work was what she had wanted and she had an abundance of it. Physically tired, emotionally worn, she didn't have the strength to remember. Kishi was the household anchor. He moved through the house and garden like a shadow—constant, indispensable but barely noticed. Sometimes Kate was stricken with guilt seeing him perform every task, every piddling detail of the day's routine, with the same wide smile, the undaunted patience.

She levered herself stiffly off the porch and went to help him sweep the littered walk.

"You and Yoshio are through for today?" he inquired, handing her an extra broom. "More sessions and shorter. He is a stubborn man, isn't he?"

"So am I," said Kate. "Stubborn. We'll get it finished."

Hiroko smiled to himself. "I have no doubt. Between the two of you, his demons have been wrestled to a standstill. You should think about taking his manuscript with you and doing a translation for the publisher. You have rare gifts to use."

Kate leaned on the broom and looked at the heaps of sweet-scented wisteria flowers. She loved their lavender color, their fragrance, but they dropped too soon, made a colossal mess. "I asked him about the possibility of an English version. I couldn't do one, though. It would take... what, at least two or three years, and his Japanese publisher would definitely want to use someone like Matsu Kenji, a top, recognized authority. Besides, Yoshio told me personally he doesn't care what happens to the book after he's gone. He just wants to see it done, hold it in his hands."

Hiroko nodded, wrinkled his eyes up. "He knows no one will make a movie of it, starring him. And he doesn't have to read it anymore."

Kate crumpled up a handful of papery flowers and blew the debris in his direction. "The two of you! You're both children."

"Bad children," chuckled Hiroko. "Ah, forgetful children, too. A letter for you. I think the mailman wants the stamps. Please save the envelope for him."

The postmark and stamp was German; the bold writing was Cass's. Kate put the envelope in her pocket as if it meant nothing and went back to sweeping. It meant too much. She wanted to be completely alone when she read it.

Hiroko rubbed his forehead with the back of his arm and left streaks of dirt. "Are you afraid to read it?" he asked, worried.

"Maybe," admitted Kate, slowly. The memories of her happiness were as real and compelling as ever. She wouldn't want anything to ruin them.

Although there was no summons from Yoshio's bell, Hiroko lifted his head and looked toward the house.

"He needs me," Hiroko said, setting aside his broom. "You don't have to finish sweeping. I will do it later."

"The bell didn't ring," Kate objected.

She got a puckish grin and a shrug. "Love calls louder than a bell," he quoted. "You are just beginning to discover that, aren't you?"

Without waiting for a reply, he ambled away. Kate scratched her nose and worked on the thought he'd left her with. Conversations with Kishi always ended on a philosophical note, no matter what they started talking about. Sometimes, he left her with a headache. Most usually, a smile.

Of the two men, she had decided Yoshio was the more unworldly, despite Hiroko's years in a monastery. There were moments lately, when Hiroko held forth on gardening and growing things, that she wondered if he wasn't aware of her anxiety and her hopes that she was pregnant.

Kate settled on a bench, taking out the envelope and tapping it with her nails. Fran had written once and her letter had evoked all sorts of unresolved feelings. The news of the Cutler was ordinary enough, the description of their second wedding, but the tone was so happy, the writing was practically luminous on the paper. Kate had been jealous.

And the clipping disturbed her. The local Riverside paper had a paragraph or two, describing the purchase of the *tan-e* with a "local boy makes good" attitude. Kate had put the letter away, overcome by longing, by remorse.

She slit the envelope carefully with her thumbnail and unfolded the single sheet of paper inside. The prose was simple and spare. The first few lines were actually terse, describing how Cass intended to have the *tan-e* sent to UCLA, his alma mater, before Sunco displayed them.

Berlin seemed almost tranquil after Tokyo. He was busy. If it was difficult for him to write—as difficult as it was for her to read such prosaic words—Kate wasn't sure. Only when she got to the end of the letter did she glimpse Cass. She read and reread the last few sentences

Everything is very different. Nothing seems quite the same but I can't explain it. I wanted to give you everything and I couldn't. What I have is without equal, without precedent in my life. I love you.

She folded the letter. Without ever reading it again, those words—like so many things he said to her—were printed in her brain and engraved in her heart. She closed her eyes for a second, dizzy, almost giddy.

The bell brought her back to reality. Yoshio needed her. And he was impatient, relentless when it came to his book, feeling the pressure and the limits closing in on him every minute, every day.

"Two more weeks," he said authoritatively, raising himself so he could transfix her with his sternest stare. "You have moved about half my mountain from here to there." He swept from the collection of jumbled writing on the bed to her neatly organized stacks on the table.

"You are very optimistic," Kate replied. "Four, let's say. I'll cable Holman tomorrow and be on the safe side."

"There is no safe side," growled Yoshio and coughed for five minutes. "I don't have four weeks. If you would stop moon-watching when we take breaks for tea, it will be done. Cass Yashima is not up on the moon, scarecrow."

"I know where he is." She picked up a chapter, prepared to work and divert the conversation. "I got a letter today."

"The letter. The letter," snapped Yoshio. "Are you going to keep everything important from me? What did it say?"

Her pencil was poised, ready to go. "I believe we were on Hiroshige's *Clear Weather after a Snowfall*. You wanted to expand on why the print is one of the apexes of his art."

Yoshio Sabusawa fell back heavily on his pillows and rolled his eyes in disgust. "I am a genius, no saint. You come in, eyes ablaze with fire, a secretive smile, and tell me nothing. I say a man's name and the green fire flares. Unless you wear a hood, you will never learn to mask your feelings."

"He said he loves me. Obviously, he has greater obligations," said Kate, doodling nervously in the paper's margin. "I thought you were the one who didn't want to waste time."

"Love is not an obligation," muttered Yoshio, fixing his eyes on the ceiling. "It is a privilege to love. I saw a man who bought *tan-e* as much for the love of a woman as for the works themselves. I saw a proud man who humbled himself when he asked two old strangers to care for her."

"You're talking too much," said Kate. She saw the scribble she made; it was a little Sunco crest. She erased it.

"Soon you will be free to go to him," Yoshio said hoarsely. "Two weeks. Make reservations now."

"I can't. I won't," countered Kate. She got up and straightened papers so she didn't have to face him with naked emotions. "I was planning to stay until . . . you leave." She hated the lame euphemism but she still stumbled over naming the demon.

"I see a too-proud woman, she who does not bend but breaks," rasped Yoshio. "My favorite student, loved but not my beloved. Ask for what you want, for a change."

"I'm not in a position to set the terms," Kate said faintly. "I signed Arnold's contract and took what I got. I agreed to 'enough' with Cass. Just enough."

"What a stupid notion," exclaimed Yoshio. "Enough love. Did the sun shine enough today? Ask a bird if she flew enough and see what answer you get." Abruptly, he picked up a page of his manuscript. "The incredible intricacy of this drawing, the detail of the procession moving up the mountainside, is balanced by the extremely simple use of color. The red of daybreak sky shading into blue, the pinkish-white cast of the snow make the work simple and harmonious and moving."

Kate ran over and started to write as quickly as she could, hoping she would find the right section later. She bent over the work, unable to face the fleeting shadow of pain on Yoshio's face or reveal the shadow of pain on her own.

Unexpectedly, Yoshio appeared to have a respite of three days where he gained strength. The remission of his symptoms allowed him relief from coughing and pain and he wanted to use every second to work. Kate understood how temporary any improvement was, so she hurried and didn't object to the schedule.

With a mild euphoria setting in, they spent the entire nights rushing through the work. His dream was rapidly accumulating, page by page, and becoming real.

Her own dream seemed possible. Every time Cass had gone away, it was with part of her. Now, day by day, she was more and more convinced that part of him was left with her, growing within her. She wanted something of him to hold forever.

She made plans, as she always did, but for now they had to be for half dream, half anticipation plans. The raise from the board, her savings would help. She never questioned what the reaction of her parents and the people close to her would be. They would understand . . . and a thirty-year-old single mother in California was pretty tame stuff nowadays.

Yes, there was a twinge of guilt when she thought about Cass. He wouldn't know. He didn't know. She had taken away his choice and would have to live with depriving him of the happiness she was hoping for.

"The sun is out," announced Hiroko one afternoon, tramping into the living room where she and Yoshio were working. "Kate should go into the garden and take the sunshine. She looks too pale."

Yoshio glanced up at Kate. "She is supposed to be pale. She is a *gajin*. Look at her calligraphy if you don't believe me."

Kate smiled faintly down at the page she was working on. Yoshio must be feeling better if he was strong enough to be sarcastic. "That's okay, Hiroko. We're almost finished with this chapter. I'll go out shopping in a while and walk around the neighborhood."

"Now," insisted Hiroko, piling up the mugs of tea and Yoshio's untouched lunch. "I'll make a nice, rich broth for this skinny fool and funnel it into him. Go!"

The unexpected order surprised Kate. It wasn't like Hiroko to insist on anything. Perhaps he did suspect her pregnancy and was concerned about the long, irregular hours, the hasty meals and the lack of sunshine. He returned her inquiring stare with a perfectly angelic smile.

"Go!" he repeated and fastened his attention to Yoshio. "You will nap after the *miso*. I will read you such a dull bit of philosophy, you will be asleep before I can turn the page."

Yoshio sneered and shrugged with resignation, waving Kate off. "We dare not argue with the mad monk. He will quit and then my bonsai trees will not bloom."

Kate raked her hair with her fingers and took a few deep, cleansing breaths of the warm air from the porch. It was a gorgeous day and she hadn't noticed before. She didn't see their visitor until after she came down the stairs. It took agility and care not to trip over the loose planking and she wasn't taking any chances on falling, lately.

He isn't there, was her first thought when she saw Cass. Too little sleep can cause hallucinations. Too much wishful thinking can trick the mind.

She blinked a time or two and shaded her eyes with her hand against the glare of sun on gravel. He was there, standing under the wisteria trellis, and he looked as tired as she felt. His face was drawn, his mouth set in a thin, pallid line.

The crunch of her footsteps on the loose white gravel alerted him. Cass saw her, smiled, and in two strides was there—really there—holding her.

A long silence passed before he said her name. "Kate, oh, Katie..." And some of the fatigue left his face.

She didn't know what to say. She wasn't sure what to do, other than kiss him and hug him as tightly as she could.

"When did you... You're in Washington, aren't you?" She finally made her mouth do something but return his kisses.

"Obviously, I'm not," he said with a short laugh. "Even I haven't mastered being in two places at one time. It would come in real handy."

"But...but what are you here for? Come on in...I'll tell Yoshio and Hiroko...oh, you must have seen him. That's why he pushed me out the door..." Kate heard herself babbling, the happy babble of a child.

Cass just shook his head from side to side until she ran down. "No, I'll see them later. I'm not going to be here for long, Kate. I have to be at the airport around eight tonight. Can we go somewhere?"

He meant the apartment. She glanced away. "Is this a pit stop on the way there? I guess it must be, if you're already talking about leaving." She looked back and met his eyes. "I don't think I want a couple of hours and another one of those killer goodbye scenes."

She started to walk down the path and he fell into step with her. "Neither do I," Cass said softly, taking her arm. "But I want you. More than ever, more than anything."

When Kate tried to move away from him, Cass grabbed her, his hands holding her head steady. Pulling her against him, Cass kissed her deeply and for a long time. His tongue sought hers and she jerked her head aside.

"Don't," Kate said angrily. Her heart was racing; it always did but she didn't want it to.

"Why not?" He wouldn't let her go, only took a firmer grip on her arms and kept his body pressed to hers.

"You can't drop in and out like this," said Kate, "that's why. It's not fair."

"It wasn't meant to be fair," Cass replied. His mouth began to descend toward hers once more. "I had to see you ... hold you. I grabbed a plane to tell you what it's been like for me—without you. Lousy! Lonely!"

Kate pushed on his chest and stepped back. He wasn't going to play fair, striking at her vulnerability, her terrible love and desire for him. Her anger, the rage, was still in her voice, but she wondered if the other emotions showed as clearly in her face or eyes.

"Yesss," she hissed. "That's what it's been like. That's what it will be like. Even after a few more hours. Especially after today. It will be like opening a wound that's barely healed. Don't ask me to go and make love with you and then bravely see you off with a wave until the next time our paths cross. I won't do it. I can't do it."

She put her hand to her mouth and turned away, unable to look at him and not want the impossible.

His voice, tight with suppressed anger of his own, lashed out at her. "You could be with me! You could go with me on that plane or take the next one or another one in a week ... whenever you could, wherever I was ..."

"I'm a curator, not a camp follower," said Kate. "You're suggesting I make you my full-time project and be your part-time ..."

"Wife," he finished for her and fell silent.

Her shoulders wilted and she struggled to keep the tears out of her eyes.

"You heard me," Cass said when she wouldn't respond. "I want you to marry me, Kate. I love you. I love you more than I ever loved anyone...or ever will. It's not over for us. It doesn't have to be.''

He ran his hand gently down her back and she was afraid she would melt, collapse at his feet, and cry, "Yes, yes." But she concentrated on keeping herself under control.

"And the terms of surrender?" she argued. "The spoils of war. I'd have to give up my work and sit in Costa Mesa or hotel rooms all over the world and wait...and wait. Or I could stay at the Cutler and have a marvelous modern marriage with a husband who was gone thirty weeks of every year. And I could raise our children alone..."

It was the wrong thing to say because it touched too close to her secret. Kate felt the tears flood her throat and choke her. She waited until the feeling passed. It was different, deciding consciously to be a single mother and to face the prospect of living, and yet not truly living, with her child's father.

"We can discuss this," Cass ground out, whirling her around to face him. "There's too much between us to let it go, there's too much ahead of us to let what we have die...I'll compromise. I'll listen to what you want—"

"You have listened!" Kate snapped. "The past few months, you've listened and been sorry and sympathized, but it can't change unless you want to change. I love you, too. I want you. But not on any terms. How long would a marriage last if I give up everything that's important to me but you? How interesting and strong a woman would you find me?"

The muscle in his jaw jumped. He took his hands off her and balled his fists at his sides. "You can't take the Cutler along with you, no. I can't give up being the president of Sunco and truck farm outside of Riverside, no. But, if you weren't so miserably rigid, you'd find a way to bend, suggest a way for me to give you—"

"I don't want to get gifts," shouted Kate, losing all hope of containing herself. "I didn't fall in love with your money or your title . . . but you. I'll compromise when you can."

Cass pulled her up to him, crushed his mouth to hers and tried to make her respond, open her lips and yield to the temptation of a kiss. She was furious but he was strong, quietly powerful when he was angry, and equally determined. She fought, but she also reacted to the sensations of having him this close, this insistent and overwhelming. He knew only too well how to move her, how to work his mouth and tongue on hers, how to slip one hand around her to caress her breast.

As abruptly as the kiss began, he ended it, leaving her still angry and now aroused.

"Goddamn it!" Cass swore but the look he gave her was one of hurt, not fury. "You're wrong, Kate. You're all wrong about me. I came here, not out of strength, but out of this weakness, this crazy need for you . . . I want a way to give you—" he put his hand over her mouth, not allowing her to object "—what you want, what you need. And I'm not smart enough to figure it out for myself. But I knew it could be done, if we wanted it badly. *We,* not just me. I wanted you to help me free myself enough to be free for you."

He took his hand away and held her shoulders, rested his forehead against hers. His voice dropped to a silken whisper. "But I'm not your prisoner. I'm my own, I guess. All I would have done is brought you into my cage with me."

Without a last kiss this time, without another word, he spun around and left her, almost running in his haste to get out of the garden.

Kate stood there for countless minutes, paralyzed and nauseated. It made sense to be sick to her stomach because she was sick at heart, hearing the echo of his voice over and over and visualizing the bleakness of his eyes staring back at her. She swallowed hard and splashed water from the hose over her wrists and face, drank and gagged and drank some more.

She had written the final lines to their story herself, she realized, and made him pay in pride and pain for something that wasn't all his fault. And there wasn't any satisfaction, any triumph. She knew she still loved him and that she couldn't be with him.

And there were no accidents, she learned that night. There was fate and fate was as unkind as rumored. It could not be coincidence that she got her period and had to deal with the loss of Cass and the loss of hope, all at once.

When Hiroko found her sobbing and washing, out in the yard at midnight, he didn't ask what was wrong. He simply stood there for a few minutes and then, helped her wring out the clothes and hang them.

"Life is what happens to you while you're making other plans," sniffled Kate, taking a clothespin from him.

"As long as it happens," said Hiroko stolidly, "it's better than missing the next spring. You never know what will grow and that makes life worth watching."

"I'm not growing anything but old," Kate said self-pityingly.

Hiroko went and carefully emptied the rinse tub over the base of his precious trees. "Being older can be a reward," he said with a twinkle. "You will have seen all the magic tricks of life once and know how they are done. You will only have to believe in the ones you like and whisper to your children and grandchildren that the rest are illusions. Oh, they won't listen, by the way."

She laughed a little, in spite of herself. "Love, huh?"

He tucked his arm in hers and turned her toward the house. "Still my favorite. I've practiced ten years and I'm still not able to disbelieve it. Attachments! Bad for the Zen monk, good for the man. Let's hurry up... Yoshio wanted me to bring you in an hour ago to work on his Kawabata critique."

She went in, ready to keep moving the mountain from one side of the room to the other. There were two more good days and then, gradually Yoshio grew weaker and sicker. Kate worked alone most of the next two weeks and bothered him only when it was absolutely necessary.

"You have your reservations?" Yoshio croaked at her one night. "We are finished here. In every sense of the word. My book is so good, I am enjoying it." He put down the last hundred pages or so and smiled.

"You're going to be famous," Kate said, grinning as she took off her glasses. "The Complete Sabusawa... it was a real privilege, *sensai*. My famous teacher."

"So are you," he said cryptically. "I will have taught the foremost Western expert on Japanese art. I will write a footnote tomorrow about my scarecrow."

She went to bed, telling him over her shoulder that she would not put any such note into the text and have to put up with a lot of teasing at conferences. There were not going to be long or sentimental goodbyes tomorrow. Yoshio would be aggravated if she carried on or thanked him for the five weeks of toil and trouble and tremendous personal satisfaction.

The Cutler was there. Fran's letters let her know she wasn't indispensable. Her whole life—the rest of it—was still waiting, too. Maybe Cass was. Maybe he wasn't. But she was going to find out and tell him it was always winter without him, for what it was worth.

"You carry on," said Yoshio in the morning.

Kate nodded, not trusting herself to speak. She watched Hiroko carrying her suitcases down the treacherous front steps. They were right; her life was on the other side of the Pacific. There was nothing left here for her to do.

"I'm tired. I'm just too tired," were Yoshio's parting words. He managed a smile. No sentimentality, no drawn-out goodbyes. She put her hand in his and let him squeeze her fingers while she kissed his forehead.

"I will see you off myself," announced Hiroko. He stumbled into the cab after her, a fat, odd looking gardener escorting her to Haneida Airport.

He joked and scolded the cab driver for going too fast, talked to all the baggage handlers and customs officials as if he were in charge of tourism or a clown in a circus.

"You don't have to wait until my plane gets off," suggested Kate. "Yoshio looked very weak this morning. I'm sure you'd rather be with him."

"I'll be with him in plenty of time," Hiroko said brightly. "He wouldn't like it if I didn't see your departure was smooth. The manuscript is on its way and you must be, too. No passport delays, no last-minute snarls. You did well, Cleary-san."

"Not in everything," replied Kate, her eyes clouded. "The book...I gave it a beginning, a middle and end. I only had to map the twists and turns of Yoshio's mind. Other things..." She broke off the thought and put it away, a jagged, sore point.

Her flight was announced with crisp efficiency. Kate held out her hand and Kishi took it in his pudgy one. Then, he bowed to her formally and gave her a wrapped package and an envelope.

"Your parting gifts," Kishi said at the puzzled look on her face. "Surely you didn't expect us to ignore custom and good manners."

"Surely not," teased Kate uneasily. She didn't want gifts. She hadn't felt like a guest. Sometimes family and sometimes Yoshio's serf, but not a guest. "Thank you and *sayonara*."

She gave and received the lowest, politest of formal bows. As the farewell promised, she hoped they would meet again. She put the gifts in her carryon as if they meant nothing, also manners.

Hiroko Kishi grinned and with a final bob, walked away to merge immediately with the crowd in the terminal. Kate saw him vanish almost magically from sight as the boarding of her plane began. This was no place for tears, she decided, and she had lots of time ahead of her. Eighteen hours away, Riverside was another world. Perhaps by the time she arrived, she would understand everything that had happened to her here.

The drone of the stewardess's mechanical safety lecture was lost in the roar of the plane's engines. Kate blocked out everything from her consciousness but the sights from her window as the jet lifted slowly from the runway. She watched until the last of the islands were far behind and there was nothing but sea and sky around them. When the passengers were lulled into quiet by food and drink, the soft constant purr of power, she brought out the package and the letter.

Reaching up to snap on the overhead light, she unwrapped the gift. The red brocade case opened at a touch and Kate blinked, awed, at the pearls. Each one was perfect, large, matched to its mates for size and flawlessness and color. She dangled them on her hand, gasping at the rose-pink blush that made the pearls look warm. The bright gold clasp was a carved rectangle depicting a stylized sun with a single diamond.

"We'll be on the ground in Honolulu in about forty-five minutes," the stewardess said softly. "Do you want to get out and stretch your legs?"

Kate looked at the sleeping couple across the aisle. "No, that's all right. I'll try to catch some sleep, too." She caressed the envelope with her fingers, put the pearls on and opened the note from Yoshio.

There were actually two letters in the envelope. One was to her, informing her that he had placed a copy of the raw manuscript in her luggage. The second was the draft of a letter Yoshio had written to his publisher, naming Kate as the translator of his choice, giving her credentials and his recommendation.

She smiled, although a tear did fall and blotch the neat calligraphy on the paper. It would take her ten years to translate the book, working part-time. It was a present, a beautiful present. Strangely, she felt happy.

In closing the letter, Yoshio had added, "Ask for what you want."

Well, she had wanted all of Cass Yashima and perhaps, she would never have more, but she felt linked to him for all time. She could not accomplish what she would like to for Yoshio but her whole life had been changed by knowing him. She had wanted a child and was coming home with a book, an embryonic masterpiece. It would have to suffice. For now.

CHAPTER FIFTEEN

JUST AS SHE HAD PLANNED, Kate spent the four remaining days of her leave with her family in San Bernadino. It was enough time to renew the bond, to fish in companionable silence with her father, and to help Elaine Cleary cut and sew a new wardrobe. They told Kate their plans to go to the Grand Canyon and Las Vegas, the panacea for retirement boredom.

She showed them pictures from Fran's wedding in Tokyo and made them laugh with anecdotes from the war with Whelan-Jones. The whole tense confrontation with the Muratas was detailed in the sunlit kitchen and Kate showed them the draft of Yoshio's precious manuscript.

The emotional and physical rigors of the trip proved an adequate explanation for her too easy tears. She did not talk much about Cass; they did not ask.

David and Fran were called and drove up from Riverside. They brought Tomadachi for Sunday dinner and a great reunion. He clung to Kate with unexpected feline affection, fatter and more loving. David looked properly harried, Fran acted jumpy, but the honeymoon glow still hadn't completely faded from their faces.

Fran got through most of the meal, worrying her bangs, but the dam of natural ebullience burst during dessert. She made a false start and pushed David's warning hand from her arm.

"Come on, David," she squealed. "I was going to hold out till she got back but it won't wait!"

"Bigger than a breadbox?" Kate raised an inquiring eyebrow. "Does it deserve a drum roll?"

David obliged with the silverware and Fran got her silliest grin. "Okay," she giggled, "but hold on to the table, everybody. I want to spoil Marcus Holman's surprise for the board meeting next week. I want to see Kate faint dead away into the peach cobbler."

Kate felt light-headed and odd before Fran got another word out, but she was sure it had nothing to do with the Cutler's director. It had to do with Cass. She knew without knowing how.

"My raise didn't go through. The *Blue-Veiled Goofup* arrived and Marcus is firing me." She filled up the space with nonsense.

"Kate!" Fran glared at her, silencing her quite effectively. "Holman got an offer from Sunco. We are going to be the recipients of the *tan-e* as permanent loan properties and a sizable check to begin a building fund program to add another wing. A... are you ready for this? Yoshio Sabusawa Memorial Wing."

She had never fainted. Never. But for one heart-stopping moment Kate saw everyone's faces blur, and their excited burst of chatter receded far, far away. She gripped the edge of the table.

"Oh, my, what a coup," trilled Elaine. "How marvelous."

Colonel Cleary harrumphed in his throat. "Generous. On the order of miraculous, really. You must be thrilled, Katie." He reached over and patted his daughter's hand.

Fran screwed up her features in disgust at Kate's lack of response. "Where's the glee? Where's the hallelujahs? God, aren't you even happy about it? Holman was leaping around his office like a bunny rabbit. He even *kissed* me, for crying out loud, right before he said he'd fire me on the spot if I leaked this to anyone."

"Kissed you?" said David archly, looking down at his wife. "Maybe you'll get a raise, too."

"I'm happy," confirmed Kate. All eyes stayed on her. "Yes, I'm delighted," she said more quickly, standing up and excusing herself. She escaped to listen to her family's noise from the safety and distance of the porch.

"Did I say something wrong?" she heard Fran say plaintively.

"I don't think so," David and her father chorused. "I think she's upset about Yoshio," theorized the colonel.

"She looks exhausted, worn out. I prescribe a couple of days more rest and readjustment," argued David. "I read this new piece on jet lag ..."

Fran said, "Maybe," in a very unconvinced way. She knows, thought Kate. She saw me force a smile once too often and shake off one too many questions.

"CAN YOU STAY a minute or two, Kate?"

The rest of the Cutler staff got up and shuffled off singly or in pairs. Kate arranged her notes carefully and slid them back in her file folder, looking up expectantly.

"Yes, sure. Anything wrong?"

The head of the museum chuckled as if she'd been unusually witty and leaned on the back of his chair. "You are kidding, I presume. Wrong? When has it gone better? I get through detailing all the advance publicity we're getting on the Sunco gift and loan and it's all due to you. Maxine reports the membership drive is practically guaranteed and you're approved for a substantial salary boost. How much better does it get?"

"Flowers from the boss," Kate said quickly. "Thanks for them. I'm sorry I'm so preoccupied. It's been rough catching up. That's probably why I didn't take time off before."

She liked Marcus Holman. Normally, she liked to banter with him. The mention of the loan, the funds, combined with the less than perfect Utamaro geisha, courtesy of Arnold, were sufficient to irritate her today. Gifts were not supposed to represent such high costs in personal terms. The price for all these gifts had been paid in emotions and it was hard for her to appreciate their real value.

She waited for Marcus to get to his point, if he had one, and wondered what it would cost her.

"Maybe I should be asking you what's wrong?" He came over and flopped heavily into a vacant chair. "Did I handle the campaign and presentation badly?"

"No, no, it's fine."

He took a stab in the dark, studying her face for clues. "Are you thinking about leaving us? I'm aware that after this trip, you might swing a position with one of the bigger museums...you have that book you want to do, too. A university offer?"

"I . . . I really don't know. I don't think so. There's a really limited market for my teaching talents." She smiled at him and laughed weakly at the dramatic sigh of relief he gave her. "I'll never get back to my office if you don't tell me why you wanted me to stay, will I?" she said straight out.

The head of the Cutler had two secretaries and had to be told what day it was, regularly. "Did I ask you...oh, yeah! This is the pièce de résistance for us." He took something out of his suit pocket. "We're in the big time."

The invitation was handsome, printed on a textured paper. The tiny woodblock logo was a sun. She covered it with her thumb and read the announcement of the press showing of the Sunco collection. It was being given at the home of the president, black tie optional.

"I don't need to preview the *tan-e*," said Kate. Her mouth was dry. She hoped whatever was in her eyes was hidden, vague. "I know what we're getting, Marcus. You love talking to the press."

"My name is on the envelope. So is yours. We are going to revel in the compliments from all the jealous losers, Kate. Hal Walters, Mark Dreger of the Winters Collection, Apkarian from the Los Angeles Journal, the ugly guy from Art News . . ."

Kate struggled to imagine herself there, taking Cass's hand, posing for pictures. She thought about talking casually and inconsequentially with him while photographers shot them against the background of four prints. She wasn't ready. She wouldn't know how to say what she wanted to.

"I don't have to go," she interrupted.

He consulted his watch, not listening to her. "I've been on a diet for three hours now. I'm going to cut a dashing figure when I rub a few noses in it. If George Hoover is there, the victory will be total. When he got the Emore Trust and the Rockefeller, leaving us out in the cold..."

"Maxine should go. She could plug the membership drive," Kate said feebly.

"You can't *not* go!" Holman was horrified. "Kate, you can deep-six that humble, self-effacing act with me. You're not in Japan right now. This is a biggie for us and we are spreading the word. A little nothing collection hits it..."

It wasn't humility. It was pride, she decided. She did know what she wanted to say. She was afraid to do it, afraid to swallow some pride and ask for what she wanted. Cass had. She remembered his face, the hurt she had inflicted on him. And yet, he had given them the *tan-e*, made a magnificent tribute to someone she loved by starting the Sabusawa addition.

Holman was working himself up, trying to wind her into his mad enthusiasm. "Think of the band-wagon effect. Everyone who is anyone will be there. I know glad handing isn't your favorite part of the job, but it *is* part of the job."

She glanced at her name on the invitation. "This is a command performance."

"And an order," muttered Holman.

"Thumbs under my sequined suspenders and my best Cheshire cat routine, huh?"

"That's it!" He smirked, totally pleased with himself and her. "We put on our show for the visiting firemen. I want the Cutler to shine, you want the

Cutler to shine. You take a bow—a small one, if you like—but a bow.''

She scribbled the date on her folder. "I'll think about it.''

"You won't," he hollered. "Why are you making a production of this? Give me one good reason."

Because I'm too proud. No, Holman would never buy it. *Because if I go, I may find out I am not too proud to beg, too proud to ask for what I want, and if I get it, you'll say goodbye to me, not good-night.* No, he wouldn't much like that one, either.

"There may be people there I'd rather avoid seeing in a social or professional context," said Kate.

"Whelan-Jones," spat Holman. "Yeah, okay, don't look at me like I made out the invitations. He gave us the Utamaro, the rumor goes, because he tried a fast shuffle once too often and thought you'd put the word out on him. Guy named LeClerc has been talking a lot lately. Don't worry. If Arnold Whelan-Jones was invited and goes, he'll get nothing but blisters from shaking hands, trying to make friends and influence people.''

Kate's eyes lingered on the *Blue-Veiled Geisha*. She was resigned to the outcome of this debate. "I think I'll have that hung on my office wall, if it's all right with you.''

"I thought you were going to store that one. No, it's fine. Take it. Okay on the showing?''

Kate rubbed the Sunco logo and smiled. "Okay, boss. I'll put in an appearance.''

"Good girl." Holman rubbed his hands together. "I'd like to treat you to a sweet roll and coffee.''

Kate gave his small paunch a significant look and got up to leave. "You are on a diet until Saturday. There will be goodies galore at the party. If you starve yourself until then, you can go berserk, devour everything that isn't covered in glass and hung on the walls."

Holman went out, reciting his hit list to himself. "Hoover, Constantino, Dreger...they'll eat their words."

"Or you will," added Kate. She stayed behind in the conference room, appraising Arnold's generous contribution and appraising her own chances for real, lasting happiness.

When she was feeling brave, she went back to her office, and stood by Fran's desk, pawing through the morning mail. As off-handedly as she could, Kate penciled in the party, place and time on Fran's master calendar.

"Well, it's not exactly a candlelit dinner for two," she said when Fran refused to do more than grin like a sheep stricken with gas.

"Oh, really!" Fran said, snatching the mail away. It flew all over the carpet and she had to scramble around the floor to collect it. "Is that the best you can come up with? Give me a break."

"That's not the best I've come up with—no," said Kate and motioned for her to close the door. "When Arnold gave us the print, it depressed me. I don't know if he thought he was buying me off or if it was a peace offering or what. But he owed me something, Fran, and Cass doesn't."

"Honey," said Fran with a slight sneer, "don't tell me you think Cass as Mr. Sunco gave us bounty because he feels guilty. It doesn't work like that. He isn't trying to atone for anything. He loves you! He would like you to be happy, without him but preferably, with him."

"It was a sacrifice," said Kate. "He knew how much I wanted the *tan-e*."

Fran's eyes were puzzled but concerned. "He wants to see you again, Kate. The road isn't closed yet. He'll explain his motives at this shindig if you ask him."

"I have some other questions, too," Kate said hesitantly. "Do you want to hear them? This is a rehearsal, I guess. If I shock or scare you, stop me anytime."

She could have been thinking aloud. Fran was so quiet for fifteen minutes, Kate could have been alone, talking to herself. When she was finished, Fran gave her a hug.

"You know my motto," Fran said. And on her way out of the office, she broke into a few high-school cheerleader steps, rooting her team on.

THE HOUSE IN COSTA MESA was long and low. Kate stopped on the blue-white gravel to admire it. Cass had complained how empty his house was, but she and the Holmans had walked a full city block of parked cars tonight before they reached the entrance.

"How do I look?" Marcus asked, tugging at the tuxedo sleeves. He was openly nervous.

"Fat," said his wife.

"Very trim," said Kate, laughing. "Three pounds can make a lot of difference. Besides, that was my line." She linked her arm through his on one side and his wife did the same on the other. At Mrs. Holman's signal, they started to half drag him toward the entrance.

"Full house," muttered Holman, surveying the assemblage of gawkers, newsmen and visitors. He paused in the arch of the living room and ran a practiced eye over the walls. "Very nice. This man is a contact to hold on to. I can't wait to meet him."

"My sentiments precisely," answered Kate. She could not find the one face in the sea of bobbing heads she was looking for.

"We look like the three monkeys posed here," snarled Mrs. Holman. "Hear no evil, see no evil…oh, there's Mary Hoover. I'm going to see if that necklace is real, Marc."

If Marcus Holman thought their pose was for effect or looked ridiculous, he didn't raise any objection. Kate wore a dress she had worn only once before; it was much more—and less—to look at than all the hand-beaded and ruffled creations floating around the enormous expanse of the living room.

The deep green of Japanese silk did an incredible job of complementing her skin and almost matched the shade of her searching eyes. The only adornment she had worn was a string of pearls; the faint blush to them was the same pink blooming on her cheeks. The massed black of her hair was softly wound at the nape of her neck, not braided. It invited the touch of a special hand to loosen it. Hadn't he said countless times how he liked to touch her hair, run his fingers through it?

"Okay," sighed Holman, sucking in his stomach, "now that we've got their attention, Kate, what will we sing? Everyone is looking up here and you were the one who didn't want a fanfare.''

She stopped craning her own neck long enough to see the swiveled heads, the admiring stares. She grew warm under so much scrutiny, but she couldn't help looking into the upturned faces for the one she wanted.

"I wonder where our host is?" she asked Holman.

"Never mind. Maybe he's still off on business," Marcus said out of the side of his mouth, keeping his fixed smile intact. "The gray-haired man rolling his eyes at you is Mark Dreger. Why don't we wander over and see how interested he is?" He nudged Kate hard and she had to take a step downward or fall.

Marcus Cutler Holman was in his element now. She saw his whole countenance change, smelling interest, smelling benefactors. He had been a pest until tonight, bothering her with schemes to turn the event to full advantage. Kate, once she decided she was going, had relaxed and worked without dwelling on what could or would happen. It had seemed pointless to write more fairy-tale scenarios; she no longer trusted the power of her dreams.

But Marcus was calm now and she was in a trance. A drink was thrust into her hand and Kate sipped at it. It had no taste so she put it down. The prints and paintings lining the walls could have been towels, for all the attention she gave them. The comments and congratulations were showering down and she responded by rote.

"In a year, I think," Kate said, squeezing someone's hand. "We might consider sending them out after a year." She smiled with the strained effort of a beauty queen candidate but it worked. "Yes, thank you."

The smiles, quips and comments for colleagues came automatically. For that facility she was grateful. She could not focus on any single face for longer than the time it took to see that it wasn't Cass. Her own laughter rang hollow in her ears. Her discussion was forced and shallow and nobody seemed to notice it or mind.

"Kate! Over here...here he is, at last," crowed Marcus with his booming heartiness, steering her and extending his own right hand. "A monumental pleasure, Mr. Yashima. I know I said it all on the phone but it bears repeating. Thank you from all of us!"

"Cass," came the resonant, low correction. Kate felt her heart strike fire at the sound—the music—of his voice. "The pleasure is all mine, Marcus."

Tonight might have meant aching emptiness. Suddenly, the night meant everything. Seeing Cass made the whole world shrink to the size of a man. Kate, motionless and mesmerized, found herself his captive once more. The last three months of her life only made sense and fell into place when she was close enough to touch him.

Marcus was being insistent and effusive in his thanks, marvelously long-winded, due to the presence of reporters. Kate was grateful; she could stand there and deal with the cruel pleasure of seeing Cass. It hurt physically after so long to look, not to reach and not to hold. She breathed, shallow and controlled, and the effort for such tight control knotted her stomach.

"And, of course, the lady who made this possible," gargled Holman, moving Kate closer into the group. "Dr. Katherine Cleary, our graphics curator and miracle worker."

Cass moved his mouth, made some reply to the newsman from San Diego, and she thought she had gone deaf. The words meant nothing; the sight of his lips made her think only of the taste and texture of his kisses. Her skin reacted the way it did when his mouth moved silently over it.

Kate rubbed her arms briskly. "Do you think I could get a refill, please, Marcus?" She realized she wasn't holding a glass as her request emerged. "A drink, I meant. Anything."

"We should pose for the pictures," he said. His voice was sharp with irritation at her lack of professionalism.

"Later," Kate said. The faint scent of a male cologne, citrus and smoke, evoked too vivid memories of Cass's body, naked and heated. The familiar fragrance had surrounded her not so long ago, clung to her skin, to the sheets.

Cass turned the dark intensity of his eyes on her and Kate looked for desire. But he swung his head back to Holman and spoke decisively.

"Yes, later," he said.

Her boss shrugged his shoulders and gave Kate a glance critical of inexplicable female behavior. He shuffled off, taking the reporter with him for a detailed report on the membership drive.

The space between them was air, inches of air that vibrated with tension. The silence bordered on oppressive before Cass spoke.

"How beautiful you are," he said softly. "I was staring at you and whatever I said to Holman probably was nonsense. I had a speech all ready to go for you. It even started with a joke. Now I've forgotten how it begins."

"I don't know my lines either," answered Kate. "We are not very good at small talk, are we?"

"We never needed it before." He took her hand and his expression said he felt what she was feeling, too. He could see the spark light, the emerald glint reserved for him. "I want to talk to you—alone—without all this competition. Come outside with me?"

She had not been aware, much less bothered, by the noise, the clinking of glasses. "Yes, of course."

People tried to stop her, tried to corral him as they crossed the room. Cass kept her walking, ignoring everyone as if they weren't there.

Herringbone decking of redwood ran in a moon-silvered strip around the entire western side of the house to face the sea toward the sunsets. Other party-goers had taken refuge for a quick breath of night air. Kate heard the hum of voices in the shadows and saw the orange glow of a cigarette.

"Why aren't you in Washington?" she asked. It was better out here, almost hidden in the darkness, calmed by the sigh of waves and cooled by the ocean breeze.

"I went. I left two key men there to take over for me."

"You did?" Kate turned completely around, pressing her back against the railed corner of the deck.

"A week ago." A fugitive from the festivities brushed by his back and Cass swayed toward her. With the other man's garbled apology came the sudden warmth of his hand on her bare arm, steadying himself, unbalancing her. "I ran on the beach, rode the horses, read a bunch of books I've been promising myself I'd get to."

"A vacation," Kate said thickly.

"A new leaf." His hand didn't leave her. The pressure of his fingers increased slightly. "I don't want to sell the house. I want to live here."

She saw the polished gleam of moonlight on his face, how close they were drawing to each other without taking a step. "That's a change since the last time I saw you," she said. "It was about change that I wanted to talk to you."

"A change of heart?" The sound of the waves almost swallowed up his question.

How reckless would she be? How much would she dare? Kate slid her hands up the front of his jacket and leaned closer to him. The very ends of her breasts brushed him and her mouth was too near to his for talking. Her lips parted to form his name, but the sound didn't emerge, crushed and held there by his kiss.

The power of their love was still there, stronger than ever. All they needed to do was touch and the high-voltage emotion surged through both of them. His arms were around her too tightly, holding Kate with a desperation that knew no limits.

Kate almost cried out from the vicelike grip, and yet she gasped, "Hold me. Hold me."

His embrace gave her the sensation of being alive, completely and achingly alive, finally.

The movement of her body against his was an offer that Cass accepted eagerly. His mouth had never been less gentle, more demanding. Kate welcomed the hunger, returning it as wildly, as fiercely, inviting him to take more.

"Kate, I'll hold you forever," he whispered. "Say you'll let me. Say you'll stay with me."

His strong fingers were gripping her, but she did not struggle at all. Being reunited with the familiar excitement his body could engender created no pain, just need, and she longed for all of him. There had never been enough of Cass to end her yearning and tonight she would have him and the answer she was seeking.

"We'll have to make changes... both of us," she murmured when he gave her a chance. "It looks as if we both made a start. You, here. Me... I have something besides the Cutler I want."

"Anything. Any changes. Name them." He nipped at her throat and then ran his tongue over the little love bites. His touch, always so gentle, was hastier, frenzied, as he rolled down the thin straps of her dress.

The ragged, harsh sound of his breath flooded her with more heat, the wildness of triumph. He still wanted her as much as she wanted him. The intricacy of the straps frustrated him and Cass became impatient, pulling at the fabric to stroke her greedily.

"Not here," Kate moaned, despite her own desire. The involuntary dance of her thighs against his, her hips tantalizing him, said there was not going to be any place or time for talking for a while.

A shudder wracked his frame when he bent his dark head to lick at the silver peaks and black shadows he had revealed.

She was dizzy, sick with excitement. Soon it wouldn't matter where they were, only that he would

love her and very, very soon, if the feeling of his hard
body, fully aroused, under her fingers was no dream.
Soon she wouldn't be able to stop touching him. The
fires inside made her crazy, bold.

"Kate," he groaned against the gleaming pearl of
her breasts. "Kate, you scare me. You make me scare
myself."

It was such a strange thing to hear him say, she
laughed softly. He was the strongest, surest person
she'd ever met. The laugh was low and throaty and
provocative; it made her sound as wanton as she felt.

"Enough to make you hang around a little more?
Enough to make this place 'home' and not just a big,
beautiful motel?"

"Yes," he said very clearly. "Enough to make sure
there are other people who take care of the business
while I take care of my life...all of it. A wife...kids."

She felt her hair begin to slip and float, loosened,
over her shoulders and back. "That's not scared," she
said. "That's loved."

His hand moved down, curved to cup the contour
beneath her dress—pressing, stroking, teasing. "You
could show me!"

"I could," she murmured. "I certainly could."

His kiss stole all other thoughts from her. She felt
him lift her and knew he was carrying her back into
the house. The darkness of wherever he took her was
warmer, deeper. The dim light that suddenly flickered
on was soft and golden, not the cool silver of the
moon.

Cass was not in her arms, and Kate's momentary
panic quelled only when she saw him. He had turned
on the small bedside lamp and through heavy-lidded

eyes, she watched him undress. Before she could hold out her arms to him, he was with her, easing her back onto the wide, pillowed bed.

She stroked fine lines down his sides and stomach, showing him and telling him how much she'd missed him, how many nights she'd thought about doing this.

"No more than I did," said Cass. "Berlin...Washington...every second I was away from you. I went through the motions, thought it would ease. I have to have you, Kate...alone, forever."

"You have me," Kate whispered, looking in his eyes and seeing not surrender but love. Not sacrifice, but love.

They couldn't be patient. Cass was fierce, insistent, pinning her with his wonderful weight until Kate writhed under him and cried his name. His knee slipped between her legs and his hands slid, hard and demanding, to cup her buttocks, to lift and open her.

"You're mine, Katie," he said hoarsely. "All mine, only mine. It was true from the first second I saw you. Tell me!"

Her hand sought him, found him and guided him into her. Her hips rose to meet him. "Yes," she moaned. "Oh, yes...yes. Hurry, hurry."

This love was better than a dream, unlike any dream. Filled with him, Kate was filled with completeness, with the union of beauty and strength. Like becoming a flowering cherry tree, she became a part of him. She gave herself up as a separate being when he fused with her, moved as one with her, and the fusion made her more, not less.

They hovered together at the one endless second of time. There was a mutual slowing of breathing and his eyes met hers in the terrible calm before the climactic storm. She saw his full and total commitment of himself beyond this moment for all time; the open promise and starkness of love stripped of any other emotion.

She would abandon everything for this feeling, this ecstasy, and for Cass. The fury of her release flooded, swept her up even as he began to move again. They did not smother or suppress the sounds of joy tonight.

It was over but not ended.

Kate lay next to him, stroking his arms and chest. When his heart had slowed and resumed its easy, quieter rhythm, Cass leaned over to see if she had fallen asleep.

"I was right to be terrified of you," he whispered with a smile looking into the banked fires in her green eyes. "You make me believe in demonic possession." He dropped a light kiss on the fullness of her mouth, touched his finger to it tenderly.

"I believe, too," laughed Kate. "I'm in a strange bedroom, stark naked. I don't remember how I got here or when I lost my shoes."

"Not stark naked," he corrected, running his hand over the pearls. "But you may have to stay a long while." He reached one arm lazily over the side of the bed and held up a limp rag of designer green for her to see. "There are at least eighty people out there who are in for a very exotic, erotic show if you insist on going back to the party."

"Pearls go with basic skin and everything else," she whispered. His fingertips left the necklace and skimmed along the entire length of her body. She shivered, feeling the stirrings so soon.

Cass kissed her eyelids closed, rocked himself a little closer.

"You are the host," Kate protested weakly. "What will they say if you aren't there?"

"I don't give a damn, Scarlett," he said, nuzzling her ear. "I have more important matters to deal with."

"Ah, yes, me. And I think I have a wonderful deal for you."

"I'll just bet you do," he agreed huskily, moving on to the valley between her breasts. "I can't be a blue-eyed blond or a starving artist for you, but I'll try anything else. What do you want?"

"I want you to be the father of my baby. I tried to make it happen, unilaterally," whispered Kate and saw his head rise at her words. "For all I know, we succeeded tonight...but I want it to be something we both want, and not just my desire."

He caressed her stomach, his eyes a dark and beautiful mystery. "Katie, to want my child and not be able to tell me..."

"I'm reckless when it comes to you," she said. "I wanted that happiness no matter what. I was lying when I said I would settle for enough. There is no limit to what I feel."

The golden light from the lamp made his face glow to match the smile he gave her. "A promise from me to you . . . not in words, not in a contract . . . a promise of a new life, a new spirit. I'd be so happy, Kate. It couldn't be too soon."

"There's more," she said. "Do you want to hear it all now?"

"Yes," he insisted, his face filled with desire and amusement. "You know me and contracts. I want to know every detail, read all the fine print. I want it iron-clad for us."

"So businesslike," chided Kate gently although what his hands were doing had no relationship to any business she'd ever worked in. "I thought I'd like to work on Yoshio's book full-time. I could translate it in two years if I gave it the attention it deserves."

"With time out for me and—" he pressed his mouth to her navel "—whoever shows up."

Kate squirmed and made a small, stifled sound. "It feels as if you're not going to waste any time getting this family started."

"I'm not going to waste another minute," he said, turning his head slightly to the side. His hard body was much more expressive than his words.

Much later, Cass sighed deeply and sat up, pulling her with him and flapping the wrinkled sheet over them. He reached and opened the drawer in the table next to the bed.

"I wrote this in Berlin. I didn't have the nerve to give it to you when I went back to Tokyo. You don't have to read it. I'll tell you what it says."

She put her head on his shoulder. "Is it a poem?" The love welled up in her heart and she felt the tears begin to spill over the rim of her eyes. Cass's lips touched her gently, brushed her ear, his warm breath a caress.

"A rain of flowers in your hair," Cass recited. "Forever lucky, forever loved."

"That's a very traditional Japanese proposal for what will be a modern Western marriage," she said. Her smile overcame her tears and she peeked up at him.

"Four, no more than five short trips a year," he said solemnly, running his finger up and down her cheek. "Maybe you'll be with me on all of them. How about a pony?"

Kate got giddy and silly with laughter. "It wouldn't fit into a suitcase."

"For our . . . oh, never mind," he growled, getting up and going to the dresser. "Are you marrying me?"

"I gave you the answer before you asked the question," said Kate, watching him pull a single gold chrysathemum from the arrangement near the mirror. "Why are you wasting my time with words? I need you."

He came back with the flower, rubbing it between his palms, and showered Kate with the fragile petals, which were like the rays of a small, fragrant sun. Then, Cass took her back into his embrace and said everything else without uttering a sound.

Harlequin
Superromance

COMING NEXT MONTH

#198 SEARCHING • Robyn Anzelon
Helping Mac Kincaid with his article on adoption
seemed simple enough to Carrie Prescott, but in the
end she is left with two choices: give up her own
search for her natural mother or give up Mac. Either
way she stands to lose....

#199 STORMSWEPT • Lynn Erickson
When Amy Slavin accompanies a rescue team to
Pearl Pass, she becomes caught up in a complicated
web of intrigue and deceit. Falling in love with a man
she can't trust is just too risky!

#200 BEYOND COMPARE • Risa Kirk
Television hosts Neil Kerrigan and Dinah Blake
disagree about everything—except the growing
attraction between them. Dinah quickly learns that
one doesn't have to like everything about a man to
fall in love with him....

#201 TWIN BRIDGES Sally Garrett
Best-selling author and recluse Laudon Brockman
and horse-breeder Michelle Innes are opposites. Yet
drawn together in the Montana Rockies they begin to
see the world with new eyes, the eyes of love....

What readers say about
HARLEQUIN SUPERROMANCE™

"Bravo! Your SUPERROMANCE [is]… super!"
R.V.,* Montgomery, Illinois

"I am impatiently awaiting
the next SUPERROMANCE."
J.D., Sandusky, Ohio

"Delightful…great."
C.B., Fort Wayne, Indiana

"Terrific love stories. Just
keep them coming!"
M.G., Toronto, Ontario

Take 4 novels and a surprise gift FREE

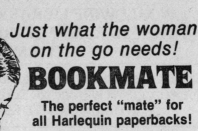
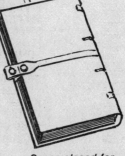